MEET THE M
THE PEA
IN THE KAN

LUKE TRAVIS: As Abilene's marshal, he cleaned up a brawling, lawless town. A man who had seen his share of frontier violence, he was ready to take on Walsh and his gang . . .

AILEEN BLOOM: A courageous frontier doctor, she had a tough skin and a warm heart—especially where Marshal Travis was concerned . . .

CODY FISHER: As Travis's young deputy, he was learning the law-and-order business fast—in a town where every day brought a deadly new lesson . . .

ORION McCARTHY: Abilene's jovial saloon-keeper was a good friend over a drink and a better one in a fight . . .

JAKE WALSH: The famed red-bearded outlaw was loyal to three things: his men, his loot, and most of all, his own hide . . .

DAN BAXTER: The white-haired federal marshal was a top-notch lawman who wore two deadly guns. And he had a personal score to settle with the bandit named Walsh . . .

MAXWELL STOCKBRIDGE: The wealthy, ruthless president of the Kansas Pacific Railroad was also a widower whose children meant everything to him . . .

DOROTHEA STOCKBRIDGE: With dark hair and flashing green eyes, she was a flirtatious beauty who feared no one—until she met real danger in Abilene . . .

Books by Justin Ladd

Abilene Book 1: The Peacemaker
Abilene Book 2: The Sharpshooter
Abilene Book 3: The Pursuers

Published by POCKET BOOKS

Most Pocket Books are available at special quantity discounts for bulk purchases for sales promotions, premiums or fund raising. Special books or book excerpts can also be created to fit specific needs.

For details write the office of the Vice President of Special Markets, Pocket Books, 1230 Avenue of the Americas, New York, New York 10020.

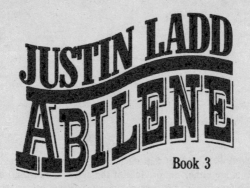

JUSTIN LADD

ABILENE

Book 3

THE PURSUERS

™ **BCI** Created by the producers of
**Wagons West, Stagecoach,
Badge, and White Indian.**

Book Creations Inc., Canaan, NY · Lyle Kenyon Engel, Founder

POCKET BOOKS

New York   London   Toronto   Sydney   Tokyo

This book is a work of fiction. Names, characters, places and incidents are either the product of the author's imagination or are used fictitiously. Any resemblance to actual events or locales or persons, living or dead, is entirely coincidental.

Another *Original* publication of POCKET BOOKS

POCKET BOOKS, a division of Simon & Schuster Inc.
1230 Avenue of the Americas, New York, N.Y. 10020

ISBN: 0-671-64899-3

First Pocket Books printing August 1988

10 9 8 7 6 5 4 3 2 1

POCKET and colophon are trademarks of
Simon & Schuster Inc.

Printed in the U.S.A.

THE PURSUERS

Prologue

———◆———

A DAY'S RIDE WEST OF ABILENE, A TRAIN PULLED BY A BIG Baldwin locomotive steamed along the tracks of the Kansas Pacific Railroad. The morning was bright and sunny, the sky high above the Kansas flatland a deep blue. Inside the cab of the locomotive, Ben Mooney rested his hand lightly on the throttle and looked out at the passing landscape.

To the north, far across the flat prairie, he could see the Smoky Hills, just anthills, really, compared to the spectacular Rockies. To the south a line of scrubby green trees and brush marked the gentle valley of the Smoky Hill River. Ahead the tracks cut through grassy plains that varied little except for an occasional shallow arroyo.

Though the flat, unchanging terrain was monotonous, Mooney did not mind it. He was a railroad man, had been for years, and was happy wherever the tracks ran. He had been driving this route across Kansas for six months, and it had been a pleasant job.

His fireman, old Cleve Bellem, opened the firebox and shoveled more coal into it. Bellem's wiry body had surprising strength for a frame that was so small and slender. Like Ben Mooney, he had been working on railroads for most of his adult life, starting back in Pennsylvania in the forties.

Bellem shut the door on the flames. He leaned against the other side of the cab and let the wind that blew in the train's open window ruffle his thin gray hair. He grinned over at Mooney as he took his cold pipe from a pocket and clamped it between his stubby teeth.

"Makin' good time," Bellem called over the roar of the engine. Both men were used to shouting.

"You bet," Mooney called back, returning the smile and pulling out his watch. He flipped open the big turnip-shaped instrument and studied the face. "We're going to make Denver ahead of schedule. Looks like we've already made up for that delay back in Abilene."

Mooney closed the watch and returned it to its pocket. Then he leaned out the big window in his side of the cab to look down the tracks. His eyes were permanently squinted from doing the same thing in countless locomotives over the years. He peered at the rails unrolling ahead of them, not expecting to see anything except the endless double line of steel.

For a moment, the spurt of flame and dust and debris that flung high in the air did not fully register on his brain. Then, over the roar of the train, he heard the blast of the explosion.

With an alarmed shout, Mooney lunged toward the brake lever. He threw his weight against it, bracing his feet and holding the metal bar tight. The earsplitting whine of the brakes shrieked across the plains. Sparks flew along the tracks as the wheels of the locomotive ground the rails in an effort to stop.

With a cold, sick feeling in his stomach, Ben Mooney knew that the train was not going to stop in time. The explosion had broken and twisted the rails and shattered the ties beneath into kindling. There was no way he could keep the train from derailing.

Frantically, Mooney glanced over at Bellem and yelled, "Get out of here, Cleve!"

Still braced against the other side of the cab, the fireman shook his head and shouted back, "I ain't jumpin' if you ain't!"

"Can't leave the train," Mooney screamed. He did not know if Bellem heard him or not. His whole head seemed to be filled with the futile shrieking of the brakes.

The locomotive hit the damaged section of track. Mooney had slowed its speed considerably, but its momentum drove it forward.

The wreck was horrible and awe-inspiring at the same time. As hundreds of tons of metal hurtled off the tracks, the locomotive tilted crazily, its cowcatcher digging its sharp nose into the dirt and ripping a monstrous furrow in the rich Kansas soil. The coal tender and first few cars followed the engine off the tracks, until at last the locomotive stopped, its massive weight embedded in the earth. Everything behind it came to a buckling, shuddering halt. The last cars of the train, still on the tracks, began to crash together, twisting and crumpling under the impact.

The hiss of steam escaping from the boiler, the rending crash of metal, the screams of the injured all blended together in one hideous cacophony of sound.

The engine had fallen completely over on its side. In the ruins of the cab, Ben Mooney swam through a fog of pain and shock. He could feel some sort of weight on him, holding him down. Forcing his hands to work, he reached up and tried to shove the thing aside. He cried out involuntarily when he realized that the burden on him was Cleve Bellem's body.

Bellem's head hung at a funny angle, and Mooney knew that the little fireman's neck was broken. His eyes were open and staring sightlessly from his coal-smudged face. For such a slender man, he was incredibly heavy.

Or maybe I am just weak, Mooney thought. He could not seem to make his left arm work correctly, and his legs felt strange. His pants were wet; part of his mind knew it was blood, but he refused to acknowledge it. All he wanted now was out.

Shuddering, Mooney worked himself out from under Bellem's body. He felt earth under his hands and began dragging himself forward. As he crawled into the sunlight, he realized that he was making his escape through a jagged hole in the roof of the cab.

The thunder of hooves made him look up in time to see riders approaching the train. At least a dozen men on horseback boiled out of a nearby wash. They rode toward the wrecked train, shouting like banshees and firing their guns into the air. In the lead was a burly man whose unruly thatch of bright red hair stuck out around the hat that was jammed on his head. The bandanna he wore over his face barely concealed a bushy red beard beneath it.

Mooney saw the redheaded giant in the forefront of

the attack, and through bloody lips he whispered, "Jake Walsh . . ."

Every railroad man in Missouri, Kansas, and Nebraska knew about Jake Walsh. He had held up trains repeatedly in all three states in some of the most daring robberies since Frank and Jesse James had taken up the gun. Walsh's description had been circulated to railroad officials and lawmen all over this part of the country. Along with the description had gone a warning: Jake Walsh was a killer.

Mooney scrabbled inside his jacket with his good arm, trying to find the pistol he carried there. He could not seem to locate it. And as he suddenly saw, it was far too late.

Jake Walsh spotted the injured engineer lying on the ground next to the destroyed locomotive. Walsh reined in, his big chestnut horse rearing slightly. Then the gun in his hand cracked twice, both bullets finding their target. Ben Mooney grunted, hunched his shoulders, and slumped, lifeless.

Walsh wheeled his horse, leveled his pistol at one of the passenger cars that was tilting crazily, and triggered several more times. He yelled at one of his men, "Get to that express car!"

There was a sporadic crackle of gunfire all along the train now. Passengers who had survived the wreck had realized that the train was under attack by bandits, and they were trying to fight back. Several of Walsh's men were pouring rifle fire into the cars.

Walsh spurred his horse toward the express car. Although heavily damaged at both ends, it was still upright. Some of the outlaws were already storming it, riding back and forth in front of the buckled door and firing through it. A few shots came from the car.

Inside, the express messenger fought desperately,

but Ernie Henson was a young man who had never before today fired a shot in anger in his life. He was stretched out on the floor of the express car, his leg throbbing from the injury he had received when the crash threw him off his feet. He did not believe his leg was broken, just badly sprained. There was a bullet gash on his forearm, but that was nothing, just a stinging annoyance.

None of that mattered. Unless something happened, he was going to be dead in a few minutes, and a twisted leg and a nicked arm would be meaningless.

Henson saw the outlaw leader galloping alongside the train and angled his pistol toward the man. If he could bring the criminal down, he thought, his death would not be in vain.

Something crashed into the other wall of the car. As Henson rolled over and jerked his head around, he saw an axhead split the heavy wood. Bitterly, he realized that the outlaws had been keeping him busy while some of their companions chopped their way into the car from the other side. Within seconds, the bandits had hacked a fist-sized hole in the wall.

Henson fired toward it, his aim good. The bullets went through the hole and at least spooked somebody on the other side. He heard a man yelp.

He had neglected the original threat, though. One of the outlaws rode close to the shattered door of the car and emptied his six-gun through it. Two of the slugs punched through Ernie's back, driving him facedown on the floor. He jerked for a moment, then lay still, his gun slipping from his fingers. A big bloodstain blossomed on his white shirt.

The second group of outlaws, led by two men with axes, burst through the wall just as Walsh and several of his men climbed into the car through the door.

Walsh frowned at the sprawled body of the express messenger. "Should've been at least a couple of guards," he growled. "Something's wrong here."

As Walsh snapped orders, his men began ransacking the car. Quite a few packages were strewn around the inside of the car, packages that had been neatly stacked until the grinding collision. Walsh's men tore through them, casting aside the smaller ones.

"Dammit!" Walsh roared when it became apparent that he was not going to find what he was looking for. "That strongbox was supposed to be here!"

One of his men looked out the door of the express car and then hurried over to Walsh. "Looks like trouble, boss," he said anxiously. There was no mistaking the worried expression in his eyes.

"What is it?" Walsh barked.

"Looks like the passengers and what's left of the crew are putting up more of a fight than we expected. Some of our men are dead out there."

Tightly gripping his pistol, Walsh turned the muzzle toward Ernie Henson's body. For a moment, he seemed on the verge of pumping more rounds into the young man, for no other reason than to vent his rage. Then, instead, he rammed his gun back into its holster.

"We've been double-crossed," he said coldly. "And somebody's going to pay for it." He turned to another of his men. "Grab that express sack. There's bound to be a few hundred dollars in it." His voice was filled with bitterness at such a small payoff.

The sounds of the fighting were growing louder. As Walsh leaped down from the express car and ran to his horse, he saw the conductor and several passengers crouching behind some of the wreckage and shooting at the gang. Walsh swung into the saddle, sent a couple of slugs whistling toward the passengers, and then spurred his mount into a gallop.

"Let's get out of here!" he yelled to his men.

The outlaws who were already mounted abruptly halted their attack and peeled away from the train. The others hurried to their horses and quickly mounted. Within moments the bandits were lost in the cloud of dust kicked up by their horses. They left their dead behind, the bloody, motionless bodies sprawled on the ground.

The conductor and the passengers fired a few more rounds at the retreating outlaws. The bald-headed conductor, his cap gone, his uniform bloody and torn, glared and cursed, knowing that the shots would not reach their targets.

Then he turned and started running toward the ruined express car. As he reached the door, he spotted the express messenger's body and cried, "Henson!"

Incredibly, the young man stirred. A cough racked him, and he moaned as he slumped back to the floor. The conductor hopped into the car, hurried to the injured man's side, and gently turned him over. From the look of the wounds, the bullets had gone right through him.

"It'll be all right, Henson," the conductor said as the express messenger's eyes fluttered open.

"I . . . I saw him," Henson gasped. "It was . . . J-Jake Walsh. . . ."

"Yeah, I saw him, too," the conductor said. "It was that redheaded louse, all right." He patted Henson on the shoulder. "You rest easy, son. I'll try to get some help for you as soon as I've checked on the passengers. We've got a lot of people hurt."

Henson clutched at the conductor's sleeve as the man started to stand up. "Good thing we got word . . .

to unload that strongbox back in . . . in Abilene. Walsh must've heard. . . ."

"Reckon he must have," the conductor agreed grimly, thinking of the fifty thousand dollars that were sitting in the Abilene depot.

When the conductor returned to the express car with a doctor, he found to his surprise that Ernie Henson appeared to be stronger. The youth had lifted himself into a sitting position and had one shoulder propped against the wall of the car.

The doctor had been a passenger and had survived the crash with only a gash on his forehead. He had been tending to the broken arm of another passenger when the conductor located him.

As the doctor began to tend to his wounds, Henson frowned. "Looks like they got the express sack," he said. "Couple of hundred dollars, maybe. Couldn't have been much more than that."

The conductor grunted. "Not much money to wreck a train and kill fourteen people for, is it?"

Henson closed his eyes for a moment, wincing in pain at the doctor's probing fingers and at horror of the news brought by the conductor. "Fourteen people dead?" he said weakly.

"So far. Probably some more of them won't make it."

"Mooney and Bellem?"

The conductor shook his head.

Henson muttered a heartfelt curse. He had known and liked both of the railroad veterans.

The conductor knelt beside him. Henson bit his lip and paled as the doctor poured disinfectant on his wounds and then began to bandage them.

"Those are clean wounds," the doctor said wearily.

"Right straight through, both of them. You were lucky that they didn't hit anything vital. You ought to live, son, if the holes don't get infected, but you'll be off your feet for a long time."

"So will this railroad," the conductor said. "We're going to have to move this train and replace a good long section of track. There's not a repair train this side of Kansas City that I know of. It's going to take days, maybe over a week, before the railroad can use this stretch of track again."

"This young man is going to be disabled a lot longer than that," the doctor snapped.

"It's all right, Doc," Henson said. He looked up at the conductor. "Walsh was after that money, wasn't he?"

The conductor nodded slowly. "And now it's going to have to stay where it is for a while." His lips pulled back from his teeth in a humorless smile. "I wouldn't want to be the law in Abilene about now."

Chapter One

———◆———

On THE DAY AFTER THE TRAIN WRECK, JUST BEFORE noon, Marshal Luke Travis stood calmly waiting on the platform of the Kansas Pacific depot in Abilene. A tall man with a drooping brown mustache, Travis had tilted his tan, flat-crowned hat to shield his eyes from the sun. His lean, muscular frame was clothed in denim, and the walnut butt of the Colt on his hip was well worn. Travis's prowess with a gun was almost legendary in this part of the country. He was every inch the self-possessed, competent lawman that he appeared to be.

The poised marshal contrasted sharply with the anxious little man who paced up and down the platform near him. The man, wearing a brown suit and a string tie, was sweating in spite of the pleasant coolness of the morning air. He mopped drops of moisture from his forehead with a handkerchief and then nervously stuffed the cloth back in his pocket. Pulling a watch from his vest pocket, he frowned as he looked at it and said, "They should have been here by now."

"Take it easy, Harve," Travis told him. "There's no hurry. That train's not going any farther until they get the tracks repaired."

"You don't understand, Marshal," said Harvey Bastrop, Abilene's stationmaster. "This is Mr. Stockbridge's private train. He's going to be furious when he finds out that the track up ahead is closed." He stared along the tracks to the east as if his doom were scheduled to arrive at any moment.

News of the derailment and the robbery had reached Abilene in the hours just before dawn. A passing cowboy had discovered the wreck and had ridden hard through the night to bring the town news of the tragedy. He had found Deputy Cody Fisher at work in the marshal's office. Cody had awakened Travis to pass along the news, and Travis had carried the word to Bastrop. The stationmaster had immediately tried to wire back up the line to alert the special westbound express, but it was too late: Maxwell Stockbridge's train had already pulled out and was on its way to Abilene.

Since then, Bastrop had worked himself into such a nervous state that Travis wondered if the man was going to fall apart completely.

Now, as they waited for the train bearing the president and chief stockholder of the Kansas Pacific Railroad, Bastrop again wiped his forehead and said for the twelfth time, "I'm just glad they unloaded that strongbox here instead of taking it on with them."

Travis glanced over his shoulder toward the station building. Hours earlier, during their first conversation, Bastrop had shown him the strongbox. It was securely locked up in the station's safe, and Travis had deputized his friend, Orion McCarthy, to guard it.

"What do you suppose is in it?" Travis had asked an already frantic Bastrop.

"I have no idea," the stationmaster answered. "Money is the most likely possibility, of course. The telegram ordering us to take it off the train and hold it here was signed by Mr. Stockbridge himself. He said he would pick it up when his train came through Abilene on the way to San Francisco."

That train was due now, was in fact a little late, as Bastrop said. But the faint sound of a shrill whistle suddenly came to the ears of the two men waiting on the platform.

"That's it," Bastrop declared.

Travis straightened and moved to the edge of the platform. Peering down the tracks to the east, he focused on the small black dot that quickly resolved itself into an oncoming locomotive. The train eased its way past the Great Western Cattle Company stockyards on the edge of town. As it slowly rolled into the station, the engineer gave another blast on the whistle.

Travis had known it was a private train and had expected that it would be different from the long cattle or passenger trains that moved through Abilene. Nevertheless, he was surprised by its appearance. This train consisted only of an engine, a coal car, and a single passenger car, which was elaborately decorated with panels of rich wood on its sides and gleaming gilt scrollwork around the windows. It was clearly the vehicle of a wealthy, powerful man.

As the train came to a halt with a squeal of brakes and the hiss of steam, a man in a spotless, carefully creased conductor's uniform hopped down from the platform at the rear of the passenger car. He carried a wooden step, which he placed on the station platform to help the passengers disembark. Swallowing audibly, Harvey Bastrop walked to the step, nervously glancing over his shoulder to confirm that Travis was following him.

The first passenger off the train was an elegant man in his mid-fifties wearing an expensive suit and a gray homburg hat. He carried a silver-headed stick in his left hand, but his tall, well-knit frame showed no evidence of needing support in walking. His thick, salt-and-pepper hair and mustache were impeccably groomed, and his dark eyes were alert and intense. There was an air about him that said here was a man who got things done. Without a doubt, he was Maxwell Stockbridge.

Following closely behind him was another man, whose lean face resembled Stockbridge's although he was only half the age of the railroad president. His features were more handsome than Stockbridge's, and his smooth hair was blond. As he gazed around the station platform, his blue eyes showed the same piercing interest.

Harvey Bastrop extended his hand to the older man and said, "This is quite an honor, Mr. Stockbridge. I'm Harvey Bastrop. I run the station here in Abilene."

Maxwell Stockbridge gave Bastrop a brief handshake. "Pleased to meet you, Mr. Bastrop. Obviously, you knew I was coming."

"Oh, yes, sir. I got your telegram regarding the, ah, item you were concerned about. I handled that matter myself."

Stockbridge nodded in satisfaction. "Good, good."

He turned slightly to indicate the younger man. "This is my son, Richard."

Richard Stockbridge smiled and thrust out his hand to the stationmaster. "Glad to meet you, Mr. Bastrop," he said heartily. "We've had good reports on your work back at the main office."

"Thank you, sir." Bastrop was trying to keep the quaver out of his voice and was not succeeding very well.

Maxwell Stockbridge peered shrewdly at the sweating man and said, "Something seems to be bothering you, Mr. Bastrop. Is there a problem?"

Bastrop nodded jerkily. "This is Marshal Travis," he said, nodding toward the lawman.

Travis shook hands with Stockbridge, noting the railroad executive's firm grip. Stockbridge's hand did not feel as though it belonged to a man who spent all of his working hours behind a desk. "Hello," Travis said, keeping his tone neutral. "Afraid we've got some bad news for you, Mr. Stockbridge."

Stockbridge frowned quickly and looked back at Bastrop. "What is it?" he asked, his voice sharper now. "Spit it out, man."

"There . . . there was a holdup west of here, Mr. Stockbridge. Outlaws blew up the track and derailed the westbound train. They robbed the express car and shot up the train."

Stockbridge's nostrils flared as he drew in a quick breath of surprise. Beside him, his son appeared equally shocked. "How much did they get?" Richard asked.

"A few hundred dollars from the express sack, I imagine." Bastrop passed a hand over his face. "But that was all the train was carrying, as far as I know. I haven't talked to the messenger or the conductor yet.

We sent out a mounted rescue party at dawn, to help the survivors, but they haven't returned yet."

Stockbridge's jaw was tightly clamped, and a small muscle jumped under the skin. Anger flared in his eyes. "What about the passengers?" he asked. "How many were hurt?"

"I . . . I don't know. The man who brought word to us said that there were over a dozen people dead out there."

Stockbridge paled, and his hands clenched into fists. "Damn," he said softly, obviously shaken by the news. He took a deep breath. "I suppose it's a good thing I wired ahead about the strongbox."

Richard put a hand on his father's arm. "What about the strongbox, Father? Didn't the bandits get it, too?"

"It wasn't on the train," Stockbridge snapped. He hesitated, then said, "I sent a telegram instructing Bastrop to have it removed from the train and placed in the safe here. We're going to take it with us when we leave."

"That's the other thing, Mr. Stockbridge," Bastrop went on. "It's going to be several days, maybe as long as a week before the track will be repaired. I'm afraid you'll have to move your train onto the siding and wait here in Abilene."

Stockbridge's face flushed a dull brick-red, and he scowled in anger. "Wait for a week?" he thundered. "My business associates are waiting for me in San Francisco, Bastrop. More important, they're waiting for that fifty thousand dollars!"

"Hold on a minute," Travis cut in coolly. "Did you say fifty thousand?"

"That's right. It's in that strongbox, and we need it

to close a right-of-way deal in San Francisco, Marshal." Stockbridge swung back to face Bastrop. "There must be some way to speed things up or get around the damaged track."

Bastrop shook his head. "I . . . I wired Kansas City to send a work train immediately. That's all I know to do, Mr. Stockbridge."

"This is incredible," Stockbridge fumed. He switched his gaze to Travis. "Has anything been done about apprehending these criminals, Marshal?"

"That's out of my jurisdiction, Mr. Stockbridge," Travis said. "But I wired the U.S. marshal's office in Dodge City to let them know about the robbery. Since the mail in the express sack was taken, the federal authorities have jurisdiction over the case."

Stockbridge nodded. "Yes, yes, I suppose you're right. But you're much closer to the scene. Couldn't you have gotten up a posse to go after the bandits?"

Travis squared his shoulders. The harsh tone of Stockbridge's words rubbed him the wrong way, but he bit back the angry retort that sprang to his lips. Instead, he said, "By the time we learned about the robbery, those bandits could have ridden fifty miles or more in any direction. Chasing them would have been a waste of time."

"Listen here, Travis," Richard Stockbridge said angrily. "It sounds to me like you just didn't want to be bothered."

"Richard!" Maxwell Stockbridge snapped. "That's enough of that. We won't get anywhere harassing the local authorities."

"Yes, sir," Richard said dutifully, but he continued to glare at Travis.

Suddenly the tense conversation was interrupted by

a sweet voice from the rear platform of the railroad car. "Excuse me, gentlemen, but is this some sort of business meeting? Or are women allowed to join in?"

Travis looked up and saw a beautiful young woman standing on the platform and smiling down at them. She wore a stylish deep-green traveling suit and had a matching green hat with a rakish feather perched on her midnight-dark curls. She held a parasol to shield her fair skin from the sun. Travis guessed that she was a couple of years younger than Richard Stockbridge, and her features strongly resembled his. Then he saw another woman move onto the platform behind her. She was younger still, perhaps nineteen or twenty, with blond hair that was cut short and no hat. While not as classically beautiful as the older woman, she was very attractive in a coltish way.

Stockbridge sighed. "Gentlemen," he said, struggling to be polite under the trying circumstances. "Allow me to present my daughters, Dorothea and Holly."

The dark-haired woman came down the steps, her green eyes boldly appraising Travis. She smiled at the marshal and extended a gloved hand to him. "I'm Dorothea," she said, "and you're the local marshal, aren't you?"

"That's right, ma'am," he said. "I'm Luke Travis." He was not used to shaking hands with women, but he took Dorothea's fingers for a moment. The blond woman, Holly, just nodded to him and said a shy hello.

Maxwell Stockbridge turned to his daughters and asked, "Where's Perkins?"

Dorothea answered, "Dear Edwin is still working, Father. I couldn't tear him away from that desk and his paperwork, even when I said I wanted him to show me around this cow town I've heard so much about."

"It looks like you'll have plenty of time, Dorothea," Richard said. "We're going to be stuck here for a week."

Dorothea looked at her father. "Is Richard telling the truth? He can't be. We can't stay in a dusty place like this for a whole week, Father. We just can't!"

"I'm afraid he's right, my dear," Stockbridge said. "There has been some damage to the tracks west of here, and we shall have to wait for it to be repaired." He shot a meaningful glance at the other men, warning them that he did not want the two young women alarmed by the full story of the robbery.

Travis looked at the younger sister, Holly, and saw that she did not seem disappointed in the delay. She was looking with interest and curiosity past the station at the row of saloons that lined the dusty length of Railroad Street. *The Elkhorn, the Pearl, and the Salty Dog must look quite disreputable to a young girl from the East,* he thought.

Stockbridge turned to Richard. "Get Perkins out here," the railroad executive commanded his son sharply. "He needs to know about this."

Richard nodded and quickly went back into the private car. He reappeared a moment later with a tall, thin, bespectacled man who was shrugging into his coat. His fingers bore ink stains, Travis noted, and his shoulders were slightly stooped.

"My assistant, Edwin Perkins." Stockbridge performed the perfunctory introduction.

"And my fiancé," Dorothea spoke up, taking Perkins's arm.

That revelation surprised Travis. Perkins was considerably older than Dorothea, probably in his mid-thirties. He had rust-colored hair and a bushy mustache, and he was hardly what anyone would call handsome. *Not the type of man you would expect to be engaged to a belle like Dorothea Stockbridge,* Travis thought.

"We've got trouble, Perkins," Stockbridge said brusquely. "I'll tell you about it in a moment." He turned to Harvey Bastrop. "Mr. Bastrop, would you mind taking my daughters into the station and making them comfortable? This dusty platform is hardly the place for young ladies."

"Of course," Bastrop agreed hurriedly. With quick, nervous movements, he ushered Dorothea and Holly Stockbridge toward the entrance of the depot.

"What's wrong, sir?" Perkins asked softly when the two young women were out of earshot.

Stockbridge told him all he knew about the robbery, including the report of injuries and deaths among the passengers.

"My God," Perkins breathed, hard hit by the news. "Those poor people."

"At least they didn't get the strongbox and the money," Richard put in.

Travis spoke up. "That's what I want to talk to you about, Mr. Stockbridge. I don't much like the idea of fifty thousand dollars sitting in the safe in that depot."

"Neither do I," Stockbridge replied. "That's why we're going to move it—as soon as I've checked it."

Travis frowned. "Where are you intending to put it?"

"I have the most modern, secure safe in the country on board that train, Marshal," Stockbridge explained. "The money will be just fine in it."

"All right," Travis agreed, nodding.

Bastrop was coming back out of the station. Stockbridge started toward him, saying over his shoulder to Richard and Perkins, "Come along, both of you."

They followed closely behind him. Travis trailed along, taking his time. Stockbridge had not asked for his help, but if they were going to move a strongbox with fifty thousand dollars in it, he was going to make certain that nothing went wrong.

Stockbridge spoke to Bastrop, and the two of them went into the station with Richard and Perkins. Travis went through the big double doors a moment later and saw the four men going behind the ticket counter and into the office area, where the station's safe was located. Orion McCarthy, whom Travis had instructed to guard the safe, was still there.

On the other side of the big main room, Dorothea and Holly were sitting on one of the long wooden benches that lined the walls of the station. Dorothea looked distinctly uncomfortable and unhappy. Holly, on the other hand, was looking around the interior of the depot with cheerful interest. She seemed a little shy with strangers, but from the look in her eyes, Travis could tell that she was curious about them.

The door on the street side of the station opened, and a middle-aged man in a rumpled coat came in. Travis recognized him as one of the local drunks who spent most of his time across the street in the Elkhorn Saloon. The man liked to wander over to the station from time to time to watch the trains. Now he was staring in openmouthed admiration at the two pretty young strangers who were sitting on the bench.

Travis moved quickly across the room and caught the man's arm. "No trains coming in or leaving now, Jeff," he said. "You might as well go look for something else to do."

"But I heard a whistle a while ago, Marshal," the man said, blinking his bleary eyes and trying to look past Travis's shoulder at Dorothea and Holly.

"That train's already in, and it's not going to be leaving anytime soon. Now you just move on, all right? I don't want to have to toss you in a cell."

"All right, all right, Marshal," Jeff muttered. "Who's the gals?"

"Nobody you need to know," Travis told him firmly. He steered the drunk out of the station.

"Thank you, Marshal," Dorothea said when Travis stepped back into the depot. "I was afraid that horrible man was going to come over and try to talk to us."

"Jeff's harmless enough, as long as you're not downwind of him," Travis said as he walked over to the two young women. "I'm sorry you've run into this delay, ladies."

"It is dreadful," Dorothea sighed. "But I suppose we shall just have to endure it. Isn't that right, Holly?"

"It's not so bad," Holly replied quietly. "I like the West, Dorothea. You just won't give it a chance."

Dorothea sniffed delicately and then smiled up at Travis. "I'm afraid my sister is a bit of a tomboy, Marshal. She fancies the rugged western way of life, and she's been trying for the longest time to get Father to move to San Francisco."

"I like San Francisco," Holly protested.

"Better than Chicago?"

"Well, yes, I do. And you would, too, Dorothea."

Travis smiled. "It's none of my business, ma'am, but I've heard that San Francisco is quite a nice town. Real civilized."

"Perhaps." Dorothea shrugged prettily. "I suppose I'll find out . . . if we ever get there. It seems as though we've been traveling forever across this wretched frontier." Her eyes suddenly lit up, recapturing the spark Travis had seen in them when she first got off the train. "Waiting here might not be so bad after all. I suppose you have all sorts of outlaws and cowboys and gunmen and Indians in the vicinity, don't you, Marshal?"

Travis's smile widened. She sounded like an excited child. "Well, ma'am, we do have some outlaws around every now and then, although I try to keep them out of town when I can. You'll see a lot of cowboys, but you won't find them as glamorous as you may have heard. They're just plain, hardworking men. And the only Indians around here are civilized ones. Hasn't been a savage on the streets since I've been here."

"Now you're making fun of me," Dorothea said, pouting, though her eyes were still smiling.

Before Travis could confirm or deny her accusation, the door of Bastrop's office opened, and the station-master called to him, "Would you mind stepping in here, Marshal?"

Travis nodded warily. He tipped his hat to the Stockbridge sisters. "Nice talking to you, ladies," he said as he turned away.

Inside the office, Stockbridge and Richard were standing beside a large open strongbox. Edwin Perkins knelt next to it, counting the money that was stacked inside it. To one side, Orion McCarthy leaned against the wall, a short-barreled shotgun cradled in his arms. He was a short, burly, middle-aged man with a grayish-red beard and a quick smile. The proprietor of Orion's Tavern, he was also one of Luke Travis's best friends in Abilene.

"Everything quiet in here, Orion?" Travis asked.

"Aye," the brawny Scotsman answered.

Bastrop went to Stockbridge's side and said, "I assure you, all the money is there, Mr. Stockbridge. No one has disturbed the box since we took it off the train yesterday."

"We're just checking, Mr. Bastrop," the railroad president replied crisply. "It's good business to be careful when it comes to money, you know that."

"Yes, sir."

Perkins looked up. "Fifty thousand, just as we packed it back in Chicago, sir."

Stockbridge nodded. "Lock it back up, Perkins."

The assistant closed the lid of the strongbox and slid a heavy padlock through the hasp. It clicked shut with a solid sound.

Stockbridge took off his coat and handed it to Richard. As Travis watched in puzzlement, Stockbridge began to roll up the sleeves of his fine white shirt. Stockbridge glanced up, met Travis's eyes, and said, "Would you mind giving me a hand, Marshal? I want to get this box onto my train."

Travis nodded and moved to the other end of the strongbox and stooped slightly to grasp the handle attached to it.

Stockbridge took the other end. "All right," he said when his grip on the handle was secure.

Both men grunted as they lifted the heavy container. The money inside was fairly weighty by itself, and the strongbox was thickly lined with metal. It was quite a burden, but nothing the two men could not manage.

As they started toward the office door, Orion stepped forward quickly. "Lemme get tha' f'ye, Lucas."

Travis shook his head. "No, thanks," he said tautly. "I've got it."

Bastrop scurried to open the door, and Travis and

Stockbridge carried the strongbox out of the office, through the depot, and across the station platform. Stockbridge backed up the steps to the private car, Travis following with his share of the load.

The interior of the car was every bit as opulent and luxurious as its exterior, Travis saw. A large sitting area with a long divan and several armchairs took up the rear section. Ornate oil lamps were mounted on the walls, and a thick rug covered the floor. A partition with a door in it separated the sitting area from the rest of the car, and through the open door Travis saw a narrow corridor that ran the remaining length of the car. More doors opened off the corridor.

Still bearing their load, the two men crossed the sitting area and went down the hall. At Stockbridge's direction they turned into one of the doors, which brought them into an office. There was a desk at one side of the cubicle, papers stacked neatly on it, and Travis guessed this was where Edwin Perkins had been working when the train arrived. The other side of the office was taken up by a massive iron safe, the intricate gilt lettering on its door declaring it to be a product of the Slesar-Malone Company.

"Finest safe made," Stockbridge grunted as he lowered his end of the strongbox and Travis did likewise. Then Stockbridge bent to work the combination lock on the safe while Richard Perkins stood in the doorway of the office.

When Stockbridge had the door open, he and Travis once again picked up the strongbox and slid it into the safe. With a sigh of satisfaction, the railroad president closed the door and spun the dial of the lock.

"That's that," he said, straightening. "Thank you, Marshal."

"Glad to help," Travis replied. As far as he could

tell, Stockbridge was not breathing very hard from his labors, though the marshal was left panting.

"What do we do now?" Richard asked.

"I suppose we might as well make arrangements to stay in the local hotel," Stockbridge said as he rolled down his sleeves and took his coat from his son. "I daresay it will be more comfortable than our accommodations here on the train."

"I wouldn't guarantee that," Travis said with a smile. "But you're welcome to give it a try, Mr. Stockbridge."

Bastrop appeared in the corridor, clearly nervous at being in this luxurious private car. "There're riders coming from the west, Marshal," he announced. "Might be the rescue party returning from the wreck."

Travis hurried out of the railroad car and strode to the end of the station platform, the other men following behind him. He peered down Railroad Street to where it merged with Texas Street, and he saw a group of men slowly riding on horseback into town. Behind them came several buckboards. The slow-moving group was raising quite a cloud of dust.

Travis spotted Deputy Cody Fisher's horse in the lead. Cody had led the rescue party that started out as soon as the news had reached them. *They must have ridden hard to be back this soon,* Travis thought. He had a feeling that they were not bringing good news.

Chapter Two

———◆———

As Deputy Cody Fisher walked his tired pinto into Abilene, he reflexively scanned the streets and buildings. Immediately he noticed the small train standing at the depot, the gilt on the ornate passenger car glinting in the midday sun. Standing next to the car was the lean, denim-clad figure of the marshal. Normally Cody would smile and wave at Luke Travis, but today the grim news he carried and the sorry procession he led weighed heavily on him.

The deputy was more tired than he had been in a very long time. He had been working an all-night shift in the marshal's office when the drifting cowboy brought word of the train disaster. He had gathered the rescue party and led the long, breakneck ride to the site of the wreck. Cody knew this country, knew the shortcuts available to horses and wagons that were denied to the railroad, and the group of rescuers had made good time. If they had only found something better when they arrived at their destination . . .

Cody had never seen a derailed train before, and the extent of the damage was astonishing to him. The train was crumpled like some discarded toy.

In one of the cars that was not too heavily damaged, sixteen bodies had been laid side by side. They were draped with sheets, coats, and anything else that could be found to cover the bloody ruins that had once been human. The engineer, the fireman, and one brakeman were among them, but the rest were all passengers.

Nothing could be done for the dead, but the many injured needed attention.

Dr. Aileen Bloom, the younger of the town's two physicians, had insisted on joining the rescue party. Cody knew that Luke Travis had started to talk her out of it, but the marshal had stopped when he realized that she would be needed. Besides, once Aileen got an idea in her head, there was no dissuading her from it.

Aileen was still out at the scene of the wreck, doing what she could for the passengers who were too badly hurt to be moved. The ones who were less severely injured had been sent back to Abilene in the wagons that now rolled down Railroad Street behind the deputy.

Cody Fisher drew his horse to a stop by the steps leading to the station platform. Dust coated his dark clothes, but he made no effort to brush it away. Instead he pushed his hat back and cocked a leg around the saddle horn to ease the strain in his muscles after the long ride.

Travis studied his deputy's grim face. "Pretty bad?" Travis asked.

Cody nodded, glancing past the marshal at the

private train and the men who were waiting with Travis. Cody recognized Orion and Bastrop, but the fellows in suits were strangers to him.

"Real bad," he said. He inclined his head to indicate the wagons that had continued past the depot down Texas Street toward Aileen Bloom's office. Her mentor, the semi-retired Dr. Levi Wright, was waiting there to receive any injured patients that Aileen sent in from the wreck. Cody went on, "By the time we got there, two more people had died. That brought the total so far to sixteen. And that train's a complete wreck."

"Good Lord," the tall, middle-aged man next to Travis breathed. His face was haggard.

"Cody, this is Maxwell Stockbridge," Travis said. "He's the president of the Kansas Pacific. And this is his son, Richard, and his assistant, Mr. Perkins. My deputy, Cody Fisher."

Cody nodded to the men, all of whom were pale and shaken by the news he brought. He wondered briefly what such men were doing in Abilene, but he was too tired to worry about that for more than a few seconds.

"We brought the express messenger in," Cody went on. "He's badly shot up, but Dr. Bloom says he'll probably be all right. The conductor wasn't hurt, so he wanted to stay out there for a while."

Travis nodded. "We'll want to talk to the messenger."

"I've already talked with him some. He says the leader of the gang that hit them was Jake Walsh."

"Walsh!" Richard Stockbridge exclaimed. "That— that bandit! When is the law going to catch up with him?"

"As soon as we can, Mr. Stockbridge," Travis said firmly. "We'd best go talk to that messenger. Cody, I know you're pretty worn out, but I've got another job for you."

Cody suppressed a groan. "Sure, Marshal. What is it?"

"There's a couple of young women waiting inside the station. They're Mr. Stockbridge's daughters, and I want you to see to it that they get to the hotel all right with their baggage. Orion will help you."

Cody opened his mouth to protest, but then the implications of Travis's words sank into his tired brain. Two young women, and daughters of a rich man, at that. He said, "I expect I can handle that."

"Figured you could," Travis said dryly.

Travis, Stockbridge, Richard, and Perkins cut across on Cedar Street to Texas Street, then followed the plank boardwalk to Aileen Bloom's office. The neat little house was set back slightly from the street, behind a well-cared-for and attractively planted yard. A sign with Aileen's name on it, indicating the location of her practice, hung by the boardwalk.

Richard Stockbridge frowned at the name. "You have a female doctor?" he asked Travis.

"You won't find a better one, male or female, in all of Kansas," Travis declared. In the time he had been in Abilene, he had continued to be impressed by Aileen Bloom, her medical skill, her humanitarianism —and her beauty.

He led the way down the walk and into the house. As they entered, all four men were struck by harsh, pain-filled sobs coming from one of the examining rooms.

Several people were waiting in the front room, men and women and a few children with bloodstained bandages or rough splints marking their injuries.

Travis's face tightened into an angry mask at the sight of them. These people were strangers to him, yet he felt a surge of fury at the outlaws who had caused their pain.

Dr. Levi Wright, a tall, spare man with gray hair and a neat beard, came out of one of the examining rooms, the room where the crying was coming from. Wright was rubbing his hands with a bloody cloth. As he looked up and saw Travis, he grunted.

"May have saved the man's life, but I had to take his leg off," Wright said. "God-awful business, Marshal. I haven't seen so many hideous injuries since the war."

"I know, Doctor." Travis nodded. "Cody said he brought in the express messenger from the train. Do you think we could talk to him?"

"No reason not to." Wright indicated the hall that led out of the front room. "He's in the second room on the right. I looked him over, but I didn't have to do anything. Aileen had him patched up just fine. Better see him now if you want any sensible answers to your questions. When I left him he was sucking on a bottle of Orion's best anesthetic."

Despite the grimness of the situation, Travis smiled slightly at the old doctor's acerbic tone. With his gruff exterior Wright was hard to get to know, but Travis knew that the gruffness was a protective shell. Levi Wright genuinely cared about the people he treated.

Nodding his thanks, Travis led the three men down the hall and rapped on the door of the room where the express messenger was resting. Without waiting for an answer, Travis swung the door open and stepped through.

A dark-haired young man with an honest, open face looked up from the bed. He was half sitting, propped up by several pillows. His torso was swathed with tight bandages. In his hand was a bottle of whiskey, and there was a bleary-eyed smile on his face.

"Howdy," he said. "You gentlemen come to have a drink?"

"No thanks, son," Travis replied. "You're the express messenger from the train?"

"That's right, Marshal. Ernie Henson's the name. I'd offer to shake hands, but it hurts a little to raise my arms too much." Despite the half-empty bottle, the young man's voice was clear, and he had his wits about him.

"That's all right, Mr. Henson. I'm Luke Travis, the marshal of Abilene. This gentleman is Mr. Maxwell Stockbridge, the president of—"

"I know who Mr. Stockbridge is," Henson cut in, turning pale. "I—I'm sorry, sir. We fought back as best we could. . . ."

Stockbridge moved to the side of the bed. "I know you did, Henson," he said sympathetically. "But the important thing now is what you can tell us about the bandits who committed this atrocity."

"I saw him plain," Henson declared. "He was wearing a bandanna over his face, but it couldn't cover up that red beard. It was Jake Walsh, all right."

"You're sure?" Richard Stockbridge asked curtly.

"I've seen plenty of wanted posters on him," Henson replied. "It was Walsh."

"Did they use dynamite on the tracks?" Travis asked.

Henson nodded. "I can't be sure, of course, but that would be my guess. It sure was an awful blast, I know that. Ben Mooney never had a chance to stop."

Perkins spoke up. "Mr. Mooney was the engineer, is that correct?"

"Yes, sir. He survived the wreck, but he was killed

in the fighting with the outlaws. I heard that Jake Walsh himself shot him."

Travis shook his head. "Sounds like Walsh. He's supposed to be pretty cold-blooded. Did you catch those bullets when they stormed the express car?"

"That's right. Walsh and some of his men attacked the door, while some others chopped their way through the back wall with an ax. I . . . I tried to stop them."

"I'm sure you did all you could," Stockbridge said.

"What happened after they looted the express car?" Travis asked.

"Well, you've got to understand that I had passed out by that time. From what I've been told, the passengers started putting up a fight. Walsh and his men hightailed it."

"Do you know what direction they were heading when they lit out?"

Henson shook his head. "No, Marshal, I don't. I imagine they went west."

Travis patted the young man's shoulder and said, "Thanks, Henson. You get some rest now, and don't go too heavy on that painkiller."

Henson grinned and then winced as he lifted the bottle. "I won't, sir."

The four men left the room, filed down the hallway, and walked out of the house and into the sunshine. When they were back on the boardwalk outside, Stockbridge sighed heavily and said, "What do you suggest we do now, Marshal?"

"There's not much you can do except wait for those tracks to be repaired, Mr. Stockbridge, and then go on to San Francisco, like you planned. As bad as this holdup was, it could have been worse. At least you've still got that fifty thousand dollars of yours."

Richard Stockbridge spoke up. "I want to talk to you about that, Father," he said sharply. "I'd like to know why I wasn't informed of the change in plans. I had no idea that strongbox was being taken off the other train and held for ours."

"It was my decision, Richard." Stockbridge's voice was cold. "We originally decided to ship the money separately for security reasons. That's also why I changed the plan, just in case anyone had gotten wind of it."

"But I'm an executive vice-president of the Kansas Pacific," Richard protested. "Surely that decision didn't have to be kept a secret from me!"

Stockbridge turned toward his son with a frown. "This is hardly the place to be discussing company business," he snapped. He glanced at Travis standing nearby.

The marshal held up his hands. "Don't mind me," he said. "I'll just take you down to the hotel," he added, gesturing toward the Grand Palace, which stood next to Aileen Bloom's office. The building did not quite live up to its name, but it was a comfortable enough place to stay.

As Travis turned away, he heard Maxwell Stockbridge saying to Richard, "There's no reason for you to get your feelings hurt. I didn't tell anyone about the change in plans, not even Perkins here. And he's my personal assistant, not to mention my future son-in-law. Your feelings aren't hurt, are they, Perkins?"

"No, sir," Perkins answered dutifully.

Travis shook his head as he started down the boardwalk. He would not want to trade places with either Richard Stockbridge or Edwin Perkins. From the sound of things, Maxwell Stockbridge was accustomed to getting his own way and having his decisions unquestioned.

Travis wondered how he treated his daughters.

After Travis, Stockbridge, and the others had left for Dr. Bloom's office, Cody turned in his saddle and spoke to the men who had come back with him. "You boys can head home now. There's nothing else you can do. Thanks for riding out there with me."

"Sure thing, Deputy," one of them replied. They nodded tiredly and turned their horses to disperse.

Cody slid from the saddle and with a practiced flick of the wrist wound his mount's reins around the hitching post next to the station building. He climbed the steps onto the platform and joined Orion McCarthy.

"I guess I'll collect the young ladies while you get their bags," Cody said to Orion.

"Aye, an' tha' decision dinna surprise me," Orion said, his tone mocking.

Cody grinned, the expression relieving the naturally grim cast of his features. A faint, jagged scar on his right cheek, the souvenir of a past battle, made him look dangerous. But with a smile lighting his face, the scar was a reminder of his brash youth.

"I just figured the young ladies would prefer being escorted by someone closer to their own age," he said smoothly.

"Aye," Orion muttered laconically, leaning the shotgun against his shoulder. But he was smiling as he turned toward the train.

Cody walked into the station building, the spurs on his boots jingling musically. He immediately spotted the two young women sitting on one of the benches.

The deputy's hand went to his dusty black hat and swept it off his head. With the smile still on his face, he said, "Howdy, ladies. I'm Deputy Cody Fisher, and Marshal Travis told me to make sure you got over to the hotel all right."

His eyes scanned the young women in appreciation. The older of the two, the one with lush black curls, returned his smile and lifted her hand, extending it to him. "I'm Dorothea Stockbridge," she purred smoothly, "and I'm very pleased to meet you, Deputy Fisher."

"Call me Cody," he said, taking her gloved hand. He wondered for an instant if he was supposed to kiss it, but he decided to shake it instead. That seemed to satisfy Dorothea Stockbridge.

"And this is my sister, Holly," Dorothea completed the introductions.

"Ma'am," he greeted Holly.

"Hello, Deputy," she replied, with a slight nod.

Holly met Cody's eyes with a forthright gaze. He imagined that she had spent most of her life in her charming older sister's shadow. But she was different from her sister and an appealing young woman in her own right. He found himself liking both of them right away.

Dorothea stood up, twirling her closed parasol in her fingers. "I suppose we should proceed to this hotel of yours, Cody. I would like to freshen up. It seems as if we've been waiting in this dusty old station for hours."

"Yes, ma'am." Cody glanced over his shoulder and saw Orion entering the station. His arms were loaded with bags, and his shotgun was tucked under one arm.

"I kinna carry all o' the valises," he announced, "but I can come back later f'the rest o' them."

"That's fine," Cody said. He offered his arm to Dorothea Stockbridge, hoping he did not smell too bad after the long ride he had just finished. "Ladies? If you'll come along with me?"

Dorothea took his arm, and Holly fell in behind them. Orion, struggling with the baggage, brought up the rear.

Following the same route Travis and the others had taken, they walked down Cedar Street toward Texas Street, Abilene's main thoroughfare. Seely's General Store and the Northcraft Drug Store were on the opposite side of the street. As they proceeded down the boardwalk on this side, they passed the town's public well.

Gesturing at the well, Cody said to Dorothea, "You've heard of Wild Bill Hickok? A few years ago, right there at that well, he and a gambler, Phil Coe, finally had it out. The bullets were flying that night, from what I've heard."

"How thrilling!" Dorothea said excitedly. "It must have been a really magnificent fray!"

"So magnificent that Marshal Hickok accidentally shot one of his own deputies," Holly put in from behind them. "I read all about it in the newspaper accounts back home."

"Oh, Holly, you're making that up," Dorothea said accusingly. "I've heard all about Wild Bill Hickok. He was a hero. He wouldn't have shot one of his own men."

"Aye, he did," Orion said. "'Twas 'afore Cody here came t'Abilene. Folks say Hickok could'na see too good by then, and poor Mike Williams came up behind him too fast." The tavern keeper shook his shaggy head. "'Twas a tragedy, all right."

"Well, I still think Wild Bill was a hero," Dorothea

said stubbornly. "I think it takes a brave man to wear a badge out here on this savage frontier." She squeezed Cody's arm meaningfully.

Cody's weariness had fled. It would catch up to him later, he knew, but for the time being, the presence of the Stockbridge sisters—especially Dorothea—had revitalized him.

Texas Street bustled with a fair amount of traffic. Wagons, buckboards, and men on horseback all moved past, some of the riders nodding to Cody. A few of the pedestrians greeted him, too. Cody maintained a firm grip on Dorothea's arm as he led her across the street to the boardwalk on the other side and continued west to the hotel.

Dorothea looked up at the sign on the building they were passing. "The Old Fruit Saloon," she read. "What a colorful name!"

"It's a pretty colorful place, too," Cody said. "Of course, a lady like you wouldn't be interested in what goes on in a saloon."

"Oh, I wouldn't know about that," Dorothea murmured.

Cody saw motion out of the corner of his eye as they passed the batwings, and he suddenly threw himself backward, pulling Dorothea with him. She gasped as a shape hurtled from the saloon, sailed across the boardwalk, and landed heavily in the dusty street.

The man who had been thrown from the saloon rolled over, groggily shaking his head. His big Stetson had come off and lay in the street beside him, and he wore filthy range clothes. Cody recognized him as one of the cowboys who regularly brought herds up the trail from Texas.

Another man swaggered through the batwings and onto the sidewalk in front of Cody and Dorothea. He laughed harshly and said, "That'll be a lesson to you, Slater. Stay the hell outa saloons where real men are drinkin'."

The cowboy in the street got onto his hands and knees and then surged to his feet. As he did so, he unleashed a stream of foul language. Dorothea Stockbridge gasped again and tightened her grasp on Cody's arm.

Cody gently disengaged his arm and stepped forward, his face hard and angry. He moved between the two cowboys and said sharply, "Here now! There's no call for fighting or cussing like that!"

The man on the boardwalk cast a rather disinterested look his way. He was a cowhand, too, but a little older than the man in the street, in his early thirties perhaps. His clothes and gear were a little better as well, indicating that he probably rode for a different outfit than the first man.

"You'd better stay out of what don't concern you, sonny," the older cowboy drawled. "This's between me and that piece of trash in the street there."

"Who you callin' trash, Garvin?" the young man named Slater demanded in a howl.

Before Garvin, the older cowboy, could answer, Cody said sharply, "This does concern me. I'm the deputy marshal here in Abilene. If you don't break this up and move along, you're both going to wind up in jail."

Garvin turned toward Cody, his eyes narrowed. He shifted the toothpick he was chewing from one side of his mouth to the other and said around the sliver of wood, "Star-packer, eh? I always did hate a man who hid behind a badge."

Cody felt his anger flaring, but he made a concerted effort to control it. He was a lawman now, not the desperado he had almost become before meeting Luke Travis. He could not go around starting fights with obnoxious cowhands. He would make one more try at settling things peaceably. "Look, I'm warning you—" he started to say.

With another growled curse, Garvin swung a meaty fist at Cody's head. Then Slater yelled, "Stay out of it, you bastard!" and flung himself at Cody's knees.

Slater tackled Cody, upsetting him and knocking him backward, causing Garvin's punch to miss. Dorothea Stockbridge screamed as the fight started. She was going to see a real frontier fracas firsthand.

Cody sent a punch at Slater's head, the fist cracking against the cowboy's jaw and knocking loose his grip around Cody's knees. The deputy rolled away from him and started to his feet, but Garvin lunged forward, wrapping his arms around Cody.

"We'll finish our fight later," Garvin grunted to Slater. "Right now let's teach this pup a lesson!"

Slater came to his feet and drove a fist at Cody's stomach. The breath puffed out of Cody's lungs as the blow thudded into his belly.

Holly Stockbridge turned to Orion with an anxious look on her face and said, "Shouldn't you try to stop them?"

"Aye, I will," Orion answered with a grin. "When an' if the lad needs me to."

Struggling in Garvin's bear hug, Cody lifted a booted foot with the spur fastened on it and raked backward. The rowel dug into Garvin's upper calf, just above the top of his boot. The man howled in pain and loosened his grip on Cody for a moment.

That was the opening Cody needed. He rammed an elbow into Garvin's middle and twisted out of his grasp, jerking his head to the side to avoid another punch from Slater. Cody's arm hooked forward, the fist sinking into Slater's belly. The cowboy's whiskey-laden breath gusted into Cody's face. The deputy grimaced and threw a hard right cross that caught the point of Slater's chin.

Cody barely noticed Slater's eyes as they rolled up in his head. By the time the cowboy fell to the boardwalk, Cody was already spinning to meet a renewed charge from Garvin. The older puncher was the more dangerous of the two, Cody realized, himself a hardened veteran of countless barroom brawls.

Cody flung up an arm and blocked Garvin's punch, feeling the impact all the way up to his shoulder. He threw a blow of his own, but Garvin was able to slip it off. For a long minute, the two men traded punches, most of them missing. The ones that did connect were glancing blows that did not do much damage.

Garvin then tried a new tactic. Ducking inside one of Cody's punches, he lifted his knee and tried to drive it into Cody's groin. The deputy twisted desperately, taking the knee on his thigh. Cody's hand flashed down and grasped Garvin's leg. He heaved up and to the side, upending the cowboy.

Garvin let out a yell as he flew backward. The cry was cut off abruptly as he landed heavily on his back, the planks of the boardwalk clattering as he crashed onto them. He landed at Dorothea Stockbridge's feet. She had both hands pressed to her mouth, and her eyes were wide and shining with excitement.

Muttering a curse, Garvin sat up and reached for his gun.

"I would'na do tha' if I was ye, laddie," Orion rumbled. He leaned forward and prodded Garvin in the shoulder with the shotgun.

Garvin froze, his hand still a couple of inches away

from the butt of his gun. He glanced up at Orion's solemn face, then looked at Cody. The deputy was poised in the gunfighter's half crouch, his hand hovering over his pearl-handled Colt. Garvin swallowed and slowly moved his outspread fingers away from his gun.

"Aye, ye'd have been dead by now, had I not stopped ye," Orion told him.

Cody drew a deep breath and forced himself to relax. He straightened and said, "Why don't you pick yourself up, mister, and apologize to the ladies?"

Slowly Garvin climbed to his feet and brushed some of the dust off his clothes. Without meeting the eyes of the Stockbridge sisters, he muttered, "Reckon I'm sorry if I offended you."

Dorothea smiled. "Oh, that's all right."

Holly said nothing.

"Now get your friend off the sidewalk and out of here," Cody went on, gesturing to the sprawled shape of Slater. The young cowboy was still out cold.

"Sure, sure," Garvin said. He went past Cody and grabbed Slater under the arms, awkwardly lifting him and steering him into the Old Fruit Saloon. Inside quite a few men had been watching the fight through the window, and now they gathered around Garvin to slap him on the back.

Cody shook his head and went over to the others. "I'm sorry you ladies had to see that," he said. "Abilene's not always so rough."

"Don't worry about that," Dorothea assured him. "It was positively thrilling. It was just like watching Wild Bill Hickok taming the town."

"Not hardly." Cody grinned. "Come on. Maybe we can get to the hotel without any more wars breaking out." As they started down the boardwalk again, Cody said dryly to Orion, "Thanks for the help back there. I mean, pitching in right away when those yahoos first jumped me."

"Ye looked like ye had the situation well in hand." Orion grinned back at him. "And I did'na let the varmint shoot ye."

Cody chuckled and rubbed his knuckles.

When they reached the Grand Palace Hotel, Cody handled the checking-in while Dorothea and Holly looked around the lobby. Dorothea was quite obviously unimpressed. She was undoubtedly accustomed to much more luxury.

Cody engaged a room for the sisters, one for Maxwell Stockbridge, and one for Richard Stockbridge. That exhausted the supply of available rooms, except for a small chamber in back of the lobby that was sometimes used for storage. There was a cot in it.

"We can take that one for Edwin," Dorothea said as she strolled over to the desk in time to hear the last of the conversation between Cody and the clerk.

"It'll have to do," Cody said.

Orion started up the stairs, carrying the bags to the rooms. Footsteps on the boardwalk outside drew Cody's attention. He glanced over his shoulder and saw Travis and the other men passing in front of the lobby window. Then they entered the lobby through the open doors of the hotel.

Maxwell Stockbridge immediately strode over to his daughters and asked, "Have the rooms been engaged?"

"Yes, Father," Holly answered. "Mr. McCarthy is taking some of the bags up now."

"Good, good." Stockbridge nodded. "You girls go on up. We'll join you later."

Dorothea turned to Cody and said, "I'm sure I'll be

seeing you later, Deputy Fisher. Be careful now. The next time you apprehend a desperado, I want to see it."

Cody grinned at her. "I'll see what I can do about that," he said.

The two young women disappeared up the stairs, and Stockbridge growled, "I could use a drink." He took a cigar from an inside pocket of his coat and placed it in his mouth, waiting for Perkins to strike a match and light it for him.

Orion was coming back down the stairs. He heard Stockbridge's statement and said, "'Tis not fancy, but me tavern serves the best Scotch whisky ye'll find, Mr. Stockbridge."

"Sounds good to me," Stockbridge said. With Richard and Perkins following him, he walked out of the hotel with Orion.

"Any trouble getting over here?" Travis asked Cody in a quiet voice.

Cody shrugged. "Not much. Little fracas with a couple of cowboys who'd been drinking too much. I handled it."

"And Miss Dorothea probably enjoyed watching."

"That she did." Cody grinned. "I think she likes me, Marshal."

Travis pushed back his hat. "I guess you know she's engaged to that Perkins fellow," he said.

Cody frowned. "Engaged?" he exclaimed. "To that jasper who looks like a pencil pusher?"

"I'm afraid so."

"Well, I'll be," Cody said, shaking his head ruefully. "You'd never know it, to hear her talk."

"Just watch your step around her," Travis warned him. "Her father's a very important man and probably expects his daughter will be treated well. I'm going back to the office now, and you'd probably better get some sleep."

"Sounds like a good idea."

Travis nodded and left the hotel lobby. Cody was a few steps behind him, and he was about to move through the doors when he heard a voice softly calling his name.

He turned to see Dorothea Stockbridge coming down the stairs. She had removed her hat and the jacket of her traveling outfit, revealing a lacy white blouse. She was thoroughly lovely, Cody thought.

As she came up to him, she said, "I was wondering if it might be possible for us to have dinner together tonight, Cody. You could tell me some more about Abilene's history and perhaps show me some of the sights."

"Well, ma'am, that sounds very nice," Cody replied, thinking rapidly. The knowledge that Dorothea was engaged and that her fiancé was only a few doors away made him uncomfortable. "But I'm not sure that would be a good idea."

"Why in the world wouldn't it be?" Dorothea demanded, looking up at him and cocking her head slightly to one side.

"Miss Dorothea, I'm not altogether sure we should even be talking like this, what with you being engaged and all. Your fiancé's right over at Orion's having a drink."

"Edwin?" Dorothea asked, waving off Cody's objection. "If Edwin is having a drink, it's probably milk. He's a dear, sweet man who will make an excellent husband for me, but he is rather boring. Not at all like you, Deputy Fisher." Her voice purred seductively as she finished. She reached out and placed a fingernail against the badge on Cody's chest.

Cody took a deep breath. He said, "I'm sorry, ma'am, but I'll just have to pass. I expect Marshal Travis will have me working tonight, anyway."

"All right." Dorothea pouted. "If that's the way you feel. There is one thing you can do for me, though— quit calling me ma'am! It makes me sound old!"

With that, she turned and flounced up the stairs.

Cody watched her for a long moment, then glanced over at the desk where the clerk was standing with a smirk on his face. "What are you looking at?" Cody demanded.

Without waiting for an answer, he turned and stalked out of the lobby.

Chapter Three

———◆———

Long shadows spilled across the covers of the narrow bed as Cody woke from a deep sleep. Turning over and looking around the little room he rented, he groaned. His sore, stiff muscles had not recovered from the arduous ride out to the train wreck and back.

Slowly he sat up, swung his legs off the bed, and went to the window, wearing only the bottoms of his long johns. As he pushed back the flap of canvas that served as a curtain, he saw that the sun was just slipping below the horizon. He had slept for only four or five hours.

That was not long enough, but as he stretched, Cody thought he might be able to function now. He would feel better after he ate a hot meal and drank some strong black coffee. He pulled on his clothes, closed the door to his rented room, and walked to the Sunrise Café.

Inside the clean, brightly lit café, the fragrance of fresh bread and brewing coffee greeted him. As he settled down at one of the tables with its red-checked tablecloth, a pretty teenage girl with softly waving auburn hair hurried over to the table. She wore an apron, and she greeted Cody with a big smile.

"Hello, Cody," Agnes Hirsch said. "What can I get for you?"

Cody grinned back her. Agnes had come to Abilene not long before he had arrived. She and her brother, Michael, were orphans, part of the group living at the orphanage established by a Dominican nun named Sister Laurel. The orphanage was housed in the big parsonage of the Calvary Methodist Church, which was pastored by Cody's brother, the Reverend Judah Fisher. Cody had known almost from the first time they met that Agnes had a crush on him. He liked her, too.

But as he looked at her eager young face, he could not help but contrast her fresh, well-scrubbed attractiveness with Dorothea Stockbridge's glamour. Compared to Dorothea, Agnes was just a pretty kid.

But Dorothea was betrothed to Edwin Perkins, and that meant Cody would have to watch his step around her. Maybe the Stockbridges would not have to wait in Abilene for long. A part of Cody hoped that would be the case.

"You just bring me a steak and a heap of potatoes, Agnes, and plenty of coffee," Cody said.

The food was good, as usual, and by the time he had finished, Cody felt revived. Agnes had had to wait on the café's other customers, but she had managed to stop by his table several times to make sure he did not need anything else.

She also asked about the train wreck, having heard

that Cody had ridden out to the scene with the rescue party. The deputy worded his replies carefully so as not to horrify the young woman too much. Agnes's life had been hard at times, and she was no stranger to violence, but the carnage at the crash site had been truly awful.

By the time Cody had paid for his meal and stepped out of the café onto the boardwalk, Texas Street was shrouded in dusk. The deputy glanced toward the marshal's office, diagonally across Texas Street, and saw the warm yellow glow of a lantern coming through the window. Travis was probably inside at his desk, and Cody knew he should walk over and relieve the marshal. Travis would be hungry and want to get some supper himself.

Before he could step into the street, someone hailed him from the next block. In the dim light Cody recognized Edwin Perkins coming toward him. The easterner had obviously just left the Grand Palace Hotel.

"Evening," Cody said pleasantly as Perkins came up to him. "You and the rest of the folks get settled in all right?"

"Yes, indeed," Perkins replied. "I'm afraid Dorothea is not too happy about the accommodations, but that comes as no surprise."

The bluntness of Perkins's statement made Cody raise an eyebrow. "I suppose she is used to better places than Abilene."

Perkins laughed and said, "Dorothea is accustomed to the best of everything, which makes me wonder why she ever agreed to marry me."

"I heard that the two of you are engaged," Cody said. "Congratulations."

"Thank you. It could be that her father had something to do with her decision. I've been working for him for a long time. Probably over the years I've saved him quite a bit of money, finding more efficient ways to do things. That's my job, Deputy Fisher. Perhaps Dorothea's hand in marriage could be regarded as a sort of bonus."

Cody frowned. "That's a heck of a way to put it," he said bluntly.

Perkins's demeanor changed instantly. "Don't get me wrong, Deputy. I care about Dorothea, I really do. I care deeply. But . . . I am aware of my limitations. I'm not a handsome man."

There was nothing Cody could say to that.

Perkins took a deep breath. "Well, I didn't stop you so that we could discuss my personal life. I wanted to ask you if the marshal has had any further word from the scene of the crash. Mr. Stockbridge is quite concerned, as you can imagine."

"I don't know," Cody told him. "I've been asleep all afternoon. I was just going to the office now. You're welcome to come along."

"Thanks." Perkins joined Cody as the deputy started across the street. The traffic on Texas Street was much lighter in the early evening, but horses and wagons still moved on the street. The sounds of laughter and music came from the saloons. Perkins went on, "Dorothea seems quite taken with you, Deputy. She told me about those inebriated cowboys and the way you handled them."

Cody shrugged. "That wasn't much of a fracas, although it seems Miss Dorothea thought it was. She's just never seen much of life outside of the East."

"Perhaps. But even Holly said that your display of fisticuffs was outstanding."

Cody shrugged but made no reply. They had reached the opposite boardwalk. He stepped up and pushed open the door of the marshal's office.

As Cody had expected, Luke Travis was at his desk. He glanced up from the pile of papers he was working on, saw who the newcomers were, and leaned back in his chair. He smiled at Cody. "Feeling better now?" he asked.

Returning the smile, Cody hung his hat on one of the hooks just inside the door. "Tolerable," he said.

"Hello, Mr. Perkins," Travis went on. "Something I can do for you?"

"Mr. Stockbridge was wondering if you'd received any further word from the site of the wreck."

Travis's face grew solemn. "As a matter of fact, I have. Dr. Bloom and the last of the injured passengers returned just a little while ago. Nobody else has died, but a few of those folks are in pretty bad shape."

"What about the other passengers?" Perkins asked.

"They came back, too, some riding on the wagons and others riding double with the men in the rescue party. Most of them are looking for places to stay, those that don't have relatives here in Abilene. I imagine you'll see some of them over at the hotel. There's going to be a lot of doubling up until we can make arrangements for them to continue on their way."

"That's one thing I wanted to speak to you about. Mr. Stockbridge would like to hire some wagons and horses and have the passengers taken to Wichita. They can catch the Missouri Pacific there and continue their journeys westward."

Travis nodded. "That's a nice gesture on Stockbridge's part."

"He feels a measure of responsibility. The bandits were undoubtedly after the strongbox that they believed to be on that train," Perkins pointed out.

Travis rubbed a thumb over his jaw in thought. "Just how do you think Walsh and his gang found out about that money?" he asked.

Perkins shook his head. "I wish I knew the answer to that, Marshal. We worked hard to keep the shipment of money a secret, but it was impossible to conceal it from everyone. Quite a few people connected with the rail line either knew what that strongbox contained or could have guessed. Perhaps we can find out when Walsh is apprehended."

"You're assuming he will be," Cody said. "Lawmen all over this part of the country haven't been able to catch him yet."

"I have confidence in the authorities," Perkins stated. He nodded to Travis. "I'll pass on this latest information to Mr. Stockbridge, Marshal. Thank you."

"Sure," Travis said easily. "Wish I could be more help."

Perkins left, closing the door behind him. Cody went to the stove in the corner of the office and filled a tin cup from the pot of coffee simmering there. He sat down in one of the straight-backed chairs and leaned it against the wall.

"Sort of a strange fellow," he said, then sipped at the coffee.

"Perkins? He's an easterner. Seems like a good enough sort, though."

Cody nodded. "I don't think he's as big a stuffed shirt as he seems. He's just got his head full of his work." The deputy grinned. "He probably ought to pay more attention to that gal of his."

Travis picked up a sheaf of papers from the desk and squared them. He frowned. "I hope you've been steering clear of Dorothea Stockbridge," he said. "Getting mixed up with a woman like that could cause you a lot of grief, Cody. Especially one who's supposed to be getting married to somebody else."

"I never broke up anybody's engagement yet, Marshal, and I don't plan on starting now," Cody assured him. "I sort of like Perkins, even if he is an odd bird."

Even as he spoke the words, though, Cody was aware of the strong attraction that he felt for Dorothea Stockbridge. He knew quite well that she was spoiled and vain and out of place here on the frontier, but at the same time, he had felt definite sparks passing between them. To her he was the embodiment of all that was glamorous and exciting about the West, and there was no denying the appeal of her beauty and charm to him.

Travis pushed his chair back, the legs scraping on the planks of the floor. As he stood up, he said, "If you're all right, I suppose I'll go get some supper. You can watch the office for a while, can't you?"

"Sure, Marshal. I ate just before I came over here."

Travis reached for his hat hanging on one of the pegs and settled it on his head. He lifted his gun belt from the same peg and strapped it around his lean hips. "I think I'll walk down to the Drover's Cottage," he said. "A juicy piece of roast beef sounds awfully good right now. That's where I'll be, if anybody comes looking for me."

Cody nodded, and Travis went out. The deputy rose and went to sit behind the marshal's desk. The stack of papers Travis had been examining lay on the desk; Cody picked them up in idle curiosity and saw that they were new wanted posters that had probably arrived in today's mail. He began to shuffle through them, his interest growing as he studied the sketches of the desperadoes depicted on them.

During the quarter of an hour that passed while he scanned the posters, there had been no visitors to the office. The cells in the cellblock were empty. The whole building was quiet, so quiet that it began to get on Cody's nerves a bit. He opened the desk drawer to put the reward posters away.

The door swung open as he did so. He caught a whiff of perfume even before he looked up to see Dorothea Stockbridge standing there. She had changed her clothes and was now wearing a stylish blue gown more suited to dining than traveling. She had rearranged her hair, the thick raven curls falling softly around her shoulders, and she wore no hat.

"Good evening, Cody," she said. She closed the door behind her and leaned back against it for a moment. A smile played over her full red lips.

Cody's eyes narrowed. "Howdy, Miss Stockbridge," he said cautiously. "Something I can do for you?"

"You can call me Dorothea. And you can tell me why you're not happy to see me."

Cody shut the desk drawer. "I am happy to see you, Dorothea. It's just that I told you earlier I'm not sure how proper it is for us to be talking together."

"What could possibly be wrong with talking?" Dorothea asked. She moved away from the door, walked slowly over to the desk, and stopped beside it. "Are you sure you wouldn't reconsider and show me what kind of nightlife Abilene has?"

"It's pretty darned rough, the nightlife we have around here, Dorothea. Nothing for a lady like you to be seeing."

She gazed down at him and said, "Do you have any idea how boring it is for other people always to be deciding what a lady should and shouldn't do?"

Cody had to grin. "No, ma'am, I don't suppose I do."

"Then take my word for it. I want to do things that are new and different and exciting!" She whirled away from him, stepping toward the open door that led into the cellblock. "Do you have any prisoners back here? Some murdering desperadoes?"

Cody stood up and closed the cellblock door before she could go through it. "I'm afraid we're a little short on prisoners right now," he said dryly. "In fact, I'm the only one here." The moment the words were out of his mouth, he saw her eyes light up and knew he had made a mistake.

"I saw the marshal walking down the street, and I thought you might be here by yourself," Dorothea said, leaning closer to him. "I was afraid you might get lonely."

A strange mixture of emotions was roiling through Cody. As he had told Travis, he did not make a practice of breaking up engagements. At the same time, propriety had never been his strong suit. Too many folks were afraid to do what they really wanted just because they worried about what other people might think.

"That's mighty nice of you," he said slowly, "but I'm used to being on duty here in the office by myself."

"I just know I would go absolutely out of my mind if I had to stay here for hours. The marshal *will* be gone for quite a while, won't he?"

Cody was not sure how to answer that. If he encouraged Dorothea very much, there was no telling what would happen. Instead of answering her question, he asked one of his own. "Just what is it you really want here, Dorothea?"

She smiled again. "You westerners can be so forthright. Very well, Cody, since you've asked me, I'll tell you what I want. Better yet, I'll show you."

With that, she moved into Cody's arms so smoothly that he almost did not know how it had happened. Her head tilted back, her arms went around his waist, and her lips lifted to his. Her mouth was sweet and wet and warm. Cody's arms tightened around her.

The kiss was long and passionate, and the heat of her body seemed to sear right through their clothes. When she finally took her mouth away from his, there was a look of satisfaction on her face. Cody did not know if the kiss had made her happy, or if she was just glad finally to be getting her own way.

"Well?" she asked softly. "Do you think I'm the most brazen hussy you've ever seen, Deputy?"

The kiss had had more effect on Cody than he realized. He had to take a deep breath before he could answer, "You're about the prettiest armful of woman I've ever seen, Dorothea. If things were different—"

"Things don't have to be different," she said quickly. "You and I are attracted to each other, and we're together right now. That's all that matters."

Cody was trying to find some way to argue with that and not having much luck when the sound of a step on the boardwalk outside made him turn around suddenly. He and Dorothea were standing where they could be seen through the window from outside. The doorknob turned and the door began to open. Cody wondered fleetingly what, if anything, the visitor had seen. If the newcomer was Luke Travis—who was as observant a man as Cody had ever known—he was confident he would soon be hearing a few choice words from the marshal.

The man who came through the door was not Travis, however. The visitor to the office was a tall, slender man in a sober dark suit and string tie. He had sun-faded brown hair and wore wire-rimmed spectacles, which gave him a bit of a studious look. In his hand was a Bible.

"Judah!" Cody exclaimed. "What are you doing here?"

The Reverend Judah Fisher frowned. "What's the matter, Cody, can't I come by to say hello to my favorite brother?"

"Only brother," Cody muttered.

"That's beside the point." As he waved aside Cody's comment, Judah turned his gaze to Dorothea. He nodded politely and said, "Hello."

The young woman smiled at Judah, not as radiantly as she had smiled at Cody but disarmingly nevertheless. "Good evening," she said.

Cody wondered if he looked as embarrassed as he felt. He said quickly, "Judah, this is Miss Dorothea Stockbridge. Miss Dorothea, my brother, Reverend Judah Fisher."

Dorothea extended a hand and murmured, "Reverend."

As he shook hands with her, Judah said, "I heard about the misfortune that struck the train on your father's rail line, Miss Stockbridge. In fact, I've just visited some of the injured passengers."

"How are they?" Dorothea asked.

"In good spirits, considering." Judah shook his head. "There are some bad injuries, I'm afraid. Whatever happens to Jake Walsh when he's finally brought to justice, he'll richly deserve the punishment."

"From the way he's eluded the law thus far, he may never be caught," Cody pointed out.

Judah glanced at his brother. "Then the Lord will have to take care of justice for Jake Walsh, won't he?"

Cody shrugged. He was not going to engage in a religious argument with Judah.

The Methodist pastor went on, "Actually, Cody, I didn't come by just to see you. Is Marshal Travis around?"

"He went up to the Drover's Cottage for supper. I imagine you can find him there."

"Thanks. I want to see him about possibly letting some of those stranded train passengers stay at the church."

"Don't you have your hands full with those orphans of Sister Laurel's?" Cody asked.

Judah just smiled. "There's always room for more. A righteous man never runs out of good works to do, Cody."

Judah tipped his hat in farewell to Dorothea Stockbridge and left the marshal's office. Outside, he turned east and started toward the Drover's Cottage. The door had hardly closed behind him when Dorothea said to Cody, "Your brother seems awfully nice."

"I guess he's not too bad," Cody said. His eyes followed Judah as he walked past the window. "Wonder if he saw anything through the window before he came in?"

"You mean like us doing this?" Dorothea asked. As Cody turned toward her, she slid into his embrace again, raising her face to his.

This time Cody abruptly broke the kiss. He shook his head. "This isn't right," he declared. "I've never worried too much about what folks think, but you're engaged to be married to somebody else!"

"And I will marry Edwin . . . someday," Dorothea said. "Until then, I don't see what's wrong with doing things that I enjoy."

Cody sensed that he was going to have about as much luck arguing with her as he usually did with Judah. Besides, he was not too sure that he wanted to win this argument.

The quick tapping of feet made him jerk his head toward the door again. It opened, and Dr. Aileen Bloom stepped into the office. Cody was immediately struck by the weariness on her face. "Hello, Cody. Is Marshal Travis here?" she said.

Frustration was building inside the young deputy. He wanted to settle this business with Dorothea Stockbridge, and he was not going to be able to as long as they were interrupted every few minutes. He muttered, "Why doesn't he just put up a sign down in front of the restaurant, announcing where he is?"

"What was that?" Aileen asked.

Cody shook his head. "Never mind. The marshal went to the Drover's Cottage for supper, Doctor. If he's not there, he'll be somewhere between there and here."

"Thanks, Cody," Aileen said. She found the energy to smile at Dorothea. "You must be one of the Stockbridge sisters. Orion told me that you and your family will be waiting here for the tracks to be repaired."

"Yes, that's right. I'm Dorothea Stockbridge," the young woman said.

"Dr. Aileen Bloom," the doctor replied. "I'm glad to meet you. I just wish it had been under better circumstances."

"How are those injured passengers doing?" Cody asked.

"We have all of the injuries stable at the moment. Dr. Wright is keeping an eye on the patients for me. I want to talk to Luke for a minute, then I'm going to try to get some sleep."

"That's a good idea," Cody said.

"Thanks again." Aileen left the office, following Judah Fisher's example.

As Cody turned toward Dorothea, she spoke before he had a chance to. "This is no place for the things we need to discuss," she said. "Why don't we arrange a meeting somewhere else?"

"I'm not sure we have anything to talk about," Cody said, knowing nevertheless that they did.

"Of course we do. You can't kiss me the way you did a few minutes ago and then say we have nothing to talk about. I know! I saw some stables down by the train station earlier. Let's meet there at midnight."

Cody started shaking his head. "I don't think that's a good idea—"

"That's exactly what we'll do. Now, I'll be there at midnight, Cody, and I expect you to be, too!" She came up on her tiptoes and brushed his lips with hers.

Then, before he could stop her, she was gone and the door was shutting behind her.

Cody stood there, his mind in turmoil. He could not run after her. And he did not doubt for a minute that Dorothea would keep her part of the bargain she had proposed. Even though it was no place for a young woman, come midnight she would be at those stables.

Come midnight, he would be, too.

Chapter Four

IN THE LONG SHADOWS CAST BY A THREE-QUARTER MOON, A half hour before midnight, six men on horseback stealthily approached Abilene. They drew up on a slight rise west of town and looked down toward the scattering of lights that were still burning. Below them, Mud Creek curved along the edge of the town, while off to the north the whitewashed walls of the Calvary Methodist Church gleamed in the moonlight. To the south, the tracks of the Kansas Pacific stretched across the prairie.

"I don't much like this, Jake," one of the men said in a quiet voice. "It's too risky."

"And I don't give a damn what you like," Jake Walsh growled in reply. The burly, red-bearded outlaw leaned forward in the saddle, his gaze intent. "I been double-crossed, and nobody's goin' to get away with that! Nobody!"

Walsh swung out of the saddle. All his men, except one, followed suit. Walsh and the others handed their reins to him.

"Take these nags back to where the rest of the boys are waiting," Walsh rumbled. "We'll meet you there before sunrise."

"What if you don't get there, Jake?" the man asked cautiously.

Walsh's laugh was short and harsh. "Then you poor hopeless bastards'll have to figure out some way to get along without me. Reckon if that happens, you'll all be hanged or in jail in six months."

A couple of the other outlaws forced an echo of Walsh's laughter. They all knew that without their leader's cunning and ruthlessness, the gang would not last long.

The man with the horses shook his head and turned. He quietly led the animals away from the gang back the way they had come. Walsh and the other men started down the hill toward Abilene. When they reached the railroad tracks, they stole along the double line of steel across the small trestle spanning Mud Creek and on into town. At this hour, most of the buildings were quiet and dark; only the saloons were brightly lit and noisy.

Walsh halted the band with an upraised hand. The outlaws were within a hundred yards of the train station now, and they could see the dark bulk of Maxwell Stockbridge's private train, which had been moved to a siding earlier in the day.

"Move quiet now," Walsh hissed to his men. "I don't reckon those folks will be expecting any trouble, but it don't pay to take chances when you don't have to."

Walsh gestured to three of his men and directed

them to move along one side of the tracks, while the remaining outlaw, a man named Kelsey, followed him down the other side. All five men had removed their spurs before reaching Abilene, and now they slithered almost silently toward Stockbridge's train. An occasional crunch of gravel under a booted foot was all that could be heard.

As Walsh and his companion reached the locomotive and began to move along the side of it, Walsh slid his pistol from its holster. He had figured that there was a good chance that Stockbridge had guards on this train, for Stockbridge either carried men with him or hired citizens in the towns where he stopped.

As the bandit leader passed the coal tender and started toward the single passenger car, he saw a dark figure lean over the railing of the platform at the back of the car. The guard had something in his hand that had to be a rifle. A cigarette butt glowed redly between his lips.

Has to be a damned townie, Walsh decided. A man who made his living guarding trains would not be so careless.

That just makes the job that much easier, Walsh thought with a grin. He had seen no one in the cab of the locomotive, and he figured that there would only be a couple of guards in the passenger car.

Walsh paused and glanced across the platform at the front of the car. One of his men on that side of the train waved a hand in a high sign. They were ready. Walsh returned the sign with a wave of his gun and hurried down the side of the car, Kelsey at his heals.

The guard reacted much too slowly to the sound of the quick footsteps. He was just starting to turn toward the steps at the side of the platform when Walsh stormed up them, viciously swinging his gun.

The barrel smashed into the guard's head with a bone-crunching thud. The man sagged, the rifle slipping from his hands and clattering to the platform. Walsh roughly thrust the guard's falling body aside, then stepped to the door and shoved it open.

Inside the car, two more men were playing cards in the light cast by one of the fancy lanterns on the wall of the sitting room. They jerked around in surprise as Walsh strode through the door, backed up by Kelsey. After a split-second hesitation, the seated men lunged for Winchesters that were leaning against the long divan.

They were too late. The other three outlaws, who had slipped into the car from the front, came boiling out of the forward corridor. Walsh had ordered his men not to shoot unless it was absolutely necessary. A blow to the head with a gun butt felled one of the guards, and the other was dispatched by a knife stuck deep in his back. The outlaw wielding the blade clamped his other hand over the victim's mouth, stifling the guard's scream.

"There's another one on the back platform," Walsh said quietly. "Get rid of all three of them. Dump 'em in one of those alleys over there."

The three men who had attacked from the front went out to the rear platform to carry out Walsh's orders. Hefting the bodies of the guards, they left the train on the side away from the depot and disappeared into the shadowy darkness of Second Street.

Walsh turned to Kelsey. "Get that firebox stoked up and the engine going. You sure you can handle it?"

"No problem, Jake," Kelsey replied, grinning. "I was an engineer back in Ohio for three years 'fore I came west. I've driven plenty of locomotives just like this one."

Walsh nodded and snapped, "Get to it, then. I'll meet up with the boys outside, and we'll be back as soon as we can."

He dropped from the platform at the rear of the train and waited, gun in hand, until his three confederates rejoined him. "You get rid of those bodies?" he asked in a whisper.

One of the men nodded. "We dumped them in some barrels out back of an old warehouse. Won't nobody find them for a while."

Walsh grinned savagely. "Let's go after that filly!"

As the outlaws moved off into the shadows, the firebox of the locomotive began to heat up as Kelsey shoveled coal into it. The steam was starting to build.

A little before midnight, Deputy Cody Fisher left the marshal's office. He walked down Texas Street. At the corner of Spruce Street he turned left. By going that way, he figured he would avoid passing the saloons along Railroad Street, where it was likely that someone would stop him and want to talk. Cody wanted to avoid that, for he did not want to be late.

Something had gnawed at him all evening. It had not helped when Marshal Travis had asked as Cody got up to leave, "Going anywhere special?"

"Just thought I'd take a walk around town while I had the chance," Cody had replied. "No place special."

The lie had come easily enough, but as he walked through the darkened streets, whatever was troubling him renewed its attack. By the time he had reached Spruce Street, Cody had admitted to himself what it was: his conscience.

But at the same time, he told himself, he could not let Dorothea Stockbridge stand around some stable by herself in the middle of the night. That would be too dangerous for a beautiful young woman like her. He had to keep the rendezvous, if only to escort her firmly back to the hotel and order her to stay there.

As the stables loomed ahead on his right, a grin stretched across his face. Maybe he would take Dorothea back to the hotel, and maybe he would not. After all, she was old enough to make up her own mind about things.

And, Lord, she was pretty.

A tune sprang into Cody's mind as he approached the entrance of the stables. One of the big double doors was open a couple of inches, and a faint yellow light from a lantern burning came through the gap. Dorothea was probably already waiting for him.

He began to whistle softly. His step was light as he pushed the stable door open a little wider and strolled in.

There was a sound behind him, and the instincts that had kept him alive this long screamed a warning to him. Cody started to spin around, his hand streaking toward his gun. Something slammed into the back of his head.

Cody staggered, pinwheels of light bursting behind his eyes. His fingers brushed the butt of his Colt, but somehow they refused to work well enough to pull the gun.

Out of the corner of his eye he saw a shape lunging toward him. Cody dropped to one knee. The man viciously swinging the gun missed. Had it connected, the blow would probably have been fatal. But Cody's move had thrown off the man's aim just enough to make the gun barrel glance off Cody's skull.

As Cody tried desperately to make his body respond to his brain's command, someone else hit him from behind. Long arms wrapped around him, pinning his own arms to his sides. He uttered a bitter curse as his pistol, which he had just managed to get out of its holster, slipped from his fingers.

The first man slashed at Cody's head with his gun. Cody jerked his head to the side and felt the barrel scrape along his cheek. In the dim light from a lantern hanging in one of the stalls, the struggle was a nightmarish one, full of flickering shadows and grunts of effort and the whinnies of nervous horses. Cody was spun around, still in the bear hug of the second man.

An image flashed in front of his eyes. For a second, he saw Dorothea Stockbridge struggling futilely in the grasp of a huge, red-bearded man. The man had one arm wrapped around her in a viselike grip, and his other hand was clamped over her mouth. Dorothea's eyes were wide and staring in terror.

Then she was gone, as Cody was whirled around some more. He suddenly realized that the man holding him intended to ram him into the wall of the stable. Cody thrust a foot back, between the legs of his captor. The man stumbled, his balance abruptly gone.

Cody tore himself from the man's grip. A ball of sickness churning in his stomach, he staggered and tried to right himself. He seemed to see two of everything, and the inside of the stable blurred before his eyes. He had only one thought: *Where is Dorothea?*

"Cody!"

The shrill cry made him snap his head around. She had managed to slip away from the big outlaw, but before she could take more than a step, the man threw himself forward and grabbed her again. She shrieked as he jerked her backward.

Cody finally saw the man's face clearly and realized

with crystal clarity that it was Jake Walsh. Only one man was that big and had that striking crimson beard.

Cody took one frantic step toward Dorothea and Walsh, and then one of the other outlaws clouted him again with a gun barrel.

He pitched forward. More bright lights danced in his head and then blinked out, one by one. He vaguely felt his face hit the ground, but he could see nothing except the winking lights.

Cody heard Jake Walsh growl, "Here! You two hold onto this hellcat! It's a good thing we spotted her slippin' in here. This is a lot easier than takin' her out of the hotel."

As heavy footsteps approached Cody, he tried to lift his head, but his strength was gone. Only a few of the dancing lights still burned.

"He still alive?" Walsh asked.

"Yeah," one of the other men grunted. "Boy's got a hard head."

"That's all right. I'll finish him off. We want to keep things quiet, anyway." Walsh's words were followed by a soft sound that Cody somehow recognized as the whisper of cold steel leaving a leather sheath.

And then there was nothing. The last light winked out.

Outside, Marshal Luke Travis moved quickly out of the shadows next to the barn. He had watched Cody's behavior earlier in the evening with growing suspicion, and the lame excuse the younger man had offered when leaving the office had prompted the marshal to follow his deputy. Now he was glad he had done so, for he had been close enough to hear Dorothea's cries.

The lookout the outlaws had posted was at the

half-open barn doors, intently watching the events unfolding inside the stable. Travis slipped silently behind him and brought the barrel of his Colt thudding down on the lookout's head. As the man slumped senseless, the marshal stormed into the stable, his keen eyes taking in everything.

The scene was a grim one. Jake Walsh stood over Cody's sprawled figure, a razor-sharp hunting knife raised to plunge into the helpless deputy's back. Two of his men stood nearby, each of them holding one of Dorothea Stockbridge's arms. A rag had been hastily stuffed into her mouth to keep her from screaming again.

Smoke and flame exploded from the gun in Travis's hand. Walsh yelped in pain as the slug burned across the heel of his hand. The knife spun crazily away, the lantern light glinting on its blade.

Travis snapped another shot at Walsh. This one narrowly missed and forced the outlaw leader to dive for cover in a vacant stall. As Travis swiveled toward Dorothea and the other two hardcases, he saw them disappearing through the open door of the tackroom. One of the men was dragging Dorothea with him while the other yanked out his gun and began to blaze away at the lawman.

"Put him down!" Walsh bellowed. "Those shots'll bring the whole town!"

That was exactly what Travis was hoping for. He had never expected to walk into a hornet's nest like this one, and as he flung himself to the straw-littered ground inside the stable and rolled rapidly to one side, he prayed that Orion and some of the other citizens would hear the gunfire and come running. But the odds were not too good.

Travis rolled behind a grain bin and crouched there.

He waited and hoped that the outlaws hiding in the tackroom would not think of using Dorothea as a shield to make their escape.

Suddenly Walsh abandoned his place of concealment in the stall and darted across the open area in the middle of the stable. He moved fast for such a big man, and the gun in his hand exploded in a flurry of shots that sounded like one mighty roll of thunder. Travis had to duck and hunt for more cover. Walsh had an angle on him.

One of the other men popped out of the tackroom, wielding a shotgun he must have found there. He threw the weapon to his shoulder and triggered both barrels, catching Travis in a cross fire.

The man with the shotgun had aimed too hastily. Most of the charge missed, but several pieces of buckshot slashed into Travis's leg. White-hot needles of pain stabbed through his flesh, and the impact spun him halfway around before he fell.

Sprawled on the ground, Travis fired once at Walsh, making the big man lunge into another stall. Then he jerked the barrel of his Colt over and blasted a shot at the man with the shotgun. The slug tore through the outlaw's upper arm and sent him staggering back into the tackroom as the shotgun clattered to the floor.

Travis tried to get up, but his leg refused to work. He could feel the steady trickle of blood running into his boot, but he could not tell just how badly he was hit. The pain had been fierce but fleeting, and now his leg felt numb above the knee.

Using his arms and his good leg, he dragged himself back behind the grain bin. It was not much protection, but it would have to do. He began sliding fresh cartridges into his pistol, glancing at Cody's unconscious form as he did so. Travis could not tell if any of the lead that had been flying around the stable had hit him.

The lookout Travis had knocked out moments before suddenly came staggering into the barn, holding his head. "Jake!" he called. "You in here, Jake? There's a bunch of people comin'!"

The dazed sentry had not spotted Travis. He stumbled closer, and for a moment the marshal wondered if he could capture the man and use him for leverage. It would not work, he decided. A man like Walsh would not care about any member of his gang who was foolish enough to get caught.

Then, before Travis could even attempt anything else, a rumble of hoofbeats filled the stable. Walsh was stampeding some of the horses, Travis realized. And Cody was out there in the middle of the runway.

Without pausing to think about it, Travis emerged from his scanty cover. Several wild-eyed horses dashed past, nostrils flaring, manes tossing as they raced out into the night. Travis had a fleeting glimpse of Jake Walsh and fired wildly at him, doubting that it would do any good. The outlaws who had Dorothea appeared for a second in the doorway of the tackroom. Then they raced from the stable using the frantic horses for cover. They were taking Dorothea with them.

Travis scuttled across the stable, dragging his bloody leg behind him. As he came closer to Cody, he saw that the deputy still seemed unhurt. Evidently the stampeding horses had veered around him.

Guns roared and bullets kicked up dirt a few feet from Travis. He grabbed Cody's shirt with one hand and began dragging the deputy. He had holstered his gun to do this, but with the confusion in the stable, he doubted he would have been able to mount an effective return fire anyway.

Progress across the runway was agonizingly slow, but at last Travis slumped into the shelter of a stall, hauling Cody with him. His strength was completely gone.

And so, it seemed, were Dorothea Stockbridge, Jake Walsh, and the rest of the outlaws.

As an exhausted Travis slumped next to the inert Cody, an almost eerie silence fell over the stable. A moment later it was broken by the concerned shouts of townspeople converging on it. Travis looked up to see Orion McCarthy running into the barn, his shotgun clutched tightly in his big fists. Travis called the tavern keeper's name.

Orion raced over to the stall and gaped at the two men lying there. "Lucas!" he exclaimed. "Wha' the devil happened t'ye?"

Beside Travis, Cody stirred slightly and began to shake his head. Then he groaned and rolled onto his side.

"You'd better get help, Orion," Travis said between gritted teeth. The numbness in his leg was starting to wear off, to be replaced by sheets of blinding agony. "It looks like . . . Jake Walsh has just kidnapped . . . Dorothea Stockbridge!"

Walsh ran hard, one big paw wrapped around Dorothea's arm as he half dragged, half carried her. Behind them came the other three members of the band. The two injured men lagged behind a bit, but they kept up as best they could. Both of them knew that Walsh would kill them rather than leave them behind to reveal what they might know of his plans.

After everything that had happened, there was no reason to be quiet and careful. Walsh and his men ran around the Kansas Pacific station, leaping over the rails of the main line as they headed for the train parked on the siding. "Kelsey!" Walsh thundered as he neared the train. "Get this thing moving!"

From the cab, Kelsey waved his understanding. He fed steam to the engine, the quiet hissing rapidly increasing in volume.

As they approached the rear platform of the passenger car, Walsh thrust Dorothea into the arms of one of his men. "Hang on to her, damn you!" the big man growled. He turned as the others scrambled on board the train, taking Dorothea with them. She was past the point of struggling now, overwhelmed by everything that had happened to her.

Walsh ran alongside the train and past it, heading toward the switch where the siding merged with the main line. The locomotive's wheels were starting to turn slowly. It built up speed, cutting down the lead that Walsh had on it.

The lever was right in front of him now. He threw himself against it, shoving hard. The switch moved with a clunk of metal. Walsh staggered back a few steps as the locomotive rolled by. It moved smoothly from the rails of the siding onto the main track and rolled on, gathering momentum, heading west toward the damaged section of track.

As the passenger car rattled past him, Walsh prepared to board. Timing his leap carefully, he threw himself forward in one smooth motion, grabbing for the railing around the platform as his booted feet found the step. Two of his men, who were waiting on the platform, grasped his arms and pulled him aboard.

"We did it!" one of them whooped exultantly. "We did it!"

"Of course we did," Walsh growled. "What did you expect?"

As he looked at the rapidly receding lights of Abilene, a savage smile of satisfaction formed on the red-bearded outlaw's face.

Chapter Five

SLOWLY CODY SWAM UP THROUGH THE BLACK VOID THAT had enveloped him. He rolled onto his back, and when his head touched the hard-packed earth, a searing pain jolted through him. He jerked his head up, and the pain throbbed more intensely.

Strong hands gripped his shoulders and lifted. A voice said, "Here, lad, le' me help ye." Cody recognized the rumbling tones and the accent of Orion McCarthy.

Blinking his eyes against the glaring light of a lantern held over him, Cody looked around. He was still in the stable. A few feet away lay Marshal Luke Travis; the right leg of his pants was heavily stained with blood, and several anxious townspeople were clustered around him.

Cody glanced up at Orion and asked, "What happened?"

Orion shook his head. "I dinna know."

Forcing away the throbbing in his head, Cody struggled to remember. He began to recall the viselike arms and the savage, spinning struggle.

"Dorothea!" he suddenly cried, looking wildly around and ignoring the pain in his head. There was no sign of her.

"She's gone, Cody," Luke Travis's taut voice told him. Cody looked over at the marshal. Travis had propped himself up on his elbows and was looking intently at Cody. "Jake Walsh and his men kidnapped her and nearly finished you off."

Cody put a hand to his head. "I . . . I remember coming into the stable, and then some fellows jumped me. Walsh had Dorothea. . . ."

"He was about to plant a knife in your back when I showed up and started trading shots with the gang," Travis said. "One of them winged me with a shotgun, and then Walsh stampeded some of the horses and got away with Dorothea."

"How long ago?"

"Just a couple of minutes."

Ignoring the pain in his head, Cody grasped Orion's hand and pulled himself to his feet. His eyes scanned the ground for his gun. To the tavern keeper he said, "Have you sent for the doc?"

"Aye. A feller's gone to fetch Dr. Bloom."

Cody spotted his Colt. He bent to scoop it up. For a moment, a wave of dizziness swept over him, but he fought it off. "I've got to go after them."

Travis began, "Cody, you're in no shape—"

The whistle of steam and the rumble of wheels cut him off. The sounds drifted in through the open doors of the stable. Cody jerked his head around. "That's got to be Stockbridge's train," he rasped.

Before anyone could stop him, Cody dashed out of the barn, his pistol gripped tightly in his hand.

The sound of the train was louder as he emerged from the building. Running across Railroad Street, he headed for the depot. This frantic action was sapping all the strength that he had, but his instincts told him that Walsh and his men were stealing Maxwell Stockbridge's private train. There was no other reason for a train to pull out of the station at this time of night. And Dorothea had to be on it with them.

Cody took the steps leading onto the depot platform three at a time. The train had already cleared the switch from the siding onto the main line, its speed increasing by the second, and by now it was a couple of hundred yards down the track.

Grimacing, Cody lifted his pistol and pressed the trigger. He fired again and again at the receding train, the weapon bucking back against his palm until the cylinder was empty.

He knew it was hopeless. The range was too great, and if the outlaws even noticed his gunfire, they were not bothering to return it.

There was nothing Cody could do except watch helplessly as the train disappeared into the darkness.

The strain of the last few days was apparent on Aileen Bloom's attractive face as she hurried into the stable, carrying her black medical bag. The circle of men around Luke Travis parted, allowing her to slip through and kneel beside the marshal.

As Travis looked up at her, he saw deep circles around her warm brown eyes and weary lines around her mouth. "Sorry to have to drag you out again, Aileen. I know you're worn out," he said.

"Nonsense," she said briskly, brushing aside his

concern. "Doctors are used to going without sleep." She took a small knife from her bag and began slitting the leg of Travis's pants. Despite her experience in treating gunshot wounds, she still paled at the sight of buckshot-torn flesh.

As she began cleaning the wounds with the disinfectant that she took from her bag, Travis grimaced and caught his breath. After a moment, he asked, "How does it look?"

"It looks bad," Aileen began bluntly. Then her voice softened. "Actually, I think it looks worse than it really is. You've lost a lot of blood, Luke, and that buckshot really tore some flesh on its way through. The wounds seem to be clean, though, so barring infection, a few weeks of bed rest ought to have you back on your feet."

"A few *weeks?*" Travis exclaimed. "I can't lie abed for that long!"

Orion McCarthy was crouching on the other side of Travis. He put his large hand on the marshal's shoulder. "Ye'd best take it easy, Lucas. You're ginna have t'take the doctor's orders, laddie."

"But—"

"Hush now," Aileen said as she began to bind up the wounds with a roll of bandage.

Cody Fisher came back into the stable, his face bleak. Travis twisted to look up at his deputy and said, "Did you see them, Cody?"

"All I saw was that train pulling out of the station, Marshal. But I know Walsh and Dorothea were on it. Nobody else would have any reason to steal that train."

"Aileen, you'd better have a look at Cody's head. He caught a pretty good wallop on it," Travis said.

Aileen deftly secured Travis's bandage, then went to the deputy and gently felt the back of Cody's skull while he fidgeted.

"You've got a pretty good lump there," she announced a moment later. "Are you having any trouble seeing?"

"Not right now," Cody said. "Earlier, when I was still fighting with Walsh's men, I started seeing two of everything for a minute. That seems to have cleared up, though."

Aileen nodded thoughtfully. "Double vision is one symptom of a concussion."

"That anything like a plain old busted head?"

"A concussion is a bruise on the brain itself," Aileen explained. "It's less serious than a skull fracture, but it's still nothing to take chances with. I'd recommend a few days of bed rest."

"Bed rest?" Cody asked incredulously.

Grinning through his pain, Travis said, "Don't take it so hard, Cody. She wants me to stay off my feet for a couple of weeks."

"At least," Aileen added firmly with a stern look.

Cody shook his head. "I've got too much to do. I've got to get a posse rounded up so we can start after Walsh and his gang."

"You'll be taking a chance with your health if you do," Aileen warned him. "But it's up to you, I suppose." She turned to the men who were gathered around them. "Some of you please help the marshal over to my office."

Orion stooped and slid a brawny arm around Travis. He lifted the marshal and supported him while another man draped Travis's arm over his shoulders.

With their help, Travis hobbled toward the open doors. Another of the townspeople said, "My wagon's parked just down the street. I'll bring it up, and the marshal can ride in the back of it."

"That's a good idea," Aileen said as she closed her bag. "The less he uses that leg, the better."

Cody fell in beside Travis and the men holding him up. "Why would Walsh risk coming into town like that?" the deputy asked. "You think he was after Dorothea all along?"

"Could be," Travis grunted. "Her father's a rich man, remember."

Cody frowned. "Seems I remember hearing Walsh say something about intending to take her out of the hotel. My brain's sort of fuzzy about that. But it sounded like he came to kidnap her."

At that moment the man who owned the wagon returned with it, and Travis was eased into the back of the vehicle. After Aileen, Cody, and Orion climbed on board to ride with him, the townsman turned his team around, drove down Spruce Street, then swung into Texas Street. The shooting at the stable and the train station seemed to have awakened at least half the town, because several dozen people stood on the boardwalks. Some of them were in nightclothes; others were cowboys, gamblers, and fancy ladies from the still-open saloons.

The wagon drew to a stop in front of Dr. Bloom's office, and several of the awakened townspeople gathered around the wagon. Lamps burned in the lobby of the Grand Palace Hotel next door. While Orion and the wagon owner lifted Travis from the wagon, the hotel doors opened, and Maxwell Stockbridge, followed by Richard Stockbridge and Edwin Perkins, walked out onto the boardwalk and over to the wagon.

All three men were in their shirt sleeves, their collars loose.

"Good Lord!" Stockbridge exclaimed as Travis was being lifted down from the wagon, his bloody pants leg in tatters. "What the devil happened, Marshal?"

"Wait," Travis said to Orion and Aileen, who were helping him. Leaning on them, the lawman went on, "I'm afraid I have some bad news for you, Mr. Stockbridge."

With a frown on his face, Stockbridge said, "I thought I heard my train pulling out a few minutes ago. What's going on?"

"Jake Walsh and some of his men stole your train," Travis bluntly told the railroad president.

Stunned, Richard Stockbridge stared at the marshal. "But . . . but where would Walsh take it? And why would he want a train?" he said.

"That's not the worst of it." Travis looked bleakly from Maxwell Stockbridge to Edwin Perkins. "Walsh has kidnapped Miss Dorothea."

"No!"

The cry was torn from Perkins. His features sagged, and his pasty face became even paler in the light coming from the hotel lobby.

Maxwell Stockbridge's hands clenched into fists, and his breath hissed through his teeth. "That can't be true," he said flatly. "Dorothea is up in her room—has been all night."

Cody shook his head. "I'm afraid not, sir. I saw her down in the stables by the train station, and Walsh was holding her prisoner then. She was nowhere to be found after he and his gang got away."

Richard Stockbridge clutched at his father's arm. "My God, Father, we've got to do something!" he exclaimed, his voice shaking with emotion.

Stockbridge shrugged off Richard's hand. "You're sure about this, Marshal?" he asked.

Travis nodded.

Stockbridge's face darkened in rage. "I'll kill the son of a bitch myself!" he suddenly thundered.

Aileen Bloom broke in, "Gentlemen, you'll have to excuse us. Right now, the marshal needs to be inside getting medical attention."

Orion and the other man started to move Travis toward the door of the doctor's office, but Stockbridge stepped forward and caught at Travis's arm. "I want to know what you're going to do about this," he demanded.

Cody moved in. "You'd best let the marshal go, mister," he said in a low voice.

"My daughter is out there somewhere," Stockbridge retorted. "She's in the clutches of that damned outlaw, and I want you people to do something about it!"

"That's just what I intend to do, Mr. Stockbridge," Cody replied. "I'll be rounding up a posse to go after them. We'll get Dorothea back." He rested his hand on the butt of his gun. "I can promise you that."

"Come on inside, Cody," Travis said. "We've got some things to talk about."

"All right, Marshal." Cody kept his cold stare directed at Maxwell Stockbridge until the railroad magnate released Travis's arm.

One of the townspeople called out, "Marshal, you want us to start gettin' our horses ready to ride after those skunks?"

"Just wait until I've talked to Deputy Fisher," Travis answered.

As the marshal was taken down the walk and into Dr. Bloom's office, Cody started to follow, but Edwin

Perkins abruptly stepped forward. "Could I have a word with you, Deputy?" he asked. His features and voice were those of a man struggling to keep his emotions in check.

"Make it quick," Cody said.

"You said you saw Dorothea at the stables. Were you there with her, sir?"

Cody hesitated and then said, "Walsh had grabbed her before I ever got there."

"That's no answer, Deputy," Perkins shot back. "On the other hand, knowing Dorothea as I do, perhaps that's all you need to say. It's fairly obvious why she was meeting you at such a late hour in a place like the stable."

"I didn't say I was meeting her—"

"You didn't say you weren't."

Richard Stockbridge angrily caught Perkins's arm. "Here now, that's my sister you're talking about!" he said hotly. "I want to know what you're implying, Edwin."

"So do I," Maxwell Stockbridge demanded, his tone icy.

Perkins shook his head. His shoulders slumped wearily. "Never mind," he said. "It's not important, anyway. What matters is rescuing Dorothea before she's hurt."

"Can't argue with that," Cody said shortly. "Now, I've got to go talk to the marshal." He turned and strode into the building. As he stepped over the threshold, he encountered Orion and the wagon driver, who were just leaving after getting Travis settled in the doctor's office.

At Aileen's orders the marshal was stretched out on the divan in the waiting room, since all the beds were presently occupied by patients from the train wreck.

She was kneeling beside him, offering him a small vial of medicine as Cody entered.

"This will help the pain, Marshal," Aileen said.

Gently but firmly, Travis pushed it away. "Maybe later," he said. "Right now I can't afford to be knocked out." He looked up at his deputy. "We've got to talk about this posse business, Cody."

"I figure we can get started in about fifteen minutes, Marshal," Cody began.

Travis started shaking his head. "You're not going anywhere, Cody. You can't go chasing Jake Walsh clear across the country."

Cody stared at him. "Why not?" he demanded. "He kidnapped that girl!"

"I know he did," Travis said patiently. "But officially, our authority ends at the town limits, Cody. You know I don't mind stretching that a little when need be, but Walsh is too far away by now."

For a long moment Cody was silent, his features tightening into an expressionless mask. "I'm going," he said, and he stalked out of the office without another word.

As he strode up the walk to the street, his mind was in a turmoil. There was no one in the world that he admired more than Luke Travis, but all of Cody's instincts screamed that for once the marshal was wrong. He did not know what Walsh had in mind for Dorothea Stockbridge, but it was surely nothing good. The only chance that woman had was for a posse to get on the trail of the outlaws right away.

Quite a few townsmen stood on the boardwalk waiting for Cody. Among them were Edwin Perkins and Richard Stockbridge. Maxwell Stockbridge was nowhere in sight.

"What about it, Cody?" one of the townsmen—a man named Flood—asked excitedly. "Are we going after Walsh?"

"Of course we are," Cody growled. Something inside him blanched at going against Travis's wishes, but at the same time he firmly believed he had no choice.

Edwin Perkins looked intently at Cody and said, "I'm going along on this posse."

Before Cody could even start to object, Richard Stockbridge declared, "I'm going, too."

Cody looked from Perkins to Richard and shook his head. "I'm not going to take a couple of inexperienced easterners," he said flatly. "Not on something like this."

"She's my sister!" Richard grated.

"And my fiancée," Perkins added, his voice trembling. "You simply cannot tell us that we can't go, Deputy. We have a *right*."

From behind Cody, a thick Scots voice said, "Aye, 'tis plain t'me the lads have the right, Cody. Let them go wi' us."

Cody turned to face Orion McCarthy. "Us?"

"Aye." Orion nodded. "Lucas is a good man, but somebody has t'go after tha' poor lass."

Cody took a deep breath. "All right. I'll be glad to have you along, Orion." His relief went deeper than this simple expression of gratitude. He was not as close to Orion as Travis was, but he knew that the burly tavern keeper was a good man in a fight and could keep his head in a tight situation.

"We ridin' out right away?" another man asked.

Cody nodded. "Orion, why don't you see about getting the men armed and mounted? Anybody who doesn't have a rifle of his own can use one from the marshal's office. There's ammunition in the storage cabinet. Meet me back here as soon as you can."

"Aye."

As Orion and the other men started to turn away, the door into the hotel lobby banged open and a lithe figure strode out onto the boardwalk. Holly Stockbridge wore a dressing gown, and her blond hair was tousled from sleep. Nevertheless, fire glinted in her blue eyes as she came toward Cody. Her father hurried out of the hotel after her.

Despite the intensity of her gaze, Cody saw tears collecting in the corners of her eyes. She faced him and said, "My father told me. You're getting together a posse, aren't you?"

"Yes, ma'am."

"Then I'm going with you."

Cody's eyes widened at this startling declaration.

Richard Stockbridge took his sister's arm. "Holly, don't be ridiculous. This isn't a job for some young girl." He looked at Maxwell Stockbridge. "Father, you forbid this, don't you?"

Holly ignored her brother and father, keeping her fiery gaze riveted on Cody. "I'm going," she repeated.

Edwin Perkins stepped in and started trying to dissuade her as well, but Holly ignored him. Maxwell Stockbridge pushed Perkins aside and thundered, "Young lady, get back to your room. I'll hear no more absurd talk about your going along with any posse!"

Holly finally tore her stubborn eyes away from Cody and looked at her father. Tears came freely now, single drops rolling down her cheeks. "But, Father, they've *got* her!" she exclaimed, her voice filled with fear and despair.

"I . . . I know. And we're going to do everything in our power to get her back."

"Look, Miss Holly," Cody said, impatient but trying to keep his tone gentle. "A posse is no place for a lady. There's going to be plenty of hard riding—"

"I can ride," Holly cut in. "I'm a good rider."

"You probably are," he agreed swiftly.

"I can shoot, too. I've used a rifle plenty of times before. A friend of mine taught me how to shoot and ride. You remember Les Aiken, Father. He was from Missouri, and we spent all of last summer riding and target shooting. I can keep up and do my part."

Cody could no longer keep the sharpness out of his voice. "Look, Miss Holly," he said bluntly, "I'm in charge of this posse, and I don't intend to be saddled with any females on a job like this. Not even a pretty little tomboy like you."

Holly's face reddened. "Pretty little tomboy?" she echoed angrily. "Why, you big . . . big . . ."

Maxwell Stockbridge took her arm and pulled her away from Cody before she could find the words she was looking for. Cody spun away from Maxwell Stockbridge and his daughter. She was one problem he did not want to deal with, and he would let Stockbridge handle her. For his part, Cody wanted to try one more time to straighten things out with Travis before he left with Orion and the other men. As he went back down the path to Dr. Bloom's office, he knew that one way or the other, he was still going.

Cody found the marshal sitting up on the divan, his wounded leg propped up on a pillow. Aileen had already found it necessary to change his bandages, but the bleeding appeared to have almost stopped. Nevertheless, there was a bleak expression on Travis's face.

Cody hooked his thumbs in his gun belt and said, "I figured you might be sleeping by now, Marshal, instead of sitting up."

From the chair where she was sitting, Aileen Bloom said dryly, "He's stubborn, Cody—just like somebody else in this office."

"She's talking about you, Cody, in case you're wondering," Travis said, his gaze intent on the deputy's face.

"I know who she's talking about," Cody muttered. He glanced at Aileen. "You've got a right to your opinion, ma'am."

"But you're going after those men anyway, aren't you?" she asked.

"Yes, ma'am, I suppose I am."

"What about your head?"

Cody forced a grin. "It hurts like the very devil, but I think it'll feel better once we've got that woman back and Jake Walsh behind bars. Or six feet under, however he wants it."

"It won't be easy," Travis warned.

"I know that."

"What about our duties here in Abilene? Who's going to look after the town while I'm laid up and you're gone?"

Cody grimaced. That same question had occurred to him. "There're plenty of good men around. You can swear in a couple of special deputies to keep an eye on things. Not everybody's going after Walsh."

"Maybe you're right. But this is still a job for the U.S. marshal's office." Travis took a deep breath. "If you go after those outlaws, son, you'll be going against the law instead of upholding it. I thought you had given that up."

From the strained tone of his voice, Cody knew that

those words were as hard for Travis to say as they were for Cody to hear. Cody also knew Travis well enough to know that he was concerned about Dorothea Stockbridge's safety, and was not the type to take kindly to being shot up. But he flatly refused to exceed his authority.

"I'm sorry, Marshal," Cody said, sighing. "If you feel that way, I'll just have to take this star off. Because I'm going after Walsh and his gang. I'm going to get Dorothea back, even if I have to take the law into my own hands."

He reached for the badge pinned on his black shirt.

"Just hold it right there, son," a new voice said from the doorway of the office. "I've got something to say about that."

Chapter Six

———◆———

A BIG MAN DRESSED IN DUSTY BLACK RANGE CLOTHES filled the doorway. He wore twin Colts, the holsters thonged down. As he stepped inside, the man swept off his high-crowned black hat and nodded politely to Aileen. "Hello, ma'am," he said with a smile. "I hope I'm not intruding."

"Who in the blue blazes are you?" Cody asked bluntly.

At first glance, the stranger's thick white hair led Cody to believe that he was old. But as the deputy looked closer, he saw that the man's tanned face was relatively unlined. He was probably not much older than Luke Travis.

He also wore a badge on his chest—a United States marshal's badge.

"My name is Dan Baxter, son," the man told Cody.

His blue eyes turned toward Travis. "And you'd be Marshal Luke Travis, I expect." Baxter strode across the room, holding his big hat in one hand and extending the other toward Travis.

Travis shook the federal lawman's hand and said, "Dan Baxter, eh? I've heard of you. You're the one who cleaned out the Mulford gang up in Montana, aren't you?"

Baxter's friendly smile widened. "I had plenty of help." He turned toward Cody, and his tone became more stern as he went on, "Now, young man, I don't know why you were about to take off that badge, but it's never a wise decision to turn your back on the law."

"I don't think that's any of your business, mister," Cody snapped.

"Does it have anything to do with Jake Walsh?" At the mention of the outlaw's name, Baxter's eyes became wintry.

"It does," Travis answered from the divan. Cody just kept glaring at Baxter.

"I've been on Walsh's trail for months now," Baxter said. "I got word that he had been spotted down here in this part of Kansas and got here at fast as I could." He glanced at Travis's wounded leg. "A little late, from the looks of things. But maybe I can lend a hand now."

Aileen stood up. "Perhaps you can, Marshal Baxter," she said. "I'm Dr. Aileen Bloom. Would you mind trying to convince both of these bullheaded men that they have to take care of their injuries if they hope to recover properly?"

Baxter laughed, a deep, hearty sound. "Well, I'll try, ma'am. Can't make any promises, though."

Aileen looked at Travis. "I have other patients to check on," she said. "I know it won't do any good to ask you not to argue, but at least try not to get too upset, all right?"

"Sure," Travis agreed. He waited until Aileen had left the room and then said to Baxter, "Walsh and some of his gang were here earlier tonight. They kidnapped a young woman and stole a train."

Baxter hooked a footstool with a boot and drew it over next to the divan. He sat down, glancing up at Cody. The deputy remained standing stubbornly.

"Walsh has held up plenty of trains," Baxter said, "but this is the first time I've heard of him stealing one. Who's the woman?"

"Her name's Dorothea Stockbridge. Her father is the president of the Kansas Pacific."

Baxter let out a low whistle. "You think he grabbed her for ransom?"

"That's the way it looks. Walsh and his men hit another train west of here yesterday. Day before yesterday, it'd be now, as late as it is. There was supposed to be a strongbox full of money on that train, but it had been unloaded here in Abilene. I think this is Walsh's way of getting even."

"He's ruthless, all right," Baxter agreed. The federal lawman looked up at Cody again. "I suppose you were about to go after them, son?"

"That's right," Cody said angrily. "Somebody's got to. I already told Marshal Travis that I'll resign and do this as a private citizen if I have to."

"Why don't you make it legal instead?" Baxter asked. He stood up and faced Cody, studying the young man's taut expression. "I can deputize you and the rest of those men I saw outside getting ready to ride. That way we can follow Walsh all the way to Mexico, if we have to."

Cody glanced at Travis and saw the approval on his face. "That would make a difference, Cody," Travis said softly.

Abruptly, Cody nodded. "All right," he said. "I accept the offer, and I know most of the other men will, too." He looked shrewdly at Baxter. "But just what makes you willing to take on a posse like this, mister?"

Baxter grinned. "Maybe I like what I see of the man who was going to lead them."

Cody snorted, then turned to Travis. "There's still the problem of keeping an eye on the town while you're laid up, Marshal."

"You said yourself I could swear in some special deputies, Cody." Travis laughed shortly. "And don't tell Aileen, but I plan to be up and around on crutches in a few days. This isn't the first time I've caught some lead. I'll be all right." The marshal's voice became more serious. "And so will Abilene, until you can get back, Cody. Just bring Miss Stockbridge with you."

Cody nodded again and smiled tightly. "You can count on it."

Marshal Dan Baxter slapped him on the back and said, "Come on, son. Let's go meet the rest of that posse of yours."

In the wee hours of the morning the posse of almost twenty men rode out of Abilene. All of them were armed with rifles, and many of them also wore handguns.

Marshal Dan Baxter rode his big white horse at the head of the posse. Cody rode his pinto beside him. He had planned on leading the group himself, but he decided to defer to the senior lawman's authority—at least for the time being.

"I've heard a lot about Baxter, Cody," Luke Travis had told his deputy in the few moments they had alone. Baxter had stepped out of Dr. Bloom's office to see to his horse before the posse pulled out. "He's been a marshal for a long time, and before that he was a rancher and a local sheriff up in Montana. They don't come much tougher."

"He doesn't look like much," Cody had replied.

"Maybe not, but I think when the chips are down, he'll surprise you."

"We'll see," Cody had said doubtfully.

Now, as he rode along next to Baxter, Cody saw that the federal marshal sat easy in the saddle and, despite the late hour, seemed to be extremely alert.

The posse followed the tracks of the Kansas Pacific, heading west toward the scene of the train wreck. Cody had been puzzling over Walsh's actions and wondering how to interpret them. He shared his thoughts with Baxter. "You suppose Walsh and his gang intend to take that train all the way to where they derailed the other one?"

"You never know with Walsh," Baxter replied. "I've been after him for a long time, and I haven't been able to figure him out yet. Whatever you don't expect from him, that's probably what he'll do. I imagine he had the rest of his gang waiting somewhere with horses, but there's no way of knowing where."

"I never expected he'd come right into Abilene like that." Cody reached up and touched the tender lump on the back of his head. The pain was still there, and every beat of his horse's hooves sent a fresh jolt of discomfort through him.

Baxter barked a short, humorless laugh. "That's what I mean about Walsh. But I'll catch up to him sooner or later, and when I do . . . Well, maybe it'll be a bullet or maybe it'll be the hangman's rope, but either way Jake Walsh will be dead."

Cody frowned and glanced over at Baxter. In the light of the setting moon, Cody could see that the white-haired marshal was staring straight ahead, his face set in a grim mask.

It sounded to Cody as if Baxter bore a personal grudge against Walsh, something that went beyond the simple pursuit of an outlaw by a lawman. Cody hoped that it would not thwart the posse's efforts to rescue Dorothea Stockbridge.

Pale streaks of rosy light spilled across the eastern horizon behind the riders as they topped a slight rise and Dan Baxter at last held up a hand to bring them to a halt. About a quarter of a mile ahead, the dark bulk of Maxwell Stockbridge's private train sat motionless on the tracks.

Richard Stockbridge and Edwin Perkins walked their horses slowly to join Cody and Baxter. Both young men wore range clothing they had borrowed from other members of the posse, instead of the suits they had worn when they arrived in Abilene. They looked uncomfortable and out of place in the ill-fitting work pants, wool shirts, and boots.

Richard straightened his legs, using the stirrups to lift himself slightly from the saddle. He grimaced in pain, obviously unaccustomed to riding. Perkins simply looked miserable. Cody was not surprised by the difficulty the two easterners were having. Their inexperience in the saddle was one reason he had not wanted them to come with the posse.

"That's my father's train," Richard said quietly.

Baxter nodded and took a small black cylinder from his saddlebags. He began to pull the sections of it out, and Cody quickly saw that it was a spyglass. Peering through it at the train, Baxter studied the scene for a long moment, then said, "Doesn't appear to be anybody around. It's hard to be sure in this light, but I think that train's been abandoned."

"But where would they go?" Perkins asked, scanning the flat, dusty plains that surrounded the railroad tracks. A few scrubby trees dotted the horizon, but it was hard to imagine a more desolate area.

"The tracks will tell us that," Baxter said.

Richard began, "Railroad tracks? I don't understand—"

"Hoofprints," Cody cut in. "The marshal and I figure that the rest of Walsh's gang was waiting with horses. With a group that large, it shouldn't be hard to spot their trail."

The sky had grown increasingly brighter as dawn began to break. Baxter leaned forward in his saddle and said, "I suppose we'd better get down there." He turned and ordered the posse, "Move out, but take it slow. We don't want to ride into any ambushes."

As they started down the rise toward the train, Cody slid his Winchester from the saddle boot and levered a shell into the chamber. Beside him, Dan Baxter did the same thing. Cody glanced over his shoulder and saw that Orion was gripping his shotgun, ready to fire. It took a strong arm to handle a shotgun one-handed, but Cody knew Orion was the man to do it.

Richard Stockbridge and Edwin Perkins both looked pale and nervous. They carried rifles, but they gripped the weapons awkwardly. Cody hoped there was no shooting, not with those two behind him.

Quietly, Baxter asked, "How far is it to where Walsh wrecked that other train?"

"I figure we're about halfway there," Cody replied. "I guess he didn't see any need to go that far out of town to meet the rest of the gang."

Baxter nodded. He signaled for the members of the posse to spread out as they closed in on the train, and then he heeled his big white horse into a trot and headed directly for the passenger car. Cody followed closely behind him.

The prairie was silent except for the sound of hoofbeats. No shots rang out from the stopped train, and Cody's tensed muscles relaxed a little as he and Baxter rode up to the platform at the rear of the car.

The door leading into the car was open. Cody peered through it, ready to snap the Winchester to his shoulder and fire if he saw any threatening movement.

Baxter slid his rifle back into its sheath and swung lightly out of the saddle. Drawing his right-hand pistol, he said to Cody, "Cover me. I'm going to take a look in there."

The marshal cautiously went up the steps onto the platform, then moved through the open door. His head swiveled from side to side as he stepped into the sitting room. Cody sat stiffly on his horse, leaning slightly to one side to watch as Baxter explored the car. Baxter went through the entire car, easing his way down the corridor and checking in all of the compartments that opened from it. Then he strode back through the car to the rear platform.

"It's empty," he announced to Cody and the other members of the posse. "No one's inside."

"The locomotive's empty, too," Orion told them as he rode back from checking it out. "'Tis plain Walsh and his men are gone."

"There's no sign of Dorothea?" Perkins asked in a voice cracking with anxiety.

Baxter shook his head. "I'm afraid not, Mr. Perkins. But that may be a good sign."

Richard Stockbridge wiped a shaking hand across his mouth. "Yes," he said harshly. "At least they didn't kill her and leave her body for us to find."

Cody shot a glance at him. None of them needed to hear that kind of talk, least of all Perkins. "Walsh doesn't have any reason to kill her," the deputy said emphatically. "Miss Dorothea's not worth a thing to him unless she's alive."

"And Walsh isn't the type to pass up a payoff," stated Baxter. "Let's see what kind of trail they left. Then I want to go back over that train and search it for anything they might have left behind."

As Cody and Baxter had predicted, it was not difficult to spot the tracks of the horses used by the gang. To Baxter's experienced eye, they told a plain story.

"Walsh had at least a dozen men waiting here with half a dozen or so extra horses. When the train reached this point, Walsh and the men with him got off, mounted the horses, and rode off that way with the rest of the gang." The federal lawman waved an arm toward the south.

"Where do you think they're going?" Richard asked.

"No way of knowing that, son. But we should be able to follow those tracks without much trouble."

Edwin Perkins said, "My God, Dorothea must be

terrified. I don't think she's ever been on a horse before." He laughed, and there was more than a trace of hysteria in the brittle sound. "She's certainly never been the prisoner of a band of ruthless outlaws before."

Cody grimaced. *Perkins's nerves are going to crack before this deadly chase is over,* he thought.

Baxter lifted his voice to address the rest of the posse. "Better dismount and give your horses a chance to rest. We'll stop here for a while."

Richard Stockbridge stepped forward, a stubborn scowl on his handsome young face. "Shouldn't we start after them, if that trail is as easy to follow as you say it is? They're getting farther away from us all the time."

Patiently, Baxter explained, "Running our animals into the ground won't gain us anything, Mr. Stockbridge. In the long run, we'll catch up to them sooner if we're not careless."

"I guess that makes sense," Richard conceded.

Baxter turned to Cody. "Come on, Deputy. Let's see what we can find in that passenger car."

Cody followed the marshal back into the car. The other men dismounted, took short drinks from their canteens, and made breakfast from a bag of beef jerky and biscuits that one of the men had brought along. Orion poured water in his big floppy-brimmed hat and let the horses drink from it.

Baxter and Cody started at the rear of the passenger car and began working their way forward. They scoured the car looking for any clue Walsh might have left behind, either accidentally or on purpose. They did not have to look long.

The sheet of paper had evidently been pinned to the

back of one of the armchairs in the sitting room, but the knife holding it in place had fallen to the floor of the coach, taking the paper with it. Cody reached down and picked up both the knife and the paper. "Look at this, Marshal."

Baxter took the message while Cody turned the knife over in his hands. Baxter read the crudely printed words aloud.

You shouldn't have taken that strongbox off the train, Stockbridge. If you want to see your precious Dorothea alive again, send one man alone into Indian Territory with fifty thousand dollars.

Baxter looked up from the paper, his thoughtful gaze meeting Cody's. Cody tapped the message with the point of the knife and said, "Here's the proof that somebody told Walsh that the strongbox would be on the train to Abilene."

"Yeah, but who?" Baxter mused. "This note was left for Maxwell Stockbridge, but it's not likely that Stockbridge would have arranged for an outlaw to steal that money. Chances are somebody in his company tipped off Walsh, somebody back in Kansas City who didn't know that Stockbridge would move the strongbox off that train."

Cody nodded. "Makes sense to me. Then, when the money wasn't on the train he wrecked, Walsh got mad and decided to grab Dorothea to make up for it."

"That's the way it looks," Baxter agreed. "We'd better get Perkins and the Stockbridge boy in here and see what they think."

As Baxter stepped to the platform to summon Richard and Perkins, Cody said, "Figuring out who was working with Walsh isn't going to help us get Dorothea back now."

"No, it won't," Baxter agreed. As he glanced over his shoulder at Cody, his eyes were cold. "But we'll be getting back to Abilene sooner or later, with or without the woman, and I intend to clean up all of these loose ends."

I'm sure you will, Cody thought.

Richard Stockbridge and Edwin Perkins came into the car after Baxter called them over. Baxter extended the ransom note toward them and said, "Take a look at this."

Richard took it from him and scanned it, while Perkins read over the younger man's shoulder. When they finished, they had puzzled frowns on their faces.

"I don't understand this," Richard said, tapping the paper. "Why does Walsh make it sound like my father somehow double-crossed him?"

Baxter shook his head. "That's not the way we've got it figured. Somebody tipped off Walsh about that strongbox, but the information turned out to be wrong. That made Walsh mad. He's striking back any way he can at your father, Mr. Stockbridge. That's why he asked for the same amount in ransom that he intended to get from the strongbox."

Perkins took the note from Richard and studied it for a moment. He rubbed his temples and frowned, as though forcing himself to think.

"Walsh knew that Mr. Stockbridge's private train was going to be in Abilene," he said slowly. "That means that in addition to knowing about the strongbox, he also knew about our travel plans."

Quietly, Baxter asked, "Can you think of anybody who could have sent word to him about all of this?"

Perkins shrugged his bony shoulders. "There were several people in our main offices who might have known. . . ."

Richard Stockbridge smiled humorlessly and said, "Or it could have been you or I, Edwin. We both knew about the money, and we certainly knew what the travel schedule was."

Perkins stared at him, his features aghast. "My God, Richard, you can't be serious!" he protested. "What possible motive could we have? Dorothea's your sister, and she's the woman I'm going to marry! We'd hardly want to put her in danger."

"I'm sure that's not what Mr. Stockbridge meant," Baxter said quickly. "But it's true that we can't eliminate anyone until we know more. With any luck, Walsh himself will tell us all about the scheme once we've got him in custody."

"That's a pretty optimistic way of looking at it, isn't it?" Richard asked.

"Don't see any point in being gloomy yet, son."

Perkins was still studying the note. Abruptly, he looked up. "The strongbox!" he exclaimed. "We've been talking about it, but I completely forgot that Mr. Stockbridge had it transferred onto this train!"

Cody swore. He should have remembered the same thing. Moving quickly, he went into the corridor. The door to the office compartment was open. And so was the door of the safe inside the office. Cody drew a sharp breath. The heavy metal box was empty.

At his shoulder, Richard Stockbridge uttered a heartfelt curse. "Walsh got the money, too!"

Baxter moved Cody aside and stepped into the office. He went to the safe and crouched beside it. He swung the door to examine the lock. "It hasn't been forced," he said. He looked up at the three men watching from the doorway and went on, "How did Walsh get it open?"

Richard swallowed. "Dorothea knew the combination. I always thought that was a mistake, trusting it to her, but Father insisted. He wanted any of us to be able to get into the safe."

"Then Walsh forced her to open it," Baxter concluded.

Perkins spoke up. "He had the money. Why would he still want to hold Dorothea for ransom?"

Baxter straightened. "I told you, Walsh isn't going to miss any chance to grab some more loot. He must have decided to double the amount he was after originally."

Cody was beginning to feel impatient. As Baxter had said, it was important to rest their mounts, but the delay was starting to chafe at him. "This is all very interesting," he said sharply, "but it's not getting us any closer to Walsh and Dorothea."

"I agree, Marshal," Richard Stockbridge added. "I think we should be riding again."

As he started to turn away, Perkins put a hand on Richard's arm. "Wait a minute. Walsh's note says for one man to go alone into Indian Territory. The whole posse can't go on. It might be dangerous for Dorothea."

"It'll be more dangerous if we don't, Mr. Perkins," Baxter told him. "Besides, we don't have the fifty thousand dollars that Walsh wants. You couldn't trust a mad dog like him to keep a bargain, anyway. The only way we're going to get the young lady back is to take her."

Perkins ran a hand over his pasty face. Then he

shook his head. "No," he said bluntly. "I won't allow it. We have to do as Walsh demands, otherwise he might . . . might kill Dorothea."

Baxter turned to Richard. "What do you think, Mr. Stockbridge?"

Before Richard could answer, Cody broke in, "Marshal! You know good and well we've got to go ahead!"

"I didn't ask you, Deputy Fisher," Baxter replied. "I'm still in charge of this posse, remember? Well, Mr. Stockbridge?"

Richard licked his lips and hesitated. Finally, he said, "I don't want to do anything to put Dorothea in more danger. But I think we've got to go on."

Perkins clutched at his arm. "But, Richard—"

"Why don't we send one man back to Abilene?" the young man suggested, ignoring Perkins. "He can take this note to my father. *He* can make the decision whether or not to give Walsh what he wants. The rest of us will stay on the trail."

Baxter nodded. "That sounds reasonable to me. What about you, Cody?"

Cody grimaced. A couple of minutes earlier, Baxter had been putting him in his place, and now the marshal wanted his opinion. He was not sure what to expect from Baxter next.

"I said all along we have to go after Walsh," Cody declared. "But I don't see anything wrong with sending the note back to Abilene."

"It's settled then." Baxter turned to Perkins. "Would you like to take the note to Abilene, Mr. Perkins?"

Perkins shook his head. "No. If you're going on, I want to go with you. I want to be there to do whatever I can for Dorothea."

"That's fine. Cody, you know these men; I don't. You pick a good man who can ride fast, all right?"

"Sure." Cody flipped the knife he was still holding, the knife that had been left behind by Jake Walsh. He caught it by the hilt, then flicked his wrist. The blade drove into the rich paneling on the wall, quivering from the force of the throw. He stalked out of the car.

Chapter Seven

———◆———

BY THE TIME CODY STORMED OUT OF THE CAR AND found Orion McCarthy, he had curbed his impatience. He quickly described the situation to Orion and with the Scotsman's advice settled on a man named Renfro to take Jake Walsh's ransom demand back to Abilene. Renfro was small and fairly lightweight, and Cody knew that he had worked as a cowhand on several of the ranches in the area. He was a good rider and would be able to cover long distances quickly without wearing out his horse.

As Renfro mounted up and spurred his horse into a gallop, Cody noticed the look of trepidation on Edwin Perkins's face as he watched Renfro ride away. To Perkins, Renfro was carrying a lot more than a piece of paper with an outlaw's crude scrawl on it: he had Dorothea Stockbridge's fate in his hands. Cody had been concerned about Perkins from the start, and what he saw now only increased his worries.

"All right, men," Dan Baxter called, swinging into his saddle, "you'd best mount up. We've got a lot of ground to cover."

As the posse members began climbing onto their horses, Orion appeared on the platform of the passenger car. He had disappeared for a few moments, Cody now realized, without any of them noticing. The burly Scotsman had a canvas bag slung over his shoulder.

Cody nudged his horse over to the platform and asked, "What the devil have you got there, Orion?"

The tavern keeper's bearded face split in a grin. "I was thinking tha' there might be a kitchen on this here fancy car." He hefted the bag he was carrying. "And I reckon I was right. It isn't much, but 'twill help wi' our supplies."

Richard Stockbridge overheard the conversation as he struggled to turn his horse around in the proper direction. He looked up, aghast. "You looted our pantry?" he asked. "But that's stealing!"

Cody shook his head, trying to get Richard's attention, but it was too late. Orion's already ruddy features darkened even more. He rumbled, "Dinna be callin' me a thief, lad!"

Dan Baxter rode over to them and smoothly inserted himself between the two men. "What Orion did makes good sense, Mr. Stockbridge. We brought supplies of our own, but the more we can stretch them, the faster we can travel. And the faster we travel, the sooner we catch up to Walsh and your sister."

"I suppose you're right," Richard said grudgingly. "I hadn't thought about it that way."

"That's the only way you *can* think about it,"

Baxter told him, his tone sterner now. "Until we get your sister back safely and have Walsh in custody, everything we do has to relate to that mission. There's no time to worry about anything else."

The white-haired marshal wheeled his horse and waved for the posse to get moving. They rode out with Baxter in the lead and Cody close beside him. The other members of the group trailed along behind them, Richard Stockbridge and Edwin Perkins bringing up the rear as they struggled to get their mounts to cooperate. Despite the momentary anger he had felt toward Richard, Orion hung back to make sure that the easterners did not fall too far behind.

The posse turned south away from the railroad line to follow the trail left by Walsh and his men. Soon they splashed through the shallow water of the Smoky Hill River. The tracks left by Walsh's gang continued on the other side of the stream, angling gradually southwest.

The day grew hot as the sun rose higher in the sky, and the heat seemed to sap the strength of some of the men. Most of them had had little or no sleep the night before. The brief rest at the abandoned train had helped, but it had not been enough to refresh them completely.

Baxter called another halt when the sun was directly overhead. "We'll stop here for an hour or so," Baxter announced as he looked around at his dog-tired companions. "As soon as you've eaten, you men had better get a little rest."

The members of the posse found some scant shade in a grove of scrubby trees and dismounted to eat the noon meal. Orion gathered enough wood to start a small fire and boil a pot of coffee. Baxter accepted a cup of coffee from Orion, along with a biscuit and a handful of jerky, and went over to sit cross-legged by Cody.

The deputy swallowed some coffee from his own cup and nodded toward the hoofprints the posse had been following. "Walsh isn't making much of an effort to hide his trail," he said. "Fact is, it looks to me like he's not doing anything to cover his tracks."

"That's an indication of how confident he is," Baxter replied. "He doesn't think we can catch him. And even if we do, he won't be scared of a posse of soft-handed townies and a couple of tenderfoots."

The marshal's voice was pitched low so that it would not carry to the other men. Cody glanced over at him and said, "You sound like you don't think much of us."

"Don't get me wrong, Deputy. I know Luke Travis's reputation. I haven't seen you in action yet, but you wouldn't be working for him unless you were a good man."

"What about the rest of them?" Cody nodded toward the other posse members.

"I'm sure they're fine citizens," Baxter said. "They may work out just fine. But none of them really understands just how good Walsh is. I went up against his gang over in Missouri with a handful of tough, seasoned deputies behind me."

"What happened?" Obviously, Walsh had gotten away, but Cody was curious about the details.

Baxter grinned thinly. "I got out of that scrape alive, but none of my men did."

Cody restrained a low whistle. "That's bad," he said quietly. "Is that why you're so determined to bring Walsh in?"

"That's one of the reasons," Baxter answered. For a moment, both his voice and his gaze were faraway, as if he were seeing something entirely different from this relatively tranquil scene. Most of the posse members had finished their quick meals and were stretched out, dozing in the shade. Richard and Perkins were lying down, too, but they were restless, and occasionally one of them would moan softly in pain.

After a moment, Cody said, "You think it's going to be pretty bad when we finally catch up to Walsh, don't you?"

"It could be," Baxter admitted. "I'd feel better if we had some more deputies with us."

"Why did you bring us, then?" Cody wanted to know.

Baxter smiled again. "Because you and your friends were the best I could do at the time, son." He laughed softly. "Don't worry. I didn't bring this posse out just to get it all shot up."

Cody finished his coffee and frowned but said nothing. He was not so sure about Baxter's last statement. He had a feeling the marshal would do just about anything to capture Jake Walsh.

Baxter let the silence stretch for a minute, then asked, "You know anything about this Indian Territory we're headed for?"

"Not much," Cody replied with a shake of his head. "I've ridden into it a time or two, but never very far or for very long." He grinned. "And usually there was somebody chasing me, so I didn't have much time to see the sights."

"Regular hellion, were you?" Baxter's tone was friendlier now.

"I got around."

"Well, I can tell you this about Indian Territory, son. There's probably more lawbreakers to the square mile there than anywhere else in the country."

"I thought it was all Indian land," Cody commented.

"It's supposed to be," Baxter said. "And there are several big reservations there. But there are several white settlements around. Ranchers have leased some of the land from the government, and they run big herds there. The Texans are always bringing cattle across, too, on their way up the Chisholm Trail to your fair city of Abilene, or to Dodge or Ellsworth or Caldwell. It may be Indian Territory as far as Washington is concerned, but there are plenty of white men there, too." The marshal bit off a chunk of biscuit and then continued, "And very little law."

"Who keeps the peace?"

Baxter shrugged. "The army, supposedly. They administer the reservations and try to keep out the whites who don't have a reason to be there. But it's a big country, boy, and not enough troops to go around. U.S. marshals from Arkansas cover the eastern part of the territory when need be, but they don't often range out to the western half. Outlaw gangs from all over use the place to hole up when the law starts to close in on them."

"Like Walsh?"

Baxter nodded. "Exactly. If we don't catch up to Walsh before he crosses into Indian Territory, we'll be riding into the biggest pot of trouble you've ever seen."

"What are the chances of catching Walsh before then?" Cody thought he knew the answer to that question, but he wanted to see what Baxter would say.

The marshal chuckled. "Very few," he declared.

Cody shrugged and said, "Well, we'll go where we have to and do what we have to do."

"That's the spirit, Deputy," Baxter said as he

slapped Cody on the back. Cody could not tell if his tone was mocking or not. Baxter went on, "I think I've bent your ear long enough. You'd better grab a little sleep while you can."

"What about you?" Cody asked.

"Oh, don't worry about me. I'll stay awake so that the rest of you don't sleep too long. We'll need to get back on the trail pretty soon."

"You'll be all right?"

"I told you not to worry about me." Baxter's voice was firm.

Cody shrugged again, leaned back against the tree under which he was sitting, and tipped his hat down over his eyes. His head still ached from the clouting it had received from Walsh's men, but when he closed his eyes, the pain seemed to recede a little. Sleep drifted in quickly as exhaustion claimed him.

The next thing he knew Baxter was prodding his shoulder. "Time to get going, Cody," the marshal said.

Cody blinked rapidly. His eyes felt as though they had been dipped in sand. He shook his head and stood up, wondering how long he had been asleep. From the position of the sun, it had not been long. Around him, the other members of the posse were grumbling and climbing to their feet. Their movements were stiff and jerky.

In contrast, Dan Baxter seemed rested and fresh as he swung up into his saddle. "Mount up, men," he called. "We'd best be riding."

"My God!" Richard Stockbridge exclaimed as he straightened up, grabbing at the small of his back as the pain of sore muscles shot through him.

"You'll get over that, son," Baxter heartily assured

him. "A few more days in the saddle and you'll feel like you were born on the back of a horse."

"I already feel like I died on one," Richard muttered. He grasped his mount's saddle horn, put a foot in the stirrup, and stiffly pulled himself up. Perkins followed suit, moving even more awkwardly.

Cody took the final half cup of coffee that Orion offered him. The black brew was strong and bitter, but it was bracing. His headache had faded even more. He was convinced that he had not been hurt as badly as Dr. Bloom had feared.

The posse moved out, riding more slowly now than they had earlier. Baxter gradually increased the pace, though, taking the lead and keeping his eyes on the tracks left by Walsh and his gang.

The afternoon wore on. Riding beside Baxter, Cody wondered how the middle-aged lawman kept going and seemed to stay fresh. Baxter had to be packing a powerful hate for Jake Walsh, something that kept the fires inside him burning brightly. That was the only explanation that made sense to Cody.

The terrain continued to be fairly flat and grassy. The posse forded a narrow, shallow stream that Cody guessed to be Walnut Creek. Far to the northwest, they could see a squat elevation that was almost too insignificant to be called a mountain. Beyond that somewhere lay Dodge City. Cody doubted that Walsh's trail would take them through the cattle town; the outlaw would probably try to avoid as many pockets of civilization as he could.

As the sun was lowering toward the horizon, Cody asked Baxter, "How long are we going to ride?"

Baxter frowned at the tracks they were following. "The moon might be bright enough tonight to allow us to read these tracks, but I suppose we'd better stop and camp. What I said about horses applies to men, too. We don't want to ride them into the ground."

"That's what I was thinking," Cody agreed.

"We'll keep going until dark," Baxter decided, "and get back on the trail as soon as it's light in the morning."

Cody nodded. He peered at a thin line of trees a couple of hundred yards ahead of them. There was probably another creek there.

As Cody looked ahead, flame winked from the shadows under the trees. It was just a brief flash, suddenly there and then gone. Then something whined through the air nearby. And a second later he heard the slap of a shot.

Cody was already jerking back on his reins. He had recognized the muzzle flash of a rifle. "Ambushers in those trees!" he shouted as he wheeled his horse.

More gunfire spat from the cover of the trees. Several members of the posse yelled, but the shouts were of alarm, not pain. So far no one seemed to have been hit. The range was long, but unless the posse was able to take cover, it was only a matter of time before the hidden gunmen were able to zero in on them.

Cody's eyes darted around, looking for any kind of shelter. He spotted a clump of small boulders at the same instant that Baxter flung out an arm to point at the rocks.

"Take cover over there!" Baxter barked, spurring his horse toward the boulders.

Cody followed closely behind him. As he rode, he slid his Winchester from the saddle boot and levered a shell into the chamber. Throwing the rifle to his shoulder, Cody steered his horse with his knees and sent a slug whistling toward the trees. From this range, on horseback, it was extremely unlikely that he would hit any of the attackers, but at least they would know that the posse was going to fight back.

The other men galloped toward the rocks, many of them leaning over the necks of their horses to make themselves smaller targets. Richard Stockbridge followed their example, but as Edwin Perkins spurred his mount, he started to slip out of the saddle.

Orion saw what was about to happen and swerved his horse toward Perkins. Just as Perkins began to fall, Orion's horse surged up alongside his, and the tavern keeper's strong hand clamped on Perkins's arm. Seemingly effortlessly, Orion boosted the easterner back into the saddle.

"Hang on, laddie!" Orion yelled. "'Tis not far now!"

Baxter and Cody reached the boulders and flung themselves from their saddles. Cody grabbed the reins of his mount and dragged down on them, forcing the animal to lie down on its side. Baxter did the same. Even if the posse members escaped from this ambush with their lives, their pursuit of Walsh's gang would be over if their horses were cut down.

Cody threw himself behind one of the small boulders and started firing at the trees. He could see movement in the shadows now and could pick out targets. A bullet smacked into the ground a few feet to his right, plowing a furrow in the dirt. That was the closest the ambushers had come so far.

Baxter had his own rifle out and was pouring lead at the trees. The other men rode into the clump of boulders and frantically dismounted. Baxter paused in his firing long enough to glance over his shoulder and shout, "Get those horses down! We don't want a stray bullet hitting any of them!"

The posse members fought with their mounts,

slowly forcing the horses down into the unaccustomed positions. Richard and Perkins had no success at all, and once again Orion came to their rescue, his brawny muscles hauling on the reins until the horses were down.

Cody's Winchester ran dry. He twisted around and reached for the saddlebags on his horse where he kept his rifle shells. As he leaned out from the shelter of the rock, something tugged at his hat, sending it sailing off his head.

Cody swore, ducking instinctively and tasting dirt in his mouth as his face hit the ground.

"Lucky shot," Baxter said coolly. "Those coyotes can't aim that good."

Cody steeled himself and reached for the ammunition again, and this time he got the box of shells. He flopped back behind the boulder and began feeding cartridges into the magazine of the rifle.

The other members of the posse were sporadically firing at the ambushers. Cody's ears rang from the blasts. He called over to Baxter, "You think it's Walsh?"

"Him or some of his men," Baxter replied. He paused in his own firing. "It's a standoff. Neither bunch can do much damage to the other one, but we're pretty well pinned down here."

The pounding of hoofbeats came to their ears almost before the words were out of Baxter's mouth.

Cody jerked his head around and saw riders galloping toward them. The men were coming from the west, seemingly out of nowhere. They had to have been concealed in some hidden draw over there, Cody realized, just waiting until the ambushers in the trees had the posse pinned down. Then the riders could sweep behind and overrun the posse, wiping them out.

And knowing that isn't going to do us a bit of good, Cody thought bitterly. Walsh's daring maneuver had doomed them.

"Behind us!" Cody yelled. He swiveled and brought the Winchester to bear on the riders. At least they would go down fighting.

He fired as fast as he could, squinting through the haze of gun smoke that drifted in front of his eyes, and saw one of the riders fly out of the saddle. Orion and several other men had heeded his warning and had turned around to confront the new threat. But the men on horseback were coming fast and furious, the pistols in their hands blazing.

Cody saw another rider fall. That cut down the odds, but it was not going to be enough. There were still half a dozen attackers raining death on them.

Suddenly, Cody heard shots coming from another direction, the north. He fired the last round in his Winchester and then darted a glance in that direction. He could not make anything out, but the shots were definitely coming from the north, and they were having an effect on the outlaws. Two more men fell from their horses, and another sagged in his saddle but managed to stay aboard. Cody slipped his pistol from its holster and began to blaze away with it. He had no idea who the newcomers were or how many of them there were, but for the moment, that did not matter. All that was important right now was that the posse had a fresh lease on life, a new chance to survive this ambush.

Cody triggered off more shots. The mounted outlaws suddenly stopped their charge and began to swerve to the south, heading for the trees as fast as their horses would carry them. The men already concealed in the trees stopped firing as their companions raced toward them.

Cody sent one last shot after them, knowing that the range was too great for a handgun now. His emotions demanded the gesture.

"Better get down, son," Baxter advised dryly. "Those fellas in the trees might try one or two shots before they pull out."

Cody sprawled behind his rock again. "You think they're going to give it up?" he asked.

"It's likely," Baxter replied. "They've lost their advantage now that their little trick didn't work." The lawman glanced toward the north. "Whoever came up on our back trail sure saved our bacon."

Cody was still watching the trees. By now the mounted outlaws had disappeared into them. Then, abruptly, there was a flurry of movement, and Cody caught a glimpse of several more men on horseback. "Looks like they're pulling out," he told Baxter.

The federal marshal crawled over to his horse and retrieved the spyglass from his saddlebags. Focusing it on the grove of trees, he nodded a moment later. "Yep, just caught a glimpse of them as they went over the rise on the other side of that creek. They did part of what they set out to do, and now they're cutting their losses." He stood up. "On your feet, men. We'll be riding again in a few minutes."

Cautiously, Cody got to his feet, as did the other men. The deputy said, "You don't think they could be trying to trick us again by leaving a few men behind with rifles?"

Baxter shook his head. "That wasn't the main bunch. Walsh probably left them behind to ambush anybody who was following him. They were supposed to wipe us out if they could, slow us down if they couldn't. Well, we've been slowed down."

Slowed down, maybe, but not damaged too badly, Cody saw as he took a look around. A couple of the men had been nicked by bullets, but none of them was seriously hurt.

Richard Stockbridge and Edwin Perkins both looked pale and shaken. Cody wondered if they had even fired a shot during the skirmish. He would ask Orion about that later, when the two easterners could not overhear him.

Baxter reloaded his rifle, then said to Cody, "We'd better check those outlaws who got hit. I don't want any wounded men left behind us."

Cody nodded. He walked alongside Baxter as the marshal strode toward the sprawled bodies. From the look on Baxter's face, Cody was not sure what he intended to do if some of the outlaws were still alive. Surely a United States marshal would not simply execute them out of hand.

They were spared that decision. All four of the fallen hardcases were dead. Baxter approached them carefully, his rifle trained on them, and turned each one over with a booted foot, nodding in grim satisfaction as he saw that none of the men was breathing.

"We're cutting down the odds a little," Baxter said.

Cody nodded toward the north. He said, "With a little help. Look there."

Baxter's gaze followed Cody's outstretched arm. He was clearly expecting to see the men who had pitched in and made it possible for the posse to beat off the attack. One rider came out of the gathering shadows of dusk.

Cody gave a low whistle. "I figured there were three

or four men at least, the way those shots were coming."

"So did I," Baxter agreed. He walked forward to meet the rider.

Cody followed. It was hard to distinguish many details now that the sun had slipped behind the horizon, but he could tell that their rescuer was slight and sat the saddle easily. A broad-brimmed hat concealed the stranger's features.

Baxter said, "Howdy," as the rider came to a stop. "Glad to meet you, mister, whoever you are. You sure came along at the right time."

Cody glanced over his shoulder and saw that the posse members were keenly watching the newcomer. They were plainly well aware of how much trouble they would have been in if this rider had not helped them.

The stranger had a Winchester balanced across the pommel of the saddle. The rider reached up, swept off the hat, and smiled as thick blond hair tumbled around her attractive features.

"You're welcome, Marshal," Holly Stockbridge said.

Cody and Baxter stared at her, speechless for a moment. The younger man found his voice first. "What the devil are you doing here, gal?" he demanded harshly.

Holly laughed shortly. "Saving your hide, from the looks of things, Deputy Fisher."

"That was you who laid into those outlaws, miss?" Baxter asked.

"I don't see anybody else around here, do you, Marshal?"

Baxter smiled. "Have to allow that I don't."

Holly looked at Cody again. "I told you I was coming along with this posse, Deputy. You should have listened to me."

Richard Stockbridge came striding forward from the crowd of surprised men. "Holly!" he exclaimed. "What . . . what are you doing here? Where did you get those clothes?"

The girl glanced down at the butternut shirt and brown twill pants. They were not designed for a woman's figure, even a relatively slender one such as Holly's, but they still looked good on her. "The clothes are from Karatofsky's store, back in Abilene," she said. "They also sold me the hat and boots and this rifle here. I brought plenty of ammunition, and more supplies, too," she added, slapping the well-filled saddlebags draped over her horse's back.

"But . . . but you can't intend to go along with us," her brother protested.

Holly turned to Baxter. "Didn't you just say that you figured I saved this posse, Marshal?"

Baxter's grin grew wider. "Reckon I did."

"Wait a minute!" Cody said, speaking up before Richard could. From the look on Richard's face, he was about to object just as loudly as Cody was. "Marshal, you know this is no job for a woman. You can't let Miss Stockbridge ride along with us."

Holly's blue eyes stared coolly at him. "I didn't notice you turning down some help from a woman," she said, nodding toward the fallen outlaws. "I think two of those men were killed by my shots."

Cody shook his head. "That's just it. You're a lady—"

"And my sister's been kidnapped by Jake Walsh," Holly cut in. "Whether or not I'm a female doesn't matter, Deputy. I'm going to help get her back. I've been trailing you ever since you left Abilene, and I don't plan to go back until we've caught up to Walsh."

Edwin Perkins stepped over to Holly's horse and reached up to take her hand. "Holly, I think this is a wonderful gesture on your part. I know how concerned you are about Dorothea, and I appreciate that. But this is simply no place for a young lady. This . . . this is a wilderness, full of ruthless men."

"Like those, Edwin?" Again, Holly indicated the dead outlaws. "I know you must think I'm awful," she went on softly. "I should be having hysterics and fainting at the mere suggestion of blood, just like any other proper, well-bred young lady. But there's no time for that. We have to think about Dorothea."

Cody glanced at Baxter. Night was rapidly falling now, and it was hard to read the older man's expression. Finally, Baxter said, "We'll push on to that creek where Walsh's men were waiting for us. That'll be a good place to camp tonight. Miss Holly, you've earned the right to come with us."

"What?" Richard Stockbridge exclaimed. "Marshal, I demand—"

"I'm in charge of this posse, Mr. Stockbridge," Baxter cut in sharply. "We've come a long way from Abilene already. We can't spare a man to take Miss Holly back to town, and I don't intend to tell her she has to ride back by herself, even if she did follow us on her own. And I'm sure not going to leave her out here to fend for herself."

"But—" Richard started again.

"That settles the matter," Baxter said flatly. He looked at Cody. "Unless there are any more objections."

Cody returned the marshal's level stare. After a

moment, a grimace pulled at the young deputy's mouth. He shrugged. "No objections," he said. "You're right, Marshal."

"Let's get moving, then." Baxter turned to the rest of the posse. "Mount up, men. I think some coffee, some hot food, and a little sleep will do all of us some good."

Cody went to his horse and swung up into the saddle. He felt eyes on him and looked over to see Holly Stockbridge regarding him speculatively. He could not tell whether she was angry with him or not, or if she simply felt vindicated by Baxter's acceptance of her demand to ride with them.

Cody heeled his horse into motion. *I'm not going to worry about Holly Stockbridge,* he told himself. But that was not true, and he knew it. He had a feeling that he was going to be worrying a lot about Holly in the days to come.

Chapter Eight

———◆———

AT THE CREST OF A RISE, CODY FISHER DREW HIS HORSE to a stop and glanced over his shoulder at the group of riders behind him. It was two days since Holly had caught up with them, and three since the posse had set out. Surveying the tired, unshaven faces of the men, he reflected that if he looked anything like them, he must be a pretty sorry sight indeed.

The exceptions to that were Dan Baxter and Holly Stockbridge. Both the marshal and the young woman somehow had managed to stay fresh during the trek from Abilene.

Baxter reined in his white horse alongside Cody and looked down the slope. In the distance, the late afternoon sun sparkled on the waters of a winding stream. "You know that river, Cody?" Baxter asked.

"It's probably the Cimarron," Cody replied. He looked over his left shoulder and pointed to a low mountain rising in the distance to the northeast. "That's Mount Jesus back there." He gave the name the Spanish pronunciation.

"We ought to be getting close to Indian Territory, then, if that's the Cimarron."

"If we haven't crossed the line already." Cody scanned the terrain across the river. While still flat, the land was growing more rugged. Low hills, gullies, and rocky bluffs marked the landscape ahead, and the trees and brush were low and scrubby.

"Not a very pretty country," Baxter commented, following Cody's gaze. "But then we're not after very pretty people, either."

Richard Stockbridge rode up beside Cody and Baxter, a frown on his face. During the last few days his face had become leaner, and he was badly sunburned, as was Edwin Perkins. Richard said, "Why are we stopping, Marshal? Shouldn't we be pushing on?"

Baxter smiled. "Well, now, Mr. Stockbridge, I guess you could say we paused for a moment's reflection. Deputy Fisher and I agree that we're about to cross into Indian Territory."

"So?" Richard asked sharply.

"So there's something the deputy and I have to do," Baxter replied. He reached up and unpinned the badge from his chest. As he stowed it in his saddlebags, he said to Cody, "I'd advise you to do the same. Where we'll be riding from now on, these tin stars will only serve as targets."

Slowly, Cody removed his badge. His reactions surprised him. There had been a time when he might have scoffed at the idea that such a thing bothered him. Now he realized that the little piece of metal meant something to him.

He tucked the badge into his saddlebags and said, "You're right, Marshal. I suppose I'd better stop calling you that, though. How's Mr. Baxter sound?"

"Make it Dan," the federal lawman said with a laugh. He turned to the posse. "Did the rest of you hear that? As far as anyone else is concerned, Cody and I aren't lawmen until we catch up to Walsh and his gang."

The posse members, including Holly, nodded in understanding.

Baxter turned to Holly. "Ma'am, you'd best be sure to wear your hat as much as you can. I don't want to advertise the fact that we've got a pretty young woman traveling with us."

"All right," Holly replied. "And thank you for the compliment." She smiled.

Cody shook his head. Holly was not the same shy young woman she had been in Abilene. She was thriving out here on the trail. Her blue eyes sparkled, her cheeks were flushed with color, and in spite of her concern for Dorothea, she seemed to be enjoying herself. Cody had run into a few women who were comfortable around guns and horses, but none quite like Holly. She radiated self-confidence. She had not complained once since she joined the posse, and she was apparently untroubled that she had killed two men in helping them fight off the ambushers.

The trail had continued southwest from the creek that had been the scene of the attack. Baxter had found the spot where the men who had ambushed them had rejoined the rest of the gang. Then the posse had followed the trail for two days, stopping to camp at night even though Holly, Richard, and Perkins were impatient to catch up with Walsh.

As Baxter had expected, the outlaws had avoided Dodge City and the other, smaller settlements, swinging around them and continuing toward Indian Territory. The posse had circled the towns as well, although Baxter had sent Orion into Dodge with money to replenish their supplies. They had also been able to shoot some game along the way, so they were in no danger of going hungry.

If they were closing in on Walsh, the tracks offered no indication. Cody thought the sign looked a little fresher, but he could not be sure.

Baxter leaned forward in the saddle now and started his horse down the gentle slope. Cody fell in beside him, and the rest of the posse trailed along behind. As usual, Edwin Perkins brought up the rear, and the vigilant Orion McCarthy rode near him.

Richard Stockbridge had adjusted to the hardships of the trail better than had Perkins. The long hours in the saddle seemed not to bother Richard as they had at first, but Perkins was still in almost constant pain from his blisters and sore muscles. Cody had been surprised that Perkins did not want to turn back, considering both his discomfort and his opposition to the posse continuing its pursuit. The deputy supposed that love could stiffen a man's backbone and enable him to ignore his pain.

The posse crossed the Cimarron River about a half hour before sunset. Baxter kept them riding, rather than allowing them to make camp by the stream. The marshal did call a brief halt to refill the canteens, but that was all.

As daylight deepened into dusk, Cody noticed a light flicker across a shallow valley ahead. Quickly, several more lights began to glimmer near it. Cody nodded at them and said to Baxter, "Looks like a settlement up there."

"It does," Baxter agreed. He reined in his horse and gazed speculatively at the lights. They were becoming more clearly visible and were growing in number as the shadows of evening gathered. After a few moments, Baxter said, "I think you and I should take a little ride, Cody."

"We going into town?"

"Walsh can't avoid civilization forever," Baxter said, instead of answering Cody's question directly. "Besides, he's across the border now. He probably feels more confident now that he's out of Kansas. These are his stomping grounds."

"And you think maybe we can find out how far ahead of us he is, maybe where he might be headed?"

Baxter nodded. "If we're lucky."

Quickly he instructed the rest of the posse to make camp. There was no stream nearby, but there was a cluster of brush that would give them some cover.

"No fires," Baxter ordered. "We'll have to make do with cold camps for a while. Mr. McCarthy, you're in charge while Cody and I are gone."

"Aye," Orion rumbled. "D'ye know how long ye'll be away?"

Baxter shook his head. "It all depends on what we find. If we're not back by midnight, though, you'd better come looking for us."

Orion nodded in agreement.

Edwin Perkins strode up to them, wincing with every step but looking determined. "I want to accompany you, Marshal," he said firmly.

Baxter looked pained. "I told you not to call me that anymore, Mr. Perkins. And whatever this settlement is, it's no place for you. Why don't you just let Cody and me handle this part of the job?"

Perkins leveled a finger at the lights of the town. "What if Walsh stopped and is still there? What if Dorothea is over there, less than a mile away?"

"Then maybe we can pull her out of there," Baxter returned. "But I really don't think that's likely, Mr. Perkins. Walsh will head deeper into Indian Territory before he stops for good—you can count on that."

"What about me, Mr. Baxter?" Holly Stockbridge asked, stepping forward. "I wouldn't mind seeing a town again."

Cody spoke up, answering before Baxter could. "You'd just draw attention to us," he said. "You're too pretty for your own good."

He had spoken the words before he had a chance to think about them. Holly looked as surprised to hear them as he was to have said them. Cody turned away quickly, glad that it was almost totally dark. The flush on his face could not be seen by the other members of the posse.

Baxter grinned at Holly. "Like my young friend says, Miss Stockbridge, I'm afraid you would attract too much attention. It's better if just the two of us go in."

Holly nodded. "All right. If you're sure . . ."

"I'm sure," Baxter told her. He mounted up again. Cody was already back in his saddle. "Let's go."

The two men rode away from the camp. Picking their way across the valley, they found their progress impeded somewhat by a couple of dry washes. Paths in and out of the steep-sided gullies had to be found and negotiated. But within half an hour, Cody and Baxter were riding down the northern end of the tiny town's single main street.

The dusty street was lined on both sides with one-story frame buildings. One false-fronted structure appeared to have a second floor, but that was simply a façade. Not surprisingly, that building was a saloon. The light cast by a lantern hanging outside the livery stable across the street allowed Cody to read the faded letters that stated that this was the Double Eagle Tavern.

The other buildings housed the usual frontier businesses. Cody saw a gunsmith's shop, a smithy, a general mercantile, and even—out of place though it was—a millinery. Cody would have been willing to bet that there was not much of a market for women's hats and dresses in a settlement like this.

There was no jail, no marshal's office. The place probably did not even have a constable. Any law would be just what the citizens made for themselves.

Baxter paused in the middle of the street. Cody reined in beside him, and the two men were silent for a moment as they surveyed the town. Quite a few of the buildings were dark, the businesses closed for the day, but lanterns burned in the saloons, the stable, and most of the residences. Baxter pointed to a sign over the livery's double doors.

"Brinson's Gap Livery Stable," Baxter read aloud. "I guess that's where we are, Brinson's Gap. Ever heard of the place?"

Cody shook his head. "Nope. Never been here, either. You suppose we ought to start with that saloon over there?" He nodded toward the Double Eagle.

"That's as good a place as any," Baxter said. "I don't know about you, Cody, but I could use a drink."

Cody grinned. "So could I—at least one."

The prospect of a drink did appeal to him, even though he knew they had come into town primarily to gather information. Baxter had stictly forbidden drinking among the posse while they were on the trail, an order that did not sit too well with the men who never went anywhere without their flasks. Cody had agreed with him: If the men were allowed to drink, discipline in the posse would suffer, and some of them might get ideas about Holly Stockbridge. It was a difficult enough task to ride herd on a group of men, and when a young, attractive woman was around, the problems were compounded.

Baxter and Cody walked their mounts over to the hitch rail in front of the Double Eagle. Quite a few horses were already tied there, but Baxter and Cody were able to find room for their animals. The two men stepped up onto the plank walkway in front of the saloon. Baxter pushed through the batwings first, with Cody close behind him.

As they stepped inside, Cody saw that the Double Eagle was identical to scores of saloons across the frontier. Several tables and chairs were scattered around the room on the sawdust-covered floor. A long mahogany bar with a badly tarnished footrail ran down the right side of the main room. The wall behind the bar was lined with shelves packed with liquor bottles, a few of them empty. Beyond the end of the bar was a closed door that probably led into an office. Two more doors were on the rear wall, one undoubtedly opening onto a room for private poker games and the other a storage room.

A thick pall of smoke hung over the tables, diffusing the light from several kerosene lanterns that hung from the beams of the low ceiling. The wall opposite the bar was decorated with several stuffed animal heads. Cody saw a shabby, dusty buffalo and several tattered deer among the trophies.

About half of the tables in the room were occupied. At two of the tables poker games were in progress. The men sitting at the other tables were drinking and smoking, half-empty bottles and glasses arrayed in front of them. Quite a few men stood at the bar, although there were gaps where a man could belly up to the mahogany. Cody and Baxter headed for an opening about three fourths of the way down the bar, moving slowly so as to look over the occupants of the saloon.

The two lawmen were being studied in return. Most of the saloon's customers were cowhands, from the looks of their clothes. Seedy-looking men dressed in frock coats ran the poker games, and a bald-headed man wearing a dirty apron was tending the bar. The only woman in the room sat at one of the tables with a couple of men in town clothes, probably the owners of two of the businesses along the street. The woman had dark hair streaked with gray and was about thirty pounds too heavy for the tight green dress she wore. She turned bored eyes toward Cody and Baxter and sipped from the glass of whiskey in her hand.

As Cody and Baxter stood at the bar, the aproned man came down to them with a surly look on his face. "Something I can do for you?" he asked.

"A couple of beers would be right nice, partner," Baxter said mildly. "Cold ones, if you've got them."

The bartender snorted. "That's asking for too much in Brinson's Gap, mister," he said. "The beer's wet, but it ain't cold."

"Just so it cuts the dust, that's all I need," Cody put in.

As the bartender reached onto a shelf behind him and picked up two mugs, which looked none too clean, he asked, "Been on the trail a long time, have you?"

"Long enough," Baxter said. He watched as the bartender filled the mugs from a keg and then slid them onto the bar. The beer foamed over the tops and made puddles on the hardwood.

"Dollar," the bartender said curtly.

"For both of them?" Baxter asked.

"Apiece."

Baxter raised his eyebrows and said, "That's a mite steep, isn't it, friend?"

"That's the going rate. You don't like it, you can do your drinkin' somewheres else."

Baxter shook his head and dropped a couple of coins on the bar. "No call to get upset. We're not complaining, are we, Cody?"

Cody picked up his mug and sampled the warm, bitter brew. He grimaced and said, "Not about the price. The quality might be another matter entirely."

The bartender frowned. "Listen, you two, if you come in here to make trouble—"

"No, no," Baxter said quickly. "My young friend here sometimes lets his mouth get a little ahead of his brain, that's all."

Cody bit back the angry retort that sprang to his lips. Baxter was right; they had not come into town to pick a fight, but to gather information about Walsh and his gang. He picked up his beer, drank from it again, and said nothing.

The bartender moved away to pour drinks for some cowhands. Cody and Baxter nursed their beers for several minutes. Finally, Baxter licked his lips, set his mug down, and said loudly, "Wish I knew whether or not Jake was here yet."

Realizing what the marshal was doing, Cody thought rapidly and then asked, "Are you sure this is where he said to meet him?"

Baxter nodded. "Yeah, Brinson's Gap is what he said, all right. I just hope we didn't get here too late." Catching the bartender's eye, Baxter raised his empty mug to signal for a refill. When the aproned man came to take the mug, Baxter went on, "Say, you see 'most everybody who comes through this town, don't you, friend?"

"What makes you say that?" the bartender asked with a suspicious frown.

Baxter spread his hands and said in an innocent voice, "Well, look at the place. There's nowhere else around here that a man would want to have a drink, is there?"

The bartender grunted. "Ain't the only saloon in town," he said.

"No, but as my friend and I were riding in, I said to him, 'Let's go over there to the Double Eagle. We don't want anything to do with those hole-in-the-wall dives.'"

"I reckon this *is* the fanciest place in town." The barkeep nodded, a gleam of pride in his eyes.

Cody looked down at his beer, trying to stifle the grin he felt threatening to break out. Baxter was a smooth one, all right, and the bartender was not very bright.

Lowering his voice slightly, Baxter said, "We're supposed to meet a pardner of ours here, and I was wondering if you might have seen him. He's a big jasper, got a red beard. He might be riding with several other men, or he might have been by himself."

"This fella got a name?"

Baxter grinned. "When he feels like it, if you know what I mean."

"Yeah, I reckon I do. But I don't recollect seein' anybody like that in the last few days, mister. He probably ain't got here yet."

"I suppose you're right. I guess we'll just have to wait for him."

Baxter sipped his fresh beer. Cody tried not to gag on what was left of his first one and cast an eye around them. The conversation had been loud enough for several of the other men at the bar to hear, but they seemed to be ignoring it.

Someone stepped behind Baxter. He and Cody turned to see a woman standing there, a smile on her heavily made-up face. "Hello, boys," she said. "How are you doing?"

Baxter smiled back at her and lifted a hand to touch the wide brim of his black hat. "Why, we're just fine, ma'am. And yourself?"

"Thirsty," she replied. "You think I could talk either of you gents into buying me a drink?"

"I'm sure my friend here would be glad to," Baxter said, grinning at Cody.

Cody's mouth tightened, but he willed himself to relax. "Sure, ma'am," he said to the woman. "I'd be right happy to."

The woman sidled in between them and leaned an arm on the bar. "Whiskey, Tom," she said to the bartender.

The man poured a small glass and handed it to her. "That'll be two dollars," he said to Cody.

Cody tried not to glare at Baxter as he dug out the coins and passed them over. The woman said, "Thanks," and tossed back the drink. When she had finished it, she placed the empty glass back on the bar and let herself sag slightly toward Cody. He felt the swell of a heavy breast pressing into his side and supposed that was in payment for the drink.

"Anything I can do for you, cowboy?" the woman asked.

Cody let his left arm slide around her waist. She was really sort of pretty, he supposed, especially for a woman in a place like this. Of course, she was also probably twice his age.

"Nothing I'd like better if we had the time, sugar," he said brightly. "But me and my pard are supposed to meet a fella here, and there's no telling when he'll show up."

"Why don't you tell me about him, honey?" she suggested. "I might have seen him. And I sure wouldn't mind getting to know *you* better, too."

Cody glanced over her shoulder. The men who had been sitting at the table with her were gone. She had obviously failed to interest either of them in shelling out any more money, so now she was trying to move on to a fresh pigeon.

"Maybe he has been here," Cody said. "Ol' Jake would sure go for a lady like you, that's certain. He's a great big fella, got a bushy red beard. Looks a little like a bear."

Following Baxter's example, Cody pitched the words loudly enough for some of the other drinkers to overhear. The woman shook her head. "I'd remember somebody like that," she said. "I haven't seen him."

"That's too bad. In that case, I guess my friend here and I better mosey on, then, and see to our horses. If we're going to be waiting around, we'll need to put them in the stable."

Baxter spoke up. "I reckon I could handle that by

myself, Cody. No need for you to go." A smile pulled at the corner of the marshal's wide mouth.

Cody, trying not to grit his teeth, thought, *Baxter is enjoying this!* Quickly, he said, "You're crazy if you think I'm going to trust you with my horse. Last man who did that wound up shot, now didn't he, you old horse thief?"

Baxter's laugh boomed out. He moved around the woman, slapped Cody on the back, and said, "I reckon you're right, son. Come on, we'll both go."

The woman, reluctant to see Cody leave, clutched at his arm for a moment before she released him. "You come on back, you hear?" she said. There was a desperate look on her fleshy face.

"Sure, ma'am," Cody said. He did not like lying to her, but he did not want to hurt her feelings, either.

"You always were quite a hand with the ladies," Baxter said loudly as he and Cody went through the batwings. Cody muttered a curse under his breath.

They went to the hitchrack and untied their horses. Cody knew they were not going over to the stable, so he gripped the saddle horn and started to put a foot in the stirrup.

Dark shapes moved out of the alley next to the saloon. Cody saw them coming and tried to turn around, but with one foot raised, he was in an awkward position. Something hard rammed into his back, and he heard the familiar, ominous click of a pistol's hammer being pulled back.

A few feet away, the same thing had happened to Baxter. The shadowy figures had moved quickly, and before either lawman had a chance to do anything, they had been taken prisoner. Five men surrounded them, guns out and ready.

"You said you were goin' to take them hosses over

to the livery stable," a low voice rasped. "That sounds like a good idea to me. Move!"

The gun barrel pressed into Cody's back was shoved in painfully for emphasis.

Baxter took a deep breath. "Reckon we'd better do what they tell us," he said bleakly.

Chapter Nine

————◆————

CODY WAS SEETHING AS HE AND BAXTER STARTED ACROSS the street toward the livery stable. For a couple of lawmen, they had been taken easily. A man was in back of each of them, a couple more flanking them. The man who had given the orders led the way.

As the group moved into the stable, Cody got his first good look at the leader. The man was of medium height and seemed to be burly, although it was hard to be sure about his build. He wore a long duster, pushed back on one side to give him easy access to the walnut-handled Remington holstered on his hip. The man's hat was black and battered.

Glancing to each side, Cody saw that the two men flanking them looked about the same, and he would have bet money that the two prodding Baxter and him with their guns were of the same sort. *Hardcases, all of them,* Cody thought. *Just the sort of men who would ride with Jake Walsh.*

He was not sure, but he thought he had seen these men inside the Double Eagle. They must have slipped out the back just as he and Baxter were leaving, then moved quickly up the alley to get the drop on them. It seemed that the questions Baxter and he had thrown out had had an effect after all.

As the group of men entered through the barn's double doors, a wizened old man came out of the livery's office. He stopped in his tracks, eyes widening as he saw the drawn guns and the hard faces. The prominent Adam's apple in his thin neck jerked up and down as he swallowed and licked his lips nervously.

"Just don't ask any questions, Pop," the leader of the outlaws said in his gravelly voice. "We want to hire your stable for a few minutes."

"Th-the whole stable?" the old man quavered.

"Told you not to ask questions. Just for that, we ain't payin' you. Now git!"

As the leader started to lift his gun, the old man scurried for the doors and disappeared into the night.

One of the other men asked, "How do you know that old coot won't go yellin' for help, Durkin?"

The leader laughed harshly. "Who's he goin' to yell to? Ain't no law in this town, and the good citizens of Brinson's Gap don't give a damn." Durkin trained his Remington on Cody and Baxter. "Now get their guns."

One of the other outlaws pulled Cody's pistol and Baxter's twin Colts from their holsters. The man moved quickly and smoothly, not giving either lawman a chance to jump him, then tossed the guns to one side.

Durkin stepped closer, an ugly smile on his beard-stubbled face. "So," he said, "you two ride with Walsh, do you?"

Coldly, Baxter said, "I don't recall mentioning any name except Jake."

"Don't know any other Jake who fits that description."

"What if we are looking for Walsh? Do you know where he is?"

Cody had to admire Baxter. Even under these desperate circumstances, the marshal was still trying to get whatever information he could.

"If I knew where he was, why would I be wastin' my breath on you sons of bitches?" Durkin demanded angrily.

Suddenly, there was a loud thump from the hayloft. Durkin whirled to face the threat, instinctively raising his gun. Cody instantly recognized what might be their only chance.

The young deputy dove toward the distracted outlaw. Slamming into Durkin's back, he knocked him to the ground. Out of the corner of his eye he saw Baxter spinning around, swatting aside one of the guns that was trained on him. Then Cody's attention was riveted on Durkin as the outlaw twisted around and tried to level his gun.

Cody lunged, his fingers wrapping around Durkin's wrist and forcing the arm down. Durkin used his other hand to smash a fist into Cody's midsection, driving the air out of his body. Bright lights danced in front of Cody's eyes as he desperately clung to Durkin's gun hand.

Other hands grabbed Cody. He heard the thud of fists on flesh, the grunts of effort, the harsh rasping breaths of battling men. Then he was being torn away from Durkin. A bony fist cracked against his jaw, knocking him back and down. Somewhere in the big barn, a gun boomed.

"Hold 'em, dammit!" Durkin howled. He loomed up in front of Cody as one of the other men hugged the deputy from behind. Durkin lashed out, his big fists plowing into Cody's belly. The deputy would have doubled over if the other man had not been holding him up. He retched.

After what seemed like an eternity, Durkin stopped hitting him. Cody's head hung limply. Slowly he forced his gaze up, blinking to clear his vision. A few feet away, Dan Baxter was undergoing a similar beating, held by one man while another worked him over. The fifth man stood nearby, holding a gun and looking as though he wanted to use it.

"That's enough," Durkin said sharply to the man who was hitting Baxter. "We don't want to kill 'em yet. They got to tell us what they know about Walsh first. That shot hit anybody?"

The man with the gun shook his head. "Naw, it just went off when we was tryin' to corral that other feller. Reckon the townsfolk will come to see what's goin' on?"

"Not if they know what's good for them," Durkin grated. He bent to scoop up the gun he had dropped. "What the hell made that noise, anyway?"

The man holding Cody laughed. "Look up there at the loft, Durkin. That's what got you so spooked."

A curse ripped from Durkin's mouth. Cody lifted his eyes and saw a big gray-and-white tomcat sitting on the edge of the loft, calmly looking down at the men, a haughty expression on its face.

"Reckon he was sleepin' in that hay, and we woke

him up," one of the men said. "He must've jumped down off of something."

Durkin's face twisted in anger. "I'll teach the furry little bastard a lesson," he snarled, jerking his pistol up.

The gun cracked, but the cat had sensed the danger and moved just quickly enough. It darted away, disappearing with an angry hiss into the deep shadows of the loft.

"Reckon if cats could shoot back, you'd be dead right now, Durkin," one of the men scoffed.

"Shut up!" the outlaw leader snapped. Turning back to Cody and Baxter, he snarled, "Now, unless you two want more of the same, you'll tell us all you know about Jake Walsh!"

Baxter somehow found the strength to grin at him. The marshal's white hair was in disarray, and several streaks of blood marked his face. But he still laughed and said, "Why are you asking us? We thought you rode with Walsh!"

Durkin shook his head. "Not hardly. He's got something we want, though. You two ain't part of his gang?"

"Seems we've all made a mistake, my friend," Baxter said.

Durkin brought up his gun, jabbed the barrel under Baxter's chin. "I ain't your friend, you stupid bastard! I want to know whatever you know about Walsh. Is he comin' here?"

From where he stood a few feet away, Cody spat blood from his mouth and rasped, "Let him alone! He's telling you the truth. We're looking for Walsh just like you are."

The man holding Cody painfully tightened his grip

as Durkin swung toward the deputy. "You're a feisty one, ain't you?" the outlaw leader growled. "Listen, mister, we want what Walsh has got, and if you don't know where he is, I ain't got one damn reason for keepin' you alive. Lord knows we don't need any more competition!"

Baxter spoke up quickly. "We may not know where Walsh is, but maybe we can help you find him, mister. We've got a score to settle with him, too."

"Forget it," Durkin sneered with a shake of his head. "You're just tryin' to save your own skin now. You got no score to settle with Walsh, you just want that money, like us. Ain't goin' to work." He leveled his pistol at Cody and snapped at his men, "Get out from behind them!"

Abruptly, the outlaws released Cody and Baxter, and the realization that Durkin was about to execute them flashed through Cody's mind. He had to do something to stop the man, anything—

An eardrum-rattling shout rang through the barn before Durkin could pull the trigger. The outlaw spun around and jerked his gun toward the open loft as a huge shape came hurtling down from the shadows. Durkin let out a yell as he triggered wildly. The Remington boomed.

Orion McCarthy's booted foot slammed into Durkin's chest, driving the outlaw to the ground. Orion's full weight came down on the man's chest, and Durkin shrieked as his bones snapped and cracked. Thrown off balance, Orion pitched forward, but he managed to hang on to the shotgun in his hands. As the other outlaws whirled toward him, he touched off both barrels.

The double charge caught one of the men in the

middle of the body and smashed him backward in a spray of blood. The outlaw sprawled lifeless on the ground.

Cody and Baxter leaped toward their guns as the other outlaws turned their weapons on Orion. Baxter snatched up his Colts. "Try to take one alive!" he rapped to Cody.

A gun blasted, the slug kicking up dirt only inches from Orion. The Scotsman dropped to the ground and rolled toward Durkin, who was still writhing in agony.

"Look out!" one of the outlaws shouted, realizing that Cody and Baxter were now armed. He and one of the other hardcases spun toward the lawmen.

Cody dropped to a knee and twisted around. An outlaw bullet whined by his head as he leveled the gun. He triggered twice, aiming instinctively.

Beside him, Baxter was firing with both hands. As each blast kicked the gun up in recoil, Baxter squeezed off a shot with the other hand.

The three outlaws still on their feet staggered back as bullets thudded into them. Their fingers yanked the triggers convulsively, spraying slugs around the barn. Then, almost in one motion, all three fell to the stable floor.

Baxter stopped firing. His face was a frozen mask as he squinted through the haze of gun smoke drifting in front of his face. He kept his guns trained on the fallen outlaws, just in case one of them still had some fight in him.

Cody moved quickly to the bodies, carefully staying out of Baxter's line of fire. "They're all dead, all right," he reported a moment later, after checking the corpses.

Baxter cursed.

Cody turned toward Orion, who was climbing back onto his feet. There was no need to check on the man Orion had blasted with the shotgun; the buckshot had practically cut the outlaw in half. Cody met the Scotsman's level gaze and asked, "Are you all right?"

"Aye. 'Tis more than I can say f'this fella." He gestured toward Durkin with the barrels of the shotgun.

The outlaw leader was lying on his back, fingers scrabbling futilely at his crushed chest. Blood dribbled from both corners of his mouth, and his eyes were wide and staring.

Cody, wincing at the pain in his belly, knelt beside Durkin. "We'll go get a doctor for you," he said.

Baxter stepped up on Durkin's other side. "Don't be in such a hurry, Cody," he said icily. To Durkin, he asked, "Just exactly what were you after, mister?"

"This man's hurt bad," Cody protested before Durkin could answer.

"Don't you think I know that? That's why I want him to talk now. How about it, Durkin? Just what do you know about Walsh?"

Durkin stared up at them. "D-damn . . . you. . . ." he gasped, his voice choked from the blood in his throat. "I hope . . . that if you get that f-fifty . . . grand from Walsh . . . that you spend it in Hell, you bastards!"

The last words came from him in a rush, and his head fell limply to one side.

"Reckon he got torn up pretty bad inside when Orion landed on him," Baxter said. He thumbed fresh cartridges into his guns, then slid them back into their holsters.

"Reckon so," Cody agreed. He stood up slowly. As

evil as Durkin was, this was still an awful way to die, he thought. Grinning wearily at Orion, Cody went on, "I'd about given up when I saw you come flying out of that loft, Orion."

"'Twas almost too late I was," the Scotsman agreed.

Baxter said, "That was you who made that noise up there a few minutes ago, wasn't it?"

"Aye." Orion nodded. "I saw all o' ye being herded in here when I came into town. 'Twas not an easy job climbing into th' loft from outside. 'Twas lucky tha' cat was up there t'fool those outlaws."

"Well, we appreciate the help—even if I did tell you to stay out at the camp with the others."

"Seemed t'me ye might need help 'fore midnight."

Baxter found his hat, knocked the dents out of it, and settled it on his head. "We'd better get out of here. We won't be learning anything else in Brinson's Gap."

Orion jerked a thumb at the sprawled bodies. "What about th' law?"

Cody shook his head. "No law of any kind. That's why Durkin and his men felt free to grab us like that."

Orion broke the shotgun open and reloaded it, then fell in behind Cody and Baxter as they left the livery stable. Cody saw quite a few people watching them through the window of the Double Eagle. Other curious bystanders stood on the boardwalks in front of the other saloons. The stable's elderly proprietor had probably spread the story of being kicked out of his place of business by Durkin's gang.

Despite their curiosity, none of the townspeople approached Cody, Baxter, or Orion as they mounted their horses and rode out of town. The three men headed north toward the posse's campsite.

As they rode, Cody mulled over what had happened, and as he pondered it, a pretty clear picture began to emerge. The conclusions he drew were not pleasant ones.

"The word's gotten out, hasn't it?" he asked as the lights of Brinson's Gap faded behind them.

"Looks like it to me," Baxter agreed. "You know how word gets around, Cody. If a no-account gang like Durkin's knows about the fifty thousand that Walsh took from the train, chances are that every outlaw in the territory knows about it, too."

"And Dorothea," Cody said.

Baxter nodded. "And probably Dorothea, too. The pretty gal and the money together like that . . . Well, they make a tempting target, Cody."

"Durkin was quick to think that we were after the money, too."

"Why not?" Baxter asked. "From here on out, every wild bunch we run into is going to think the same thing. And they're going to be on Walsh's trail, just like we are."

"Tha' is going t'make it harder," Orion put in.

"Yes." Baxter nodded. "It sure will. But all we can do is go ahead."

Cody laughed abruptly, but there was no humor in it. "Shoot," he said. "I don't know what you two are worried about. The odds against us have only increased a couple of hundred or so. That's all."

Chapter Ten

━━━◆━━━

As Cody, Baxter, and Orion approached the camp, they suddenly heard a voice call out, "Hold it, you men! We've got you covered!"

Cody recognized the voice of Flood, one of the posse members. He said, "Take it easy, Flood. It's just me and Baxter and Orion."

Several dark shapes emerged from the brush, rifles in hand. They clustered around the men who had just returned from Brinson's Gap. Flood pushed back his hat and said, "Sorry, Cody. In the dark like this, we couldn't tell who you were. We heard all that shooting in town a little while ago, and I guess we got a little spooked."

The man sounded nervous, and Cody realized once again that this posse was made up of inexperienced townsmen from Abilene. It was surprising that they had come this far without anyone complaining too much or wanting to turn back.

Edwin Perkins emerged from the shadows as the trio dismounted. "What did you find out?" he asked anxiously. "Had Walsh been there? Did you hear anything about Dorothea?"

"Hold on there, Mr. Perkins," Baxter said. "I think Walsh went around that town, just like he has all the other settlements we've passed. I think he's got a particular destination in mind, and he's not going to stop until he gets there."

"But what was the shooting?" one of the other posse members asked.

"Some other hardcases grabbed Cody and me," Baxter explained. He tiredly rubbed a hand along his jaw. "It looks like the word has gotten out about that money Walsh stole from the train. We're going to have some competition from here on out."

Richard Stockbridge pushed forward. "You mean other outlaws are after the money?"

Baxter nodded. "They'll figure that they might as well collect that ransom instead of Walsh's having it."

"That's awful," Holly burst out. "What are we going to do now?"

"Same as we've been doing," Baxter said flatly. "We'll stay on the trail and see what happens."

As Holly turned away, her features drawn, Cody thought, *Her worry over Dorothea is starting to get to her.*

Baxter, Orion, and the deputy sat down to eat a late supper. After all the punches Cody had received in the belly, he figured he would not be hungry, but he surprised himself by eating several cold biscuits and strips of jerky. Some of the men, wanting to know the details of the fight in town, crowded around them.

Baxter sketched it for them, dwelling for the most part on Orion's daring rescue of Cody and him. The burly Scotsman received several slaps of congratulation on the back.

Cody wished he could have a cup of hot coffee, but he understood Baxter's reason for ordering a cold camp. It made more sense than ever, now that they knew other outlaws were prowling around, looking for Jake Walsh.

Baxter assigned men to stand watch during the night, and then the rest of the posse rolled up in their blankets to get some sleep. After what had happened in town, neither Cody, Baxter, nor Orion would be taking a turn at guard duty. Cody was grateful for that: A full night's sleep would help.

This long chase was starting to wear on all of them.

The next morning the posse continued south. Once the sun was up, it was easy to see where Walsh's gang had swung around Brinson's Gap. Following the tracks, the posse soon found that Walsh had shifted direction somewhat, veering toward the southeast and heading into the wildest section of Indian Territory.

Late in the morning, Cody suddenly felt a cool breeze on his back. He looked over his shoulder, frowning at the clear blue sky. Despite the absence of clouds, there was a definite chill in the air.

Riding beside him, Baxter spoke up. "Yeah, I feel it, too. We're due for a storm, I'm afraid. We've been lucky so far, but I knew it couldn't last."

Cody shook his head. "I don't see a cloud in the sky," he said.

"They're back there, though, and they're coming. I thought I smelled it in the air when we got up this morning."

"Rain'll wash out the tracks," Cody pointed out.

Baxter nodded. "It sure will. But we've a pretty good idea which direction Walsh is headed in. I don't think he's going to start getting fancy now."

"Hope not," Cody grunted.

He heard the other men muttering as the chilly wind began to pick up. It was not cold, by any means, but Richard Stockbridge and Edwin Perkins broke out their jackets and shrugged into them.

Orion moved up alongside Cody. The stiff breeze was fluttering the brim of his hat. "We're in for a bit of a blow, lad," he said.

"Yep," Cody agreed. He glanced over his shoulder again. A low line of swiftly moving clouds now stretched across the northern horizon, and they were coming closer by the second. "We'll just keep on the way we're going," Cody said. "Try to ride it out—that's all we can do."

The horses became more nervous as the storm began to overtake them. The low rumble of thunder became audible, and the air seemed charged with electricity.

Cody remembered a time when he had been riding in the high country of Colorado and a thunderstorm blew up suddenly. Sparks had jumped around his horse's ears, and there had been an eerie feeling in the air that still made him shudder when he thought about it. This storm would not be that bad, he thought, since they were a long way from any mountains, but that strange sensation prickled along his spine anyway.

The first drops of rain fell, fat and heavy and stinging when they hit. The posse members began pulling slickers from their saddlebags.

That was one item that Holly Stockbridge had

neglected to bring in her hurry to leave Abilene. Seeing that she still wore only her butternut shirt and pants, Cody dropped back and fell in beside her. He held out his slicker to her. "Here, you'd better take this."

Holly shook her head. "It's my own fault I didn't bring one with me. I'm not going to take yours."

"I don't like to see a lady having trouble. Goes against my grain not to do something about it."

She smiled. "Thanks, Cody, but I meant what I said."

"All right, if you're going to be one of those durned stubborn females," he muttered.

"That's all I know how to be."

Cody shrugged into the slicker, then opened his saddlebags once more and pulled out a folded piece of oilcloth. "Wrap this around you," he said, extending it to Holly. "It'll be better than nothing."

"Sure. Thanks." She took the oilcloth and deftly fashioned a cape with it. Looking at her, Cody wondered if she would wind up staying drier than the rest of them.

A sudden shout jerked his attention away from Holly Stockbridge. He looked at Baxter and saw that the marshal had brought his mount to a halt. Baxter held one hand up to stop the posse, while the other rested on the butt of one of his Colts.

The sky had grown dark, making midday look more like dusk. Ahead of the posse, a figure on horseback slowly rode out of the gloom. The slicker-clad figure had a rifle in his hand, but the barrel was pointed up and a white rag was tied to it.

"Flag of truce," Baxter muttered as Cody quickly joined him at the front of the posse. "Wonder what this is about?"

"Could be a trap set by Walsh," Cody suggested.

Baxter shook his head. "Not likely. That's not his style. He'd rather fight you face-to-face than sneak around."

"He's tried to ambush us before," Cody reminded him. "Remember back there at that creek."

"I remember. This just doesn't feel like a trap to me, though."

Cody hesitated. Knowing how veteran lawmen developed an instinct for trouble, he recognized and trusted that instinct in Baxter. But anybody could make a mistake, and an error in judgment here could cost all of them their lives.

"We'd better go see what he wants," Cody finally said. "Just you and me. The others will stay here."

Baxter nodded. "Doesn't hurt to be careful." He turned in his saddle and called to Orion, telling him to see that the posse stayed where it was.

"Aye," Orion acknowledged. He had draped the tail of his slicker over his shotgun to protect it from the rain, but the deadly weapon could be out and blasting in a split second, if need be.

Baxter heeled his horse forward toward the oncoming stranger. Cody followed close behind him. The man carrying the flag of truce plodded steadily toward them. Baxter called to him, "That's far enough!"

Cody and Baxter met the man about fifty yards from the posse. The stranger brought his horse to a stop facing them, rain dripping steadily from the brim of his hat. He had a lined, middle-aged face with a ragged mustache over his thin lips.

Eyeing the way Cody and Baxter kept their hands on their guns, the man made a small gesture with the rifle and said to the older of the two, "This here means I don't want no shootin', mister."

"I know what it means," Baxter said coldly. "What do you want?"

"You folks come down here from Abilene?"

"What if we did?"

"Walsh said one man was to come with the ransom. You ain't too good at follerin' directions, are you, mister?"

Baxter pulled his gun out of its holster and drew a bead on the man's face. "What happens if I blow you out of the saddle?"

Cody tensed, unsure of what Baxter intended to accomplish.

The stranger grinned, but his eyes darted nervously. "Oh, I reckon Jake'd just figure you didn't intend to pay up. Then he wouldn't have any reason to keep that gal alive and unhurt. He'd probably turn her over to the boys for some fun 'fore he killed her."

Slowly, Baxter lowered the pistol. His blue eyes glittered dangerously, and his jaw was tightly clenched. "All right. Just so we know where we stand. Say what you've got to say and don't try anything funny, or I'll shoot you and take my chances."

"It ain't *your* chances you got to worry about, mister. It's that gal's." Seeing the look on Baxter's face, the man hurried on. "Walsh said for me to find out if you've got the money with you."

As Baxter shook his head, his stony eyes never left the stranger's face. "It's on its way from Abilene. It shouldn't be more than a day or two behind us."

"Better not be. Jake's gettin' a little antsy." The stranger squared his shoulders. "Now listen close. Here's the way it's goin' to be. When you get that ransom money, you bring it to a place called Elysium. That's a little town 'bout thirty miles south of here. Ghost town, now, at least when we ain't there."

"So that's Walsh's hideout," Baxter commented.

"One of 'em." The man grinned. "You sound like a lawman, mister. Reckon you star-packers ought to know by now that you ain't never goin' to catch Jake Walsh. He's too damned smart for you."

"Just say what you came to say," Baxter advised. The gun was still in his hand.

"You bring that money to Elysium, and you send it into town with one man. You got that, lawman? One man. Any more'n that come ridin' in, that gal is dead."

Baxter nodded. "I understand."

The hardcase gave a curt nod in return, then wheeled his horse and spurred it into a gallop. Cody and Baxter sat still on their mounts and stared after him until he had disappeared into the rain and gloom. Then they turned and rode slowly back to the posse.

Richard and Perkins, too impatient to wait for them to return, urged their mounts forward despite Orion's telling them to stay where they were. "What was that about?" Richard demanded as he drew his horse to a halt in front of the two lawmen.

"Was that man a messenger from Walsh?" Perkins asked.

Baxter nodded. "Walsh sent him, all right. He had orders for us."

When Baxter paused, Richard burst out anxiously, "Well, what did he have to say? Is Dorothea all right?"

"I think she's fine," Baxter said. "I didn't ask. I wouldn't trust that fella too much. I'd rather just believe your sister is all right until I know differently, Mr. Stockbridge."

Tightly, Perkins asked, "What does Walsh want?"

"We're supposed to take the ransom money to a ghost town south of here called Elysium." Baxter had raised his voice so it would carry over the sound of the rain to the rest of the posse, which had ridden up slowly to join them. "Walsh probably isn't too happy that the whole group of us came after him, but he still says he'll release the girl if one man brings the ransom into Elysium."

Perkins leaned forward in his saddle. "That's what we're going to do, isn't it? I'm sure that Mr. Stockbridge sent it on immediately when he got that note Walsh left on the train."

Cody thought Perkins was being overly optimistic. There was no guarantee that Maxwell Stockbridge had decided to pay the ransom for Dorothea. Even if he had, there was certainly no way of knowing how far behind them the money was—or whether it would end up anywhere near Elysium. It might be days before it arrived.

If it ever did . . . With the whole territory up in arms, that money might be stolen before it ever caught up with the posse.

From the thoughtful look on Baxter's face, Cody had a feeling that the marshal's thoughts were running along the same lines. After a moment, Baxter said, "We can't assume anything, men. The best thing we can do now is continue on to this Elysium place. Once we get there we'll decide what to do."

"But . . . but Dorothea—" Perkins began.

"I said, we'll decide what to do when we get there," Baxter said firmly. He wheeled his horse. "And we're wasting time right now."

Cody turned his mount and fell in beside Baxter. Behind them the other posse members urged their horses into motion. Perkins and Richard sat still, looking angry and confused. Holly rode up beside Perkins and put a hand on his arm. "Come on,

Edwin," she said softly. "We have to push on. Like Mr. Baxter said, it's all we can do right now."

Perkins sighed heavily. "I suppose you're right." Wearily, he heeled his horse into a walk.

Cody turned in the saddle to check that the posse was following. They were spread out somewhat, as usual. Even in this miserable rain, Richard Stockbridge was proving to be a better rider than Perkins. He rode along with several of the men from Abilene, muttering complaints to them about the way Baxter and Cody were handling things. Though Cody could not make out the words clearly, he sensed what the young man was doing. It had been plain from the start that neither Richard nor Perkins had been happy with the posse's leadership. Perkins had suffered in silence, but Richard was not the type to do that. As Cody studied the men, the thought of going into battle with this bunch at his back made him very uneasy.

In a low-pitched voice that the others could not hear over the steady sluicing of the rain, Baxter said, "I guess you know I'm not going to give Walsh that money, Cody, even if it does show up."

Cody kept his eyes forward, not looking over at the marshal. The slanting rain made the whole world wet and gray. "Don't think it'd do any good to pay Walsh," the deputy said slowly. "Chances are he'd kill Dorothea anyway, along with the man who delivered the money."

"That's exactly what he'd do. The only chance that young lady has is for us to get her away from Walsh before it comes time to deliver the ransom. One thing's for sure—I'm not going to let scum like Jake Walsh get away with hurting innocent people." Baxter's voice was every bit as cold as the rain falling from the leaden skies. "I'll stop him one way or another, if it's the last thing I do. And then he'll be where a murderer like him belongs—at the end of a rope!"

Cody said nothing for a long moment. He looked over at Baxter and saw that the marshal's face was set in an expressionless mask despite the vehemence in his voice. Baxter's hate for Walsh seemed to run awfully deep, deeper than a lawman's feelings toward an outlaw normally did.

It seemed to Cody that Dorothea's life was not the most important thing to Baxter. She was only an excuse for the lawman to go after Jake Walsh again.

"I think I'll go talk to Orion for a few minutes and see if he knows anything about this part of the country," Cody finally said.

"Good idea." Baxter nodded.

Cody turned his horse's head away from Baxter and rode back toward the rest of the posse. He spotted Orion and dropped back until he was riding beside the Scotsman.

Nodding toward Perkins, Cody asked, "How's the tenderfoot doing?"

"'Tis a good, big heart the man has," Orion replied. "But he has no business being out here. I'll be keeping an eye on him."

"I appreciate that." Cody took a deep breath. "I want to talk to you about Baxter, Orion."

Orion glanced shrewdly at him. "Something about the man troubles ye?"

Quickly, Cody explained his feeling that Baxter was more interested in catching Walsh than he was in saving Dorothea. He finished by saying, "I'm afraid that when it comes down to it, Baxter might sacrifice

Dorothea if it meant he'd get a chance to face down Walsh."

"Aye, I can see how tha' would worry ye. If it comes to tha', lad, what are ye ginna do?"

Cody grimly stared into the rain. "I'll stop him," he said flatly. "Somehow, I'll stop him."

Chapter Eleven

THE RAIN STOPPED IN MIDAFTERNOON AS THE STORM moved away from them to the south. The posse members were glad to see it go, for there was nothing more miserable than riding in a soaking downpour.

Cody shook the rain off his hat and jammed the soggy item back on his head. Remembering that Holly Stockbridge had been forced to make do with the piece of oilcloth to protect her from the elements, he turned his horse and rode back along the line of men until he reached her.

She had undraped the oilcloth and was folding it up as he approached her. She looked up at Cody with a grateful smile. "Here," she said, holding the cloth out to him. "I appreciate it, Cody. It worked just fine."

Indeed, as Cody had suspected, Holly did not look any wetter than the rest of them. If anything, her head was a little drier. She shook it, dashing a few droplets of water from her blond hair. The clouds overhead were parting in places, letting the afternoon sun shine through, and the rays struck highlights in Holly's thick hair.

"How long do you think it'll take us to get to this Elysium place?" she asked.

"Walsh's man said it was about thirty miles south of where we met him. We can't cover that much ground today, but we ought to get there sometime tomorrow, by the middle of the day if we're lucky."

Holly nodded. The smile had vanished from her face, replaced by a solemn look. "I'll be glad when we get there," she said. "Dorothea must be having an awful time."

"I don't think they'll hurt her," Cody tried to assure her. "She's no good to them unless she's alive."

Holly shot him a meaningful glance. "That doesn't mean they have to return her in the same condition she was in when they took her."

"That's true enough," Cody said. For some reason, he did not feel like lying to Holly.

"Besides, even if we try to pay the ransom and get her back that way, what are the chances that Walsh will just kill her anyway?"

Cody did not tell her that he and Baxter had discussed that possibility and found it highly likely. Instead, he smiled thinly and said, "Well, I don't think we'd let Walsh do that. He's up against a posse of good men here."

"Maybe." Holly did not sound convinced. "But you and Marshal Baxter and Mr. McCarthy are the only ones who have much experience with outlaws like Walsh. Edwin and my brother had never even been on horseback before all this."

Cody glanced at Perkins and Richard Stockbridge, who were riding several yards ahead of them. Perkins seemed to be sitting his saddle a little better; he knew now that Dorothea was only a short distance away, and that knowledge seemed to have strengthened him. He was no longer dragging at the rear of the posse.

"They'll be all right," Cody said. "Both of them really love Dorothea."

"Edwin does," Holly admitted. "I'm not sure Richard really loves anything except money and power, and Father doesn't allow him a great deal of either."

Cody looked at Richard Stockbridge and asked, "If that's true, why did he come along with us?"

Holly shrugged prettily. "I'm not sure. I suppose his feelings for Dorothea could be stronger than I thought. Or it could be that he's just angry that anyone would dare to attack the Stockbridge family this way."

Cody hesitated and then said, "And why did you come, even after I told you you couldn't?"

"Maybe I just wanted you to know you can't push me around," Holly replied with a grin; then the quick grin faded, and she became more serious. "Dorothea is my sister. I love her, and I have to help her if I can."

"From what I saw back in Abilene, it can't have been easy all the time, being Dorothea's sister, I mean." Cody realized that he was venturing into matters that were none of his business, but he liked Holly and found it easy to talk to her. He was honestly interested in what she had to say.

Holly looked thoughtfully at him for a moment. "If you're saying that I had to spend a lot of time in her shadow," she said, "you're right. I was never the belle of the ball like Dorothea. But I never wanted to be.

The things she took such a great interest in, like clothes and parties and boys . . . well, I was happier concerning myself with other things."

Cody was unsure how to reply to that, so he said nothing. It was hard to believe that a young lady as attractive as Holly had not had some suitors. She might not be as flirtatious as her sister, but she was nowhere near as flighty.

He looked again at Edwin Perkins. The easterner was moving his head slowly from side to side, alertly scanning the horizon ahead of them. As Cody studied his profile and saw the intensity on the man's features, he was struck by the depth of feeling that Perkins carried for Dorothea.

Cody grimaced. Now that he understood things a little better, he was sorry that he had even briefly considered a liaison with Dorothea Stockbridge. She had easily manipulated him, just as she had done with every man she had met.

After a moment, Holly went on, "Don't get me wrong, Cody. I like men just fine. It's just that I got bored pretty quickly with the kind of boys who were always flocking around Dorothea."

Cody looked over at her and met her eyes. There was admiration in them, and maybe a hint of something else, too.

"I think I'd better get back up to the front with Baxter," he said quickly, turning his eyes away from hers. "I'm never sure what's going on in that old boy's brain."

"What do you mean?" Holly asked with a frown.

Cody shook his head, not wanting to share with her problems he had already discussed with Orion. "Nothing for you to worry about," he said as he heeled his horse into a trot.

When he reached the head of the posse, he posed the same question to Baxter that Holly had asked him. "When do you think we'll get to Elysium?"

"If we stop and camp tonight, like we've been doing all along, it'll be tomorrow sometime," the white-haired marshal replied.

Something in Baxter's tone made Cody glance at him sharply. "You're thinking about not stopping?"

"Before, we stopped and camped because we needed the daylight to follow Walsh's tracks." Baxter nodded toward the muddy ground over which they were riding. "Well, there're no tracks to follow anymore. If the clouds break up enough, the stars will keep us heading south. And Walsh probably isn't expecting us until tomorrow."

"So we ride on through the night?" Cody asked.

Baxter said slowly, "I'm thinking about it. Haven't made up my mind for sure yet. What do you think, Cody?"

The deputy considered the possibilities for a long moment. What Baxter had said made sense. "Sounds like that might be the best thing for us to do. But you've got to remember, if we don't make camp, we're going to have a bunch of tired men and horses when we finally get to the place."

"True enough. We'll need to take a short rest along about sundown, maybe. Let the men get a little sleep and some grub. Think that might work?"

Cody nodded. "It's probably the best we can do."

He wondered, as he rode along, if that best would be good enough to save Dorothea Stockbridge's life.

The posse pushed on through the afternoon, their progress slowed by the mud that the storm had left in its wake. Several of the creeks and gullies that lay across their path were full of fast-running water, and the posse had to ford them carefully.

As Baxter had hoped, the thick bank of clouds continued to move to the south. By the time the sun was lowering toward the horizon, the sky overhead was clear and bright. During the night the posse would be able to chart its course by the stars.

Baxter held up a hand to halt the riders behind him. He turned in the saddle and said, "We're going to stop for an hour or so. Get something to eat, try to catch a little sleep if you want to. But then we're going to ride on."

A murmur of protest ran through the posse. The men had complained very little so far, but with every grinding hour spent in the saddle, they drew closer to the end of their reserves of strength. One man called out angrily, "Baxter, these horses can't go on all night. They've got to get some rest!"

"Listen, you men!" Baxter's harsh voice cut through the grumbling. "Walsh won't be looking for us to reach that ghost town until tomorrow sometime. If we ride hard tonight, maybe we can get there by dawn. We can surprise those renegades, maybe wipe them out if we're lucky!"

The vehemence of the marshal's words drew mutters of approval from some of the men, but others still thought he was asking too much of them. Edwin Perkins urged his horse to the forefront of the group and demanded, "Do you mean to attack the town as soon as we reach it, Baxter?"

"I haven't decided that yet," Baxter replied coolly. "But I don't mind having that choice to make, rather than letting a skunk like Walsh call all the shots."

"You'd take a chance on getting Dorothea killed, then!"

Leveling icy blue eyes at him, Baxter leaned forward in his saddle and said, "Mr. Perkins, there's been a chance of that ever since Walsh dragged her out of Abilene. You've known that all along."

"But you said you'd wait for the ransom money to arrive!" Richard Stockbridge cried.

Baxter shook his head. "I don't recollect saying that, Mr. Stockbridge. And even if I did, things sometimes change. We have to follow whatever plan the circumstances dictate."

Cody watched the exchange with interest. What Baxter said made sense, but Cody could not shake the feeling that the lawman had another priority—to get Jake Walsh in his gunsights any way he could.

Looking over the posse and trying to read the expressions on the faces of the men, Cody sensed that a good number of them agreed with Baxter. That could cause trouble if Cody had to oppose the marshal. He was sure Orion would back him up, but there was no way of being certain what the other men would do.

"We're wasting time right now," Baxter said firmly. He glanced at the setting sun, its red glare lighting his face. "Like I said, take a rest for a while." He swung down from his saddle and led his horse to a clump of grass. The animal started to graze contentedly.

The other riders followed his example, and within a few minutes all had dismounted. As the sun set, they broke out a little food from the meager store they had left and began to eat.

Cody looked around for Holly and found her sitting with her back against a scrubby tree. He joined her, noting that the tree was on a slight mound of earth where the ground was not quite as wet as the surrounding area. Holly was chewing on a stale biscuit, and she offered what was left of it to Cody.

He shook his head and lifted the saddlebag he had taken off his horse. "I've got some left," he said. "Be glad to share them with you."

"No, thanks," Holly said. "I'm not very hungry."

"Thinking about your sister?"

"We're closer to her now than we've been before," she said softly. "Another day—or less—and it will all be over."

"This trip hasn't been easy for you, has it? No matter how you made it look."

She shook her head, not meeting Cody's eyes. "I keep remembering those . . . those men that I shot. I had never shot at a man before that day, Cody, let alone killed somebody." She took a deep breath. "But I'd do it again. For Dorothea . . . and to help save the rest of you . . . I'd do it again."

"I know," Cody said quietly. "I suppose most of us thought it didn't even bother you."

"It did." Holly's voice was so soft that Cody could barely hear the words.

He said nothing more, content for the moment just to sit beside her and eat. Then, as the shadows deepened, an abrupt movement startled him. He turned to see Holly slumping toward him, her eyes closed. Her head fell against his shoulder, and in her sleep she instinctively nestled a little closer to him.

Cody smiled warmly. The rigors of the pursuit had finally caught up with her.

He stayed there without moving, letting Holly sleep peacefully with her head resting on his shoulder. Finally, as he listened to her gentle, rhythmic breathing, he dozed a little himself.

* * *

Cody was unsure of how much time had passed when his eyes suddenly snapped open. The little grove of trees where the posse had stopped was draped in deep shadows, but as Cody glanced toward the west, he saw that a pink glow still tinged the horizon. The sun had been down for less than hour.

He did not move. Holly's head was still resting against his arm, her breathing deep and regular. Cody glanced around the camp and saw that all of the other posse members seemed to be asleep as well. Even the dark shape that Cody was fairly sure was Dan Baxter was unmoving.

He wondered what woke him. Some instinct alerted him that something was wrong. But what? The answer came suddenly in the thunder of hooves, the shouts of men, and the sharp crack of gunfire.

Cody leaped to his feet, his hand reaching for his gun. As he pulled the Colt, he scanned the shadows, searching for the attackers. All around him other startled members of the posse were leaping up and yelling questions.

Beside him Holly was struggling to her feet and frantically clutching at his arm. "What is it?" she cried.

Cody saw darting shapes at the edge of the camp. The posse's horses suddenly stampeded wildly through the scrubby woods and into the scattered group of half-awake men, causing their owners to fling themselves desperately out of the way. Behind the animals men on horseback, yelling and shooting, rode toward the heart of the camp. The night was lit by the flashes of their weapons.

Pushing Holly behind him, Cody fired at the attacking men. He felt the Colt buck in his hand every time a shadowy figure loomed before him.

The ambushed posse slowly began to fight back. Double flashes of gunfire coming from twin Colts identified a nearby shadow as Dan Baxter, and the shotgun blast that blew one of the marauders out of the saddle came, Cody knew, from the bulky shape of Orion McCarthy. Several other men from Abilene got their guns out and started firing.

The darkness and the confusion limited their effectiveness. It was hard to know which figures to shoot at or even how many of the attackers there were.

"Walsh's men?" Holly asked Cody during a lull in the deafening explosions, after the riders had stormed on through the camp.

Cody shook his head. "More likely some other owlhoots out to get the money." He crouched beside the tree where he and Holly had dozed, peering into the shadows. Judging by the sounds that came to his ears, the riders were turning their horses out in the darkness, no doubt regrouping for another charge.

"Cody!" Baxter's soft call came floating over from a nearby tree. "You all right?"

"For now," Cody replied. "How about you?"

"I'm fine. But they ran off the horses!" Baxter's voice shook with anger. "They'll be coming back in a minute."

"I know. Orion, you there?"

The burly Scotsman rumbled, "Aye, lad."

Quickly, Cody called out to each of the other men. Everyone answered, including Edwin Perkins and Richard Stockbridge. *Perkins and Richard sound frightened, but then so do the rest of them,* Cody thought. They were in a bad spot.

He bent down and felt around on the wet ground until he found the saddlebags he had dropped earlier. He reached inside for a box of shells, and as his fingers found the bullets, he wondered if he might not be able to make better use of them by doing something other than simply firing them from his gun.

As the idea took shape, he moved rapidly. Desperately he yanked the bandanna from his neck and spread it over one hand, while with the other he opened the box of shells and began twisting the lead bullets from their casings with his teeth. The slow work seemed to take forever, but gradually he built up a good-sized pile of black powder on the bandanna.

Holly frowned at him, saying, "Cody, what are you doing?" He was sure his actions made no sense to her, but he had no time to explain. Hoofbeats told him that the attackers were on their way back.

He raced into the small clearing through which the outlaws had charged earlier. The attackers were close now, their guns blasting. A bullet sang by Cody's head.

He threw the bandanna to the ground, and yelled, "Baxter! Orion! Close your eyes!" He hoped that the other posse members would hear and understand. The attackers would be not able to distinguish his words over the thunder of their horses' hooves.

Cody's hand darted into his pocket and brought out a sulfur match. Flicking the lucifer into life with his thumbnail, he dropped the flame into the pile of black powder, then lunged away as one of the outlaws nearly rode him down.

The powder ignited with a whoosh and a brilliant glare. The marauders' horses reared frantically away from it, and Cody knew that any man who had been looking was momentarily blinded. He rolled as he landed in the mud and came up firing.

The blasts from Baxter's guns and Orion's shotgun told him they had heard and understood his hastily shouted order. Other members of the posse were firing, too, and this time their shots were having an effect. Now it was the attackers who were confused and disoriented.

The intense heat of the blazing powder had started a small fire in the damp brush. In its light, Cody could see that Richard Stockbridge and Edwin Perkins had found handguns and were firing at the outlaws. Richard was on one knee, calmly squeezing off shot after shot. Perkins stood beside him, using both hands to fire. As Cody watched, each of them downed an outlaw.

The attack had been blunted, its back broken. Shouting curses, the remaining attackers wheeled their horses and fled. Cody fired at their retreating shadows as Baxter ran up beside him with both guns blasting. The shooting gradually died away once the shadowy attackers were gone.

Looking around the chaotic camp, Baxter snapped, "Anybody hurt?"

A quick check showed a few men had received bullet burns and one man a messy but not serious wound in his arm. Orion began binding it up in the light of the still-burning brush.

Cody turned to Baxter and asked, "You don't think that was Walsh, do you?"

Baxter shook his head. "Walsh doesn't have any reason to attack us like that. No, it was another bunch of hardcases who want that money for themselves and don't want anybody else to get it. I'm a little surprised we haven't been hit more often now that we're in Indian Territory."

"What do we do now?"

Baxter's face was bleak as he said, "We start trying

to round up our horses. No telling how far they ran after those outlaws stampeded them."

"This is going to slow us down."

"Nothing we can do about it."

Cody nodded. Baxter was right. He thumbed fresh shells from his belt into his gun and sighed. They had just lost the element of surprise.

Chapter Twelve

———◆———

THE DRIVING RAIN THAT HAD DRENCHED JAKE WALSH and his men all afternoon continued as they approached Elysium at the end of the day. Walsh heard the grumbling and complaints of the riders but paid no attention. He was not going to worry about a little rain when he had fifty thousand dollars in his saddle-bags and, riding beside him, a pretty little ticket for that much more. Walsh had been in a good mood ever since Hedges, the man who had delivered the instructions for the ransom payoff to the posse, had returned from his errand. The outlaw leader could almost taste that extra fifty grand.

As the rain began to slacken around dusk, Walsh looked appraisingly at Dorothea Stockbridge and said with a grin, "For a wet rat, you look pretty damned good, girl."

Dorothea, removing the hat Walsh had ordered one

of the men to give her, shook the raindrops from her thick black hair, which the dampness had caused to curl into a mass of dark ringlets. She looked haughtily at Walsh and snapped, "If you had any consideration, you'd have found some shelter and let us stop when that storm came along."

"You don't reckon that posse back there stopped, do you? If that white-haired bastard Hedges told us about is who I think he is, a little rain's not going to slow him down."

The gang pushed on, and as the dusky shadows deepened, they climbed a hogback ridge. When they reached the top of the slope, Walsh reined in and pointed a blunt finger at a small dot of light across a valley, several miles away.

"That's Elysium," he said. "I told the old man who looks after the place for me to keep an eye out for us. Looks like he left a light in the window."

As thunder from the retreating storm rumbled in the distance, Dorothea said, "What a ridiculous name for a town out here in the middle of this wilderness! What sort of place is it, anyway?"

"It's deserted now," Walsh answered. He shifted in his saddle and spoke to the dozen or more men in his gang who sat waiting for his orders. "We'll push on. No point in stoppin' when we're this close."

One of the men said, "That's all right with us, Jake. We'd all like to get dried off and warmed up."

Walsh spurred his horse forward and picked his way down the slope. He held the reins of Dorothea's horse, so it had no choice but to follow. Dorothea's hands were untied. There had been no need to bind her once they were away from Abilene, for out here she could go nowhere without Walsh and his men finding her rapidly.

As he rode, the outlaw said, "The way I heard the story, there was some sort of sickness hit Elysium. Smallpox, some folks said. All I know is that it wiped out more than half the town, and them that was left decided they didn't want to live there no more. Can't say as I blame 'em. So they up and left. I come along a year or so later, needin' a place to hide out over here in Indian Territory. Seemed like a good place to me."

Dorothea shuddered. "I would think you'd be worried about contagion."

Walsh shook his head. "Shoot, anything in that town that'd make folks sick is probably gone by now. I left an old-timer who used to ride with me there to watch it, and he ain't been sick a day, far as I know."

"It still doesn't seem like a good name for such a place."

"Hell, gal, I don't even know what the name means. I suppose you do."

Dorothea lifted her chin. "Indeed I do. Elysium is a name from classical mythology. It refers to the abode of the blessed dead—heaven, if you will. We did not neglect the classics at Miss Sinclair's Finishing School."

"'The abode of the blessed dead,'" Walsh echoed with a laugh. "Don't know how blessed they was, but there was plenty of folks dead." His tone took on a dangerous edge as he continued. "Could be there will be again, if that posse tries anything stupid."

Less than an hour later a weary, bruised Dorothea was led into Elysium. The once-beautiful dress she wore was now a soggy, soiled ruin. She shuddered in the chill night breeze that blew against her damp clothes and skin. Her initial terror of the burly redheaded Walsh and his rough men had faded to be replaced by outrage, but during the long ride her angry demands had brought only laughter and ridicule. At last, too tired to struggle with the impossible situation, she had resigned herself haughtily to make the best of it.

Now, as she followed Walsh out of the endless wilderness and into the town, she began to take in her surroundings. The pinpoint of light she had seen from across the valley was cast by several lanterns burning inside a large two-story building that stood in the middle of the abandoned settlement. Other structures lining the broad main street were dark, and she could just make them out as she rode past them. Those that once had housed the town's businesses seemed in fairly good shape, but the private homes were shabby, and it looked as though their walls and roofs were starting to collapse.

The riders passed one or two narrow cross streets before Walsh led them to the front of the large building. As Dorothea drew closer to the brightly lit structure, she saw a big dilapidated sign on the front that read The Applegate Hotel, Thomas Applegate, Prop. She wondered what had become of Thomas Applegate but did not dare ask Walsh. He would only offer some gruesome explanation she just did not want to hear.

Dorothea saw a man push through the double doors of the hotel and move onto the porch. He was holding a lantern high above his head, so that his bald pate shone in its light. A bushy beard covered most of his face. He wore a storekeeper's apron and carried a rifle in the other hand.

"Howdy, Jake," he greeted the outlaw leader as the gang halted in front of the hotel.

"You let it rain some, didn't you, Starnes?" Walsh replied with a grin.

"Don't blame that on me," the old man shot back. "You get what you were after up there in Kansas?"

Dorothea cringed as his eyes played curiously over her.

"And more besides," Walsh said as he dismounted. "Come on, gal."

Awkwardly Dorothea got down from her horse. The long days of riding had been pure agony, especially at first. She had never been on horseback before and had no idea how to go about lessening the bruising and chafing she received from the animal. Walsh had not provided her with a sidesaddle, of course, so she had had no choice but to pull up her skirts and ride astride, leaving her calves shamefully exposed to the lustful glances of the outlaws. Dorothea was not bothered by the lustful glances—she was accustomed to them—but the pain had been very bad. No matter what happened here in Elysium, she was relieved they had reached their destination.

Walsh roughly grasped her arm and led her onto the hotel porch. With a shove, he turned her over to Starnes and said, "Keep an eye on her."

"Glad to, Jake," Starnes replied. He licked his lips.

"And keep those paws of yours off her," Walsh snapped. "Take her into the lobby."

Warily Dorothea followed Starnes into the hotel. She remained near the still-open glass doors, listening carefully as Jake Walsh issued orders to his men.

"All right, you know what to do," Walsh said. "Get those horses in the stable and take good care of them. I don't want to have to ride out of here in a hurry on wore-out animals. Once you've got that done, some of you can come back here for a drink and some sleep." He pointed to four of the men. "You boys will stand guard, two at each end of the street. Maybe that posse will bring the ransom money and send it into town like they're supposed to—or they may hit us and try to take the girl. Either way, we've got to know when they're coming. Got that?"

"Sure, Jake. We understand," one of the men answered.

"You'll be relieved later. Now get moving."

The heavy pounding of booted feet told Dorothea that Walsh had finished with his men and was now crossing the wide plank boardwalk toward the hotel. Instinctively she drew away from the doors toward the center of the lobby, then glanced apprehensively at Starnes, who was leaning against the counter where guests had once signed in. The bald old man was leering at her, and she realized that her damp dinner dress clung revealingly to her body. She quickly looked around the lobby to conceal her revulsion.

The departed Thomas Applegate had worked to make his hotel attractive. On the floor of the lobby lay a thick rug that had probably been beautiful once, though now it was stained and the edges tattered. The shattered remains of once-elegant crystal chandeliers hung from the ceiling, and big urns that had held potted plants now stood empty in the corners.

Dorothea turned to see that Walsh, his Winchester on his shoulder, was inside the lobby. "You got rooms ready for us, Starnes?" he asked, closing the doors noisily.

"Sure. Best in the house," the old man cackled. "You want me to call a boy to fetch your baggage?"

Walsh patted the saddlebags slung over his shoulder

and then took Dorothea's arm. "Reckon this is all the baggage I've got that means anything," he said with a grin.

He led Dorothea across the lobby and through an arched entranceway into what had been the hotel's barroom. Starnes followed them and went behind the mahogany bar, which ran along the back wall and was now scarred from hard use.

Several tables were scattered around the room, but only one of them had chairs around it. Pulling out a chair with his booted foot, Walsh said with mock courtesy, "Have a seat, ma'am."

Dorothea eased herself into the crude ladderback chair while Walsh sat down across from her, laying the Winchester on the table and placing the saddlebags beside it. Dorothea frowned at him and said, "I thought once we got to town I'd be allowed to get out of these wet clothes."

"Another few minutes won't hurt you," Walsh told her. "Starnes, bring a bottle over here."

The bald-headed man reached behind the bar and brought out an amber bottle. He carried the whiskey over to the table and set it down. "Sorry we don't have any fancy glasses for the lady, Jake," he said.

"Doesn't matter." Dorothea stared with revulsion as Walsh scooped up the bottle, pulled the cork with his teeth, and spat it out. He raised the bottle to his lips, his throat working as he took a long swallow of the fiery liquor. He set it down and shoved it across the table toward Dorothea. "There. That'll warm you up, wet clothes or not."

Dorothea hesitated, then abruptly picked up the bottle and tilted it to her mouth. She drank, flinching only slightly. Then she replaced the whiskey bottle on the table.

"Feel better now?" Walsh asked.

Dorothea nodded. Her throat seemed to be on fire, and there was a raging inferno inside her belly, but for the moment she was able to take comfort from the sensations.

The clumping of boots and the jingle of spurs made her turn her head and look toward the lobby. The members of Walsh's gang, with the exception of the four men assigned to keep a lookout, had entered the hotel and were approaching the barroom.

Walsh picked up his bottle again and took another drink as his men moved up to the bar and began raucously demanding drinks from Starnes. The old man busily handed over bottles of whiskey, grumbling as he did so.

Raising his voice, Walsh called, "Hedges!" The thick-bodied, middle-aged man who had carried the message to the posse grabbed one of the bottles being passed around and came over to the table.

Pushing back his soggy hat, he asked, "What can I do for you, Jake?"

"Don't get too drunk tonight, that's what you can do," Walsh said. "That posse's back there somewheres, and it's goin' to be up to you to meet them before they get here. I guess it's safe enough tonight, but early in the morning I want you out on the trail."

Hedges took a long swig from the bottle and wiped the back of his hand across his mouth. "Hell, Jake, can't somebody else do that?" He looked down meaningfully at Dorothea, letting his dark eyes linger on the thrust of her breasts against the wet fabric of her dress. "I thought you might let some of the boys have a little fun whilst we're waitin'."

Dorothea tried not to shudder as Walsh laid his hand on the Winchester on the tabletop. "Forget it,

Hedges," he said coldly. "That ain't the way it's goin' to be. You got your orders."

Hedges took an involuntary step back from Walsh's glare. "Sure, Jake," he said hastily. "No offense."

"Just remember what I said. If that posse rides in here without us bein' warned ahead of time, I'll make sure that you don't ride out alive."

"Sure." Hedges bobbed his head and backed away.

Dorothea took a deep breath as the impending violence in the air slowly died away. In a low voice, she said, "You really rule with an iron hand, don't you?"

"These are strong men, and the only thing they respect is somebody stronger. But they're good hombres. I'm glad they're goin' to finally get a really big payoff." Walsh smiled across the table at Dorothea. "Thanks to you, little lady."

Dorothea decided to return the smile. She had been wondering about something, and given Walsh's current expansive mood, she decided this would be a good time to ask him about it.

"You didn't seem surprised that the entire posse came after us," she began. "After all, you did leave that note ordering them to send in just one man with the ransom."

Walsh waved a hand. "Aw, hell, I didn't expect whoever was leadin' that posse to pay any attention to the note. No lawman would. This is all just part of the game they play."

Dorothea shivered. "I'm afraid it's not much of a game."

Walsh grinned cockily. "I wouldn't say that. That marshal Hedges said was ramroddin' the posse sounds like a fella named Dan Baxter. Baxter's been after me for nigh on two years now. It's been pretty entertainin', runnin' rings around him."

Dorothea thoughtfully studied the outlaw leader's bearded face. "I think you want him to come into town and try to rescue me," she said shrewdly.

"Don't reckon I'd mind too much, at that." Walsh's grin widened. "It's gettin' time to go ahead and kill the bastard."

As a cold chill ran up her spine, Dorothea held out an unsteady hand for the whiskey bottle. "Can I have some more of that?"

Walsh pushed it across the table to her and said, "Sure, darlin'."

While she lifted the bottle to her lips, her mind raced. She drank deeply, then lowered her green eyes as she placed the bottle on the table and said softly, "I want to go to my room now. I have to get out of these clothes and dry off."

Walsh shoved back his chair, picked up the Winchester and saddlebags. "Sure. Come on. And bring the bottle!"

Dorothea picked up the bottle and swayed seductively as she preceded Walsh out of the barroom. There were some catcalls from the men, but she ignored them. She turned and smiled at Walsh when they reached the staircase, and he nodded for her to go ahead of him. Under her weight, the stairs squeaked and sagged, making her nervous, but they held up all right.

Walsh had picked up the lantern from the counter in the lobby, and as they reached the second floor it cast long, flickering shadows down the hall.

"Second door on the left," Walsh grunted. "It's the room I always use when I'm here."

Dorothea looked over her shoulder at him. "I'm honored," she said throatily.

She walked down the corridor, hips swaying. Walsh followed close behind. When Dorothea reached the door, she tried it. Finding it unlocked, she swung it open and stepped inside.

Starnes had not gone to a lot of trouble, but the room had been prepared for occupancy. There were blankets on the iron bedstead's mattress. A jug of water and a basin sat on a scratched dressing table, and some of the dust had been wiped off the fly-specked mirror above it. A torn piece of canvas had been hung over the room's single window.

"Like Starnes said, the best room in the house." Walsh laughed as he heeled the door shut behind him.

Dorothea turned to face him with a solemn expression on her features. "It's good enough," she said softly. "We're alone finally, and now we can do what we've been wanting to do ever since we left Abilene." Her hands went to the buttons of her dress and began unfastening them.

Walsh watched coolly as the garment slipped from Dorothea's shoulders and fell around her feet. She stepped out of it, wearing a shift that was as soaked as the dress. A glance in the mirror told her that the outline of her breasts showed plainly through the thin fabric, as did the large dark nipples crowning the swells of creamy flesh. Dorothea stepped toward Walsh, her head tilted back, her eyelids drooping closed.

Walsh slid his free arm around her, pulling her tightly against him as his mouth came down urgently on hers. For a moment her lips remained closed, but then they parted, opening to his rough kiss. Her arms went around him, the fingers clutching at the duster he wore, roaming all over his back in demanding caresses. Then her probing fingers brushed back the skirt of the duster and closed over the hilt of the Bowie knife sheathed at Walsh's waist.

Suddenly Walsh tore her away from him, causing Dorothea to cry out in pain and shock. He gave her a hard shove that sent her staggering across the room, and the side of the bed caught her in the back of the knees. She sprawled across the thin mattress with a flash of milky-white thigh.

The barrel of Walsh's rifle came down to line on her fallen form, and he levered a shell into the chamber with a snarl. "You damn slut!" he barked. "I've been waitin' ever since we left Abilene, all right—waitin' for you to pull some stupid stunt like that! You high-and-mighty rich girls think you can always have whatever you want, just for the askin'. And if that don't work, you just take what you want!"

Tears sprang to Dorothea's eyes as she covered her face with shaking hands. "No, Jake, you don't understand!" she wailed in protest. "I never met a man like you before, not a real man—"

"Shut up!" Walsh cut in. "Don't make it worse, you bitch. You figgered you could flaunt that body and that smile at me and get me to do whatever you wanted. But then you got impatient and decided to finish the job yourself by guttin' me with my own knife. Well, I was ready for that! And even if you had managed to stick me, where the hell were you goin'? Ain't no place in this territory where my men couldn't find you."

Dorothea just shook her head and kept her face covered. Her fear, carefully held in check all during the long ride south, now blossomed into pure terror, leaving her speechless.

Walsh moved closer to the bed, and Dorothea

cringed. His eyes were shining with excitement as he surveyed her quaking, half-nude figure. "Not that I wouldn't like to finish what we started," he breathed harshly. "You may have been actin', gal, but that kiss packed plenty of punch anyway." He dropped the saddlebags at the foot of the bed and laid the rifle on the floor. Bending over Dorothea, he went on, "Maybe when we get this ransom business over and done with, there'll be some time for you and me to have a little fun. Hell, when I get through with you, you may not want to go back to your daddy no more."

With a wicked grin on his face, he opened the saddlebags and took out a short length of rope. It caught on one of the packets of money that had come from the safe on Maxwell Stockbridge's private train, and it brought the stack of bills tumbling onto the floor. Walsh picked them up, riffled a thumb along the edge, and then stuffed them back into the pouch.

"Yeah, when this is all over . . ." he mused.

Then he lashed the rope around Dorothea's wrists and began tying them to the bedframe. The evil smile never left his face.

Chapter Thirteen

———◆———

IT WAS LATE AFTERNOON OF THE NEXT DAY WHEN THE posse approached Elysium. It had taken a whole night of hard work to round up the horses that had been scattered by the outlaws' attack. Cody looked at the men: If they had been gaunt and haggard before, worn down by the rigors of the pursuit, now they looked even worse.

· Cody did not know how far from the town they were, but they had to be getting close. They had been in the saddle since just before dawn, being pushed on relentlessly by Dan Baxter. The U.S. marshal had not smiled all day, his normally hearty cheerfulness having deserted him to be replaced by a grimness that set his features in a hard mask.

As the posse rode up the long slope of a hogback ridge, Cody glanced over his shoulder at the straggling line of men. They had been lucky and had recovered all of the stampeded horses except for one. Two of the men had doubled up, which ordinarily might have slowed the posse, but all the men and animals were so exhausted that they could not in any case maintain a fast pace.

Cody's gaze rested on Holly Stockbridge, and she smiled tiredly at him. Her features had become lean during the long chase, making her high cheekbones even more prominent. He was amazed that she had held up so well under all the hardships the posse had suffered.

But she had held up, and so had Edwin Perkins and Richard Stockbridge. Both men had proven to be effective fighters during the battle the night before. They were drawing on reserves that their soft eastern life had never even touched before. *But how long can those reserves hold out?* Cody wondered.

When Baxter reached the top of the ridge, he reined in. Cody came to a stop beside him as Baxter reached into his saddlebag for the spyglass. "You see something?" Cody asked.

"I think there's something over there across that valley," Baxter replied, opening the telescope to its full length and lifting it to his eye. He squinted through the lens, and after a moment grunted, "Yep, there's a town over there, all right. It's got to be Elysium."

He passed the spyglass over to Cody, who peered through it. Details of the scene across the valley leaped at him, and he could see the main street, dominated by one large structure. Because there were no horses and no movement, it looked like a ghost town.

"You sure they're there?" he asked.

"They're there." Baxter nodded. "Walsh is just lying low and waiting for us. Chances are some of his men are still sleeping off a drunk. At least we can hope so. That'll help even the odds."

Cody gave the marshal a quick glance. During the long, hard pursuit, they had never discussed what they would do once the posse reached Elysium. From the way Baxter had spoken, he had planned all along to storm the town immediately.

Handing the spyglass back to him, Cody asked, "What now?"

Baxter closed the glass and stowed it away. "We go get that lady back, that's what we do now," he said sharply. He urged his horse into motion.

A rifle cracked, the bullet kicking up dirt several feet in front of Baxter's horse.

With one hand Baxter jerked the animal to a stop, while his other hand flew to his Colt. Just behind him Cody was doing the same thing. All along the line the posse members reached for their weapons and scanned the valley in front of them for the attackers.

No more shots broke the silence around them. Baxter had crouched slightly over his horse's neck to make himself a smaller target. Slowly, he straightened, his eyes searching the valley before him.

"Just stay where you are! Don't move, mister!"

The call came from a clump of trees about fifty yards down the slope. As Cody, Baxter, and the other posse members watched, a man on horseback emerged from the trees and rode slowly toward them. There was something familiar about the man, and as he drew closer, Cody recognized him as the messenger Walsh had sent to meet them earlier.

The stranger had his rifle in his hands, and he held

himself stiffly, his tension obvious even at a distance. Cody had to give the man credit for having the courage to ride up to an armed posse like this.

The man approached to within twenty yards, then pulled up and regarded them over the muzzle of his rifle. He asked, "You got that ransom money?"

Baxter shook his head. "Not yet. We're still waiting for it to catch up to us from Abilene."

"You sure about that?" the hardcase demanded with a frown. "Seems to me it should've been here by now."

Baxter rested his hands on the pommel of his saddle and leaned forward. "Seems like it to me, too," he said bluntly. "But I've got no control over that, mister."

"You could send a rider back, have him check on it," the man suggested.

Baxter shrugged. "I could. But that'd mean cutting my force. I don't want to do that, even by one man, not with Jake Walsh around."

The outlaw forced a grin. "Jake will play square with you, mister. Don't you worry about that."

"I know how Walsh plays the game," Baxter shot back harshly. "Say what you came to say."

The man nodded. "All right. You just stay right here. Don't come no closer to Elysium. If all of you try to ride in, that lady is dead, make no mistake about it. When the money comes, you pick a man to bring it in and then fire three shots. That'll let us know he's comin'."

Baxter regarded him for a long moment without speaking. Cody glanced from the marshal to the outlaw and back again and waited for Baxter's reaction to these orders. Cody believed it would be out of character for the lawman simply to accept them, but he was uncertain.

Abruptly, Baxter nodded. "We'll do as you say," he told Walsh's messenger.

The man squinted suspiciously at him. "You don't intend to raid the town?" he demanded.

"You've got my word on it," Baxter said levelly. "We won't attack the town. We'll camp right here and wait for the ransom."

Cody heard some of the posse members breathe sighs of relief. He turned to see that a look of gratitude on Edwin Perkins's face had replaced the haggard mask he had worn. Holly's eyes glistened with tears, and a little smile played at her lips.

"All right, mister," the outlaw said. "You'd best remember what was said here."

"Oh, I'll remember, don't worry about that," Baxter promised.

A dubious look still on his face, the hardcase wheeled his horse and put the spurs to it, galloping away down the slope. He kept casting glances over his shoulder, as if he was afraid that the posse members would try to shoot him in the back.

Some of them probably would like to do just that, Cody thought. *Jake Walsh's greed has put a lot of people in danger during the last week.*

Baxter sat motionless in his saddle, his unreadable eyes following Walsh's man until the messenger had disappeared into the trees. Then the marshal turned and called to the posse members, "You heard what the man said. We might as well all get down and make ourselves comfortable."

Cody watched as Baxter swung down from the saddle, and then he slowly followed the older man's example. The other men were dismounting, as well, and Holly Stockbridge slid from her saddle, gratefully stretching to unkink the muscles in her back.

Cody stepped over to Baxter as the others began tending to their mounts. Looking intently at the marshal, Cody said, "You don't really intend to make camp here, do you?"

"Of course I do," Baxter insisted. For the first time today, his face began to reveal his thoughts, and a trace of a smile played around the corners of his mouth. "I just never said how long we'd stay here."

Cody inclined his head toward the trees where the hardcase had vanished. "This is for his benefit, isn't it, just in case he's keeping an eye on us?"

"That's right, son," Baxter replied softly. "Come dark, we'll do what we have to do."

Cody took a deep breath. "You gave him your word."

"That's right. I gave my word to an outlaw, a no-good criminal. You think that means anything?" Baxter shook his head without waiting for Cody to answer. "Well, I don't. I'll tell a skunk like that anything as long as it helps me get my hands on his boss."

Baxter turned away, abruptly dismissing Cody. Enraged, the young deputy struggled to control his feelings as he watched Baxter issue orders to the men to begin setting up a camp. The group cheered vigorously when Baxter told them they could start a fire.

"Hot coffee again!" one man said fervently. "It's been too dang long."

Eagerly, the men stripped the saddles from their mounts and gave water to the horses. There was plenty of grass for the horses to graze on, but rations for the members of the posse were scarce, so Baxter detailed two men to shoot some rabbits or prairie hens. Two more men were put on guard, just in case another gang came along and ambushed them.

Cody watched the hubbub with mixed emotions and churning thoughts. Clearly Baxter had told him that he would not honor his promise not to attack Elysium. Right now he was just putting on a show in case Walsh's man was still observing them from some hiding place. When the concealing darkness of night fell, Baxter could put his own plan into motion. And there was a good chance that his plan would get Dorothea Stockbridge killed.

At the same time, Cody had felt from the first that they could not afford to trust Jake Walsh. Walsh had been too slippery for too long. To turn over the money and hope that Walsh would release Dorothea was asking for too much; the bandit would never do it.

That was why, Cody at last decided, he and Baxter had to work together, had to come up with some other plan, some scheme that might get Dorothea out alive.

As several men built a small fire and got a pot of coffee simmering on it, Cody caught Orion's eye and then strolled over toward Baxter. The shrewd, burly Scotsman, sensing that something was up, followed along behind.

"I want to talk to you, Marshal," Cody said as he approached Baxter.

The lawman was leaning against a large rock that stood several yards beyond the campsite. He had slipped one of his guns from its holster and was examining its action in the fading light. Without looking up from his task, he said, "I thought I told you not to call me that anymore, Cody."

"Don't guess it matters now. Walsh knows we're here. He probably knows that you're in charge of the posse, too. His man probably went right back to him and described you."

Baxter closed the cylinder of his Peacemaker. "I imagine you're right," he admitted. "Walsh knows me, that's for sure. He's known all along that I was after him, and he knows I'll get him one of these days. It's going to be soon now; I can feel it in my bones."

Cody hooked his thumbs in his belt and stood in front of Baxter. "What are you going to do?" he asked flatly.

Baxter finally looked up. He slid his fingers along the ivory butt of the Colt and then slipped it back in its holster. He said, "I'll leave a couple of men here to make it look like we're camped, just like we're supposed to be. Then the rest of us will slip into town and hit Walsh while he's not expecting it. We'll get that woman back, and the money, too."

"What if it doesn't work?" Cody demanded. "What if Dorothea gets killed in the fighting? Have you even thought about that?"

"Of course I have," Baxter replied, his tone sharper now. "I'm not a reckless fool, son, no matter what you may think."

Cody shook his head. "I'm not accusing anybody of anything. I just think it would be a good idea if we worked out a better plan."

"Better plan?" Baxter snorted. "What sort of better plan?"

Cody thought quickly, trying to come up with something that might work. He said, "If you all go riding into Elysium, Walsh won't wait to see what's going to happen. He'll just kill Dorothea out of hand.

But a couple of men might be able to slip into town, find out where she is, maybe get her free."

"A couple of men?" Baxter boomed incredulously. Several startled posse members stopped what they were doing to pay attention to the conversation between the two lawmen. "Two men wouldn't stand a chance if Walsh got his hands on them!"

Cody tried to speak softly, but he realized that he was getting louder, too. "Maybe not," he said, "but Walsh wouldn't be as likely to kill the girl, either, if only two men were found in town. You take the whole bunch, and he'll kill her as soon as he knows you're coming."

"Who says he'll know we're coming?" Baxter asked angrily.

Cody laughed bitterly. "You think you can take a posse of greenhorns right into an outlaw hideout without anybody knowing about it?"

As soon as the words were spoken, Cody regretted them. Hearing angry mutters from the posse members, he knew that his brashness and impulsiveness had just made him some enemies among the townsmen from Abilene. *But it's true!* he thought. For all their courage and perseverance, these men were not experienced fighters like those in Walsh's gang.

The more levelheaded men among them realized that and agreed with Cody. Orion swung to face the posse and said boomingly, "Aye, the lad's right. 'Twill do no good t'raid Walsh's town."

Edwin Perkins stepped forward. "I agree, Mr. McCarthy. Marshal Baxter, you promised that man we'd stay here until the ransom money was delivered. I believe we should wait."

"Waiting won't do anything but get your fiancée

killed," Baxter replied angrily. "And a promise made to scum like Walsh and his men doesn't mean anything!" He started to push past Cody. "Now get your horses ready to ride."

Cody angrily reached out to stop him. His hand clamped on Baxter's upper arm and swung him around. Baxter was suddenly furious as Cody confronted him.

"Wait just a minute here!" Cody demanded. "What is it you're really after, Baxter? Do you want to get Dorothea back safely, or are you just after Walsh?"

A shudder went through Baxter as he glared at Cody. With the eyes of the entire posse on him, he paled in rage. "I've been after Walsh for a long time, boy," he rasped, his voice little more than an emotion-choked whisper now. "I'm not going to let him get away again, not when I'm this close to him."

"Why?" Cody prodded, his own temper barely under control now. Finally, the questions and doubts that had plagued him ever since the posse left Abilene were bursting out into the open. It was time to clear the air. "Why is it so important that you get Walsh?"

"Why?" Baxter repeated. "I'll tell you why, Cody. . . . Because the bastard killed my wife!"

Cody rocked back as if he had just been struck by a fist. He had suspected that Baxter had some sort of personal grudge against Walsh, but he had not expected the tragedy that Baxter now revealed.

"Walsh and his gang hit the bank in a little town in Missouri a couple of years ago," Baxter went on, the words sounding hollow. "They didn't get much. Walsh probably doesn't even remember it. But as the gang was riding out, they traded shots with the local sheriff and a couple of deputies. Nobody was hit—

except one woman who happened to be unlucky enough to be walking down the boardwalk to the store."

Cody licked his lips, which had gone dry. He said, "I'm sorry, Marshal. I didn't know——"

"Of course you didn't. But that doesn't change anything. I've been after Walsh ever since that day, and I won't rest until I've brought him to justice."

Baxter turned away, but again Cody reached out and stopped him with a hand on his arm. "You're right, Marshal. That doesn't change anything. I'm sorry about what happened, but that doesn't mean you're right about this plan to attack the town."

For a long moment the two men stood facing each other, Cody's hand on Baxter's arm. Their stubborn gazes locked while the posse members watched the two determined men. Several of the men were making comments in support of either Cody or Baxter.

Richard Stockbridge pushed out of the cluster of men. "I agree with Marshal Baxter," he announced loudly. "I think we have to hit the town while Walsh isn't expecting us."

Orion flung his arms out. "Dinna be daft, man! D'ye think Walsh is a fool? O' course he'll be ready for some sort o' raid!"

"That's right," Perkins echoed. "Please, Richard, I know how worried you are about Dorothea, but we have to wait——"

"No!" The word ripped from Baxter's mouth. He tore his arm from Cody's grasp. "I'm in charge here, and I say we attack!"

Cody tried to move in front of him, all too aware of the tension around him. The posse was split, and if they were not careful, they were going to wind up fighting among themselves. Pushing toward Baxter, Cody said, "Hold it, Marshal—"

His face contorted in fury, Baxter lunged, launching a punch at Cody's head.

Reacting instinctively, Cody blocked the punch. Before he knew what he was doing, he had thrown one of his own. His fist caught Baxter on the jaw, knocking the marshal backward. One of Baxter's boots hit a rock, tripping him. He sprawled on the ground.

An angry shout went up from the men who had supported Baxter, answered by warning growls from those who had agreed with Cody. Men clenched fists and squared off, ready to strike. Within seconds the camp would break apart in a full-fledged brawl.

"Hold it!"

The shouted command came from Dan Baxter. The marshal slowly climbed to his feet and rubbed his already swelling jaw. He grimaced, and then surprisingly, a smile slowly spead across his face.

"That's quite a punch you pack, son," he said to Cody, who stood tensely, waiting to see what would happen next.

"Sorry I had to do that, Baxter," Cody said tightly.

Baxter shook his head. "Don't be. You were right." He raised his voice. "Did all of you men hear that? Cody's right. We can't afford to take chances with the young lady's life, and we sure can't afford to waste energy fighting among ourselves. There'll be no brawling in any posse I'm in charge of. Is that understood?"

There were murmurs of agreement from the men, who slowly began to relax.

"We'll work out some other plan," Baxter went on. "That all right with you, Cody?"

Cody nodded. "That's all I wanted."

"Fine. Right now, I think I want some of that java

before this jaw gets too sore for me to enjoy it." Baxter headed for the coffeepot, grinning at the men who were going back to their tasks.

The crisis appeared to be over. But for some reason, Cody was still worried. Too many things could still go wrong.

Chapter Fourteen

———◆———

Dorothea Stockbridge's eyes were dry. She had cried all the tears that were in her during the course of this long day. Even though her arms ached from being pulled over her head and tied to the bed, her face showed no pain: She refused to give Jake Walsh the satisfaction of seeing her hurting.

Walsh sat in a chair near the bed, smoking a cigarette and taking sips from a bottle of whiskey. Although he had occasionally run his hands over her body during the day, he had not molested her in any other way

He had talked plenty, though, rambling about his plans once he had that extra fifty thousand dollars. Together with what he had taken from the train, it added up to a cool hundred grand, more money than he had ever seen before. Of course, his men would have to have their shares, but he intended to come out with at least half.

"Reckon fifty thousand ought to buy me a pretty damned good hacienda down Mexico way," he said now. He had pushed back the canvas over the window, and he smiled at the soft light of dusk. "A man'd need a good woman to help him enjoy a place like that."

Dorothea said nothing. She turned her head away to avoid looking at him.

"It'd be up to you, of course. You could come with me, lady. We could have us a right nice time down there south of the border. You best think about it and make up your mind, 'cause that ransom money's probably goin' to be here sometime tonight or early in the mornin'."

Dorothea sighed. She would make the effort one more time. . . . She asked, "Why can't you just let me go back to Abilene like you said you would if the ransom was paid?" Her voice was hoarse, for she had had little to eat or drink during the day.

Walsh shook his head. "I never had me a lady like you before. I figger if I'm goin' to retire from outlawin', I need something special to take its place. You're it."

Bitterly, Dorothea said, "Last night you called me a bitch and a slut."

"Well, I reckon that's what you are. But you're awful pretty, too, and I reckon I can tame you down some." Dorothea could not see him, but she could almost feel Walsh's leer as he went on, "Hell, that might be fun by itself."

She shuddered, hating herself because she knew he was watching her reaction.

The worst of it, she told herself, *is my utter power-lessness in this situation.* There was nothing she could do to help herself. She had tried the night before, and the effort had brought her nothing but more abuse.

There was one hope that she nurtured. From what she had overheard, a posse from Abilene was supposed to be somewhere close by. That young deputy Cody Fisher was probably with them, assuming he had not been hurt too badly during the fight with Walsh's men at the stable in Abilene. She cringed at the ghastly memory of those ugly moments.

That posse was her only hope. It was a long shot, she knew. With Walsh and his men expecting trouble, they would be ready to thwart some kind of rescue attempt. But hope of deliverance was all she had to cling to.

Someone will come for me. Someone will rescue me.

Dorothea closed her eyes and began to pray.

As evening shadows began to fall on the campsite, Cody stood up and walked away from the remains of his supper and the dregs in his coffee cup. He had spent a quiet hour sorting his thoughts and eating his meal. Now, he decided, it was time to approach Dan Baxter and work out a new plan to save Dorothea.

The evening meal had been pretty skimpy—a couple of rabbits and a handful of stale biscuits—but the chance to drink hot coffee had cheered the men a little. Many had gathered around the fire, talking in low voices and laughing from time to time. A few sat apart, like Richard Stockbridge and Edwin Perkins. Although their lack of complaining and their surprising coolness under fire had won the grudging respect of the other posse members, everyone knew that the two easterners would never really fit in here.

Holly had chosen a spot a little away from the fire, too. As Cody passed close by, she looked up and smiled at him. He wished he could sit down with her and enjoy a few minutes of peace again, but he had to settle things with Baxter. He just smiled and nodded and went on to the edge of the camp, where the federal marshal was checking on the horses.

"Everything all right?" Cody asked softly, not wanting to spook the animals.

"All quiet," Baxter replied.

"That's good. I figure we need to talk about the situation."

"It's a stalemate, Cody, you know that. Walsh isn't going to move, and neither are we."

"Somebody's got to do something."

Baxter nodded. "You said something about a couple of men slipping into town. . . ."

"That's right," Cody said quickly, keeping his voice down so that the discussion would not drift to the ears of the rest of the posse. If there was another argument, he did not want it spreading again. "I think two men could get in and out of there pretty easy. Once we've got Dorothea, all of us could light out for Kansas. Walsh might come after us, but we've got enough men to hold him off."

"It's chancy," Baxter said slowly, "but then what isn't? Who do you think should be the two men?"

"I'm one of them," Cody declared flatly, his tone brooking no argument.

"And the other? It ought to be your choice, since your neck's going to be on the line."

"I was thinking about Richard Stockbridge."

Baxter frowned. "Stockbridge? Why him? Why not me or Orion?"

"You and Orion need to stay with the posse. They'll

still have to have a leader, no matter what happens in town. That's you. And Orion's probably the best fighting man in the group, next to you and me. Stockbridge handled himself well enough when those owlhoots hit us last night."

"But he's a tenderfoot—"

"Maybe when he started out," Cody said. "I think this experience has toughened him up considerably."

"Well, maybe . . ." Baxter sounded doubtful. "Like I said, it's your choice. When do you figure to go?"

"When do you think would be a good time?"

Baxter thought a moment, then said, "Dawn is still the best time to surprise somebody. Folks just aren't as watchful then. Might be your best bet."

Cody nodded. "Sounds good to me."

Baxter clapped Cody on the shoulder. "Good luck, son. You're going to need it. Why don't you get some rest now? I'll talk to Stockbridge for you, find out if he's willing to go along with the plan."

"All right. Thanks, Marshal."

Baxter moved off toward the other men. A moment later, Cody saw him sit down next to Richard Stockbridge and begin talking earnestly to the young man. Cody found a good, comfortable spot next to a tree, leaned back against it, and tilted his hat over his eyes. Lack of sleep and the weariness of the long chase caught up with him rapidly, and a peaceful, dreamless sleep claimed him almost immediately.

A strong hand pulling at his shoulder roused him from a deep slumber. Cody blinked at the darkness and looked up to see a large shadow looming over him.

"Ye'd better get up, lad," Orion rumbled. "There's something strange going on."

Cody sat up quickly. Orion was kneeling beside him, and close by was another figure, this one slender, with the light of the waning three-quarters moon reflecting on blond hair. Holly . . .

"What is it?" Cody rasped. Every instinct suddenly screamed that something was wrong.

"Some of the men are gone, Cody," Holly said in a low, urgent voice. "Mr. McCarthy and I didn't notice them leaving, but they're not here, and we can't find Marshal Baxter anywhere—"

Enraged, Cody surged up onto his feet. Without even thinking about it, he knew exactly what had happened. "That old double-crosser!" he exclaimed.

"Wha' d'ye mean?" Orion gripped Cody's arm. "Ye dinna think the marshal is going to attack the town?"

"That's exactly what I think."

"Oh, no!" Holly gasped as Cody hurried past them. The deputy cast his eyes around the camp. In the moonlight he could count the sleeping figures of only half the posse members.

"On your feet, men!" he called, his voice ringing through the camp. "We've got trouble!"

As the groggy men began rolling out of their blankets, Cody ran to the other side of the camp where the horses were tied. As he had suspected, about half of the mounts were gone. The men were calling confused questions after him. As he turned back to face them in the faint light given off by the embers of the campfire, his features were taut and grim.

"Baxter and some of the men have slipped away," he announced. "I think they're going to try to raid that town and rescue Miss Stockbridge."

Mingled among the surprised cries of the posse members, Cody heard Holly exclaim, "Richard! Where are you, Richard?"

Edwin Perkins moved into the glow of the dying campfire, still rubbing at his eyes. He blinked sleepily and peered around. Holly caught him by the arm and asked urgently, "Edwin, where's Richard?"

"Why . . . I assumed he was here—"

"He's gone, too," Cody said sharply. "Baxter was talking to him just before I dozed off. He must've sold Richard on the idea of raiding the town."

"Wha' are we ginna do, Cody?" Orion asked. His shotgun was in his big hands, and he stood tensed and ready for trouble.

Cody took a deep breath. For the first time since leaving Abilene, Dan Baxter was not around to be consulted. In fact, this time Baxter was the problem. In the heat of the moment immediately after Dorothea's kidnapping, Cody had been more than ready to lead the posse. Now that the time had come to make a decision that could affect a great many lives, his confidence in himself wavered. He had been on his own for a long time, but this was a responsibility he had never faced before.

Luke Travis never would have taken me on as a deputy if he hadn't thought I could do the job, Cody thought. *Now I have to live up to that faith.*

"We'll go after them," he said. "Get mounted."

Quickly he bent to pick up his tack and began saddling his own mount. A few feet away, he noticed Holly Stockbridge preparing to hoist her saddle onto her horse's back.

"Wait a minute," Cody said sharply. "You aren't going with us, Holly."

Stunned, she turned toward him angrily. "Not going with you? Of course I'm going with you! Why do you think I came all this way?"

"We agreed to let you come along, but nothing was

ever said about your doing any of the fighting. I don't know what Baxter intended to do about you, but I'm in charge now, and I say you stay here."

Holly stared at him, obviously surprised by his decision. After a moment, she wheeled to Orion and said, "Mr. McCarthy, can you talk some sense into Cody's head?"

Orion grinned as he secured the double girths on his saddle. "Ah, 'tis not likely, lass. Folks have been known t'try 'afore, wi' a notable lack o' success!"

"You probably agree with him, don't you?" Holly snapped accusingly. "You think I should stay here where it's safe!"

"Aye, lass, tha' I do."

Holly turned to Edwin Perkins and appealed to him. "Do something, Edwin."

Perkins grimaced and slowly said, "Ah . . . I doubt that the deputy is going to listen to my opinion on the matter, Holly. After all, he *is* in charge now, since Marshal Baxter is nowhere around."

Cody had worked furiously during Holly's appeals and was now ready to go. He swung into the saddle. "I'm sorry, Holly," he said sincerely. "But you're staying out of harm's way, and that's final."

She glared up at him. "And what if you don't come back? What if you all get killed?"

Cody shrugged. "If I were you, I'd head back toward Abilene as fast as I could. You've got your rifle and quite a bit of ammunition, and you'd stand a good chance of getting back all right."

"And leave Dorothea behind?"

In the dim light of the fire, Cody met Holly's eyes and said softly, "If we don't come back, she won't either."

As she absorbed his words, Holly swallowed.

"I . . . I know." She nodded, then stepped over next to Cody's horse. "Be careful, all right?"

"Sure." A grin broke across his face. He suddenly leaned down from the saddle and kissed the startled Holly on top of her blond head. *It never hurts to kiss a pretty woman,* he told himself.

Then he put the spurs to his horse and galloped out of the camp, the rest of the posse trailing behind him.

There was enough moonlight for Cody to pick his way across the valley toward Elysium. He and the others could not maintain a fast pace over the entire distance because the terrain was very rugged in places, but neither did he and the posse waste any time.

Cody used the light he could see in the town—no longer abandoned since Jake Walsh and his men had arrived—as a beacon guiding him to his destination. When he judged that they were a mile from Elysium, Cody reined in, holding up a hand to halt the others. Gradually they came to a stop, bunching up close behind him.

Cody turned his horse around to talk to the other men in low-pitched tones. "The town's up ahead. I'm a little surprised we haven't heard any shooting so far, but if Walsh hasn't been alerted, there's no need to tip him off now. We'll ride on, but take it slow, easy, and *quiet.*" He paused, then added, "And keep your hands close to your guns."

Turning his horse, he began quietly to pick his way toward Elysium. His stomach was doing some sort of anxious dance as he rode. Cody would have matched his nerves and gun speed against almost any man alive, but this skulking around in the dark and not knowing what was going to happen next gnawed at him.

The posse had ridden perhaps another hundred yards when the silence of the night was shattered by a barrage of gunfire.

Cody slapped the reins on his horse's neck, bracing himself for the animal's surge of speed. "Come on!" he yelled. "That's got to be Baxter!"

Caution and silence were discarded now. The pounding of hoofbeats blended with the continuing roar of shots in a hideous melody as the posse raced toward the sounds exploding in Elysium.

In the forefront of the hard-riding men, Cody found himself following a trail that gradually widened into the main street of the town. He could see the darkened buildings lining the street. Brilliant muzzle flashes came from the shadowy hulks.

Suddenly, flames erupted toward the far end of the street. The blaze lit up most of the street, exposing the knot of men on horseback—Baxter and the others— who were desperately fleeing from the trap into which they had ridden.

Seeing the trap close on the hapless men, Cody grimly appreciated just how well prepared for trouble Jake Walsh had been. One of the outlaw's men must have touched off the brush that had been piled at the approach to the town—for just this purpose. Baxter and the posse members who had accompanied him on this ill-advised rescue attempt were now paying the price.

Cody saw one of the possemen go down, flung from his saddle by the storm of lead. He could not tell who it was, but one thing was sure—caught in that cross fire, the casualty would be the first of many.

Yanking his horse to a sliding stop at the end of the street, just outside the glare cast by the bonfire, Cody threw himself down from the saddle. He wrested his Winchester from his saddle holster and dropped to one knee as he levered a cartridge into the chamber. "Give them some covering fire!" he yelled as he snapped the rifle to his shoulder and pressed the trigger.

He fired as fast as he could work the lever, the blasts assaulting his ears and the gun smoke stinging his eyes. The other men had dismounted as well and were pouring lead into the buildings on both sides of the street.

Given a momentary respite, Baxter and his men gathered themselves for another dash. They spurred their horses into motion and fired wildly as they galloped down the still-muddy street.

The arrival of Cody and the rest of the posse had distracted the outlaws enough to allow several of Baxter's group to break past the bonfire and head for the relative safety of the darkness. Baxter, however, was hanging back slightly, firing with both guns at the buildings as he raced past.

Cody's Winchester clicked empty. Rather than reload it, he stood up and palmed out his Colt. Most of the possemen were out of Elysium now, but he could still see Baxter by the nightmarish glare of the fire. Then he saw the marshal suddenly rock back in the saddle and clutch at his shoulder. As his horse seemed to run out from under him, Baxter crashed to the ground in the middle of the street.

Cody started to lunge toward his horse. *Trying to save the ornery old coot will probably just get me killed,* he thought, *but I have to try.*

Before Cody could reach his mount, another horse pounded past him. He looked up and saw to his surprise that Edwin Perkins was on the back of the animal. Leaning far forward in the saddle, Perkins was lashing it to greater speed with the reins as he hurtled toward the bonfire.

Perkins is trying to get to Baxter, the deputy realized with a shock.

"Cover him!" Cody yelled as he spun around to follow Perkins's progress.

The possemen fired their rifles furiously, and as the men who had ridden with Baxter rejoined their comrades, they rolled from their saddles and added their efforts to the covering fire. Unaware as they fled that Baxter had fallen, they were confused at first by Perkins's daring ride, but they started shooting anyway.

Perkins still showed the awkwardness in the saddle that had plagued him all the way from Abilene, but in this desperate moment he somehow found the strength and know-how to pilot the plunging animal down the street past the bonfire. Baxter had twisted around and was still firing at Walsh's men with his good hand. The horse's shadow suddenly loomed over him as it came to a halt, and he instinctively jerked the gun around, ready to fire. He held off at the last second.

Gripping the reins tightly in one hand, Perkins dropped from the saddle. He bent and slid the other arm around the stunned marshal, hoisting Baxter to his feet. Baxter staggered slightly, then gained his footing. Slugs plowed into the dirt of the street and cut the air around them as Baxter, with Perkins's support, got his foot in the stirrup and pulled himself up.

Baxter took the reins from Perkins and was turning the horse even as the easterner scrambled on behind him. Hunched forward in pain, Baxter spurred the horse as soon as Perkins was mounted. Perkins held on for dear life as the horse sprinted down the street.

Angered that Baxter was getting away, some of Walsh's men came to the edge of their hiding places and fired at the fleeing men. The men in Cody's group peppered them with shots, making them dive back into the abandoned buildings. The horse carrying Perkins and Baxter pounded past the bonfire and on down the street out of town.

"Get mounted!" Cody ordered his men. "Keep shooting so those men are covered, but get ready to ride!"

A moment later, foam trailing from its mouth and flecking its sides, Perkins's horse with its double burden came racing up. From his own mount, Cody called to Perkins, "Keep going! Get back to camp! All of you men, pull out!"

The posse turned their horses and started back across the valley. Cody hesitated, watching as Walsh's men ventured farther from the buildings to send a few parting shots after them. The flames of the bonfire had begun to die down a little, but there was still enough light for Cody to see the four unmoving bodies sprawled in the street, unmoving, their clothes bullet-torn and blood-soaked.

Four men almost certainly dead, Baxter wounded —God knows how badly—and Walsh probably madder than a hornet that somebody had dared to defy his orders. This rescue mission had fallen apart in a hurry, Cody thought bitterly. Then he turned and rode hard into the night, to see if he could salvage any of it.

Chapter Fifteen

————◆————

AT THE TOP OF THE RIDGE FROM THE CLUMP OF TREES where they had camped, a slender rider worked the horse nimbly down the slope toward the valley floor. In the moonlight her blond hair shone, and the barrel of the rifle she carried shimmered. When she noticed the riders approaching, she reined in and raised the rifle, pointing it at the lead rider.

Cody spurred his horse ahead the moment he spotted Holly, holding up a hand and calling her name so that she would not mistake them for some of Walsh's men. As he reached her, she lowered the rifle and demanded anxiously, "Cody, what happened? I heard all the shooting—"

Cody shook his head. "I don't know all of the story yet, but what we saw was a nightmare, Holly. Baxter and the men who went with him were trapped by

Walsh. He was ready, Holly, must've been waiting for them. Still, we managed to get most of them out."

"Most of them?"

"We lost four of them," Cody told her.

"Richard . . . ?"

The deputy shook his head and said softly, "Don't know yet. I haven't had a chance to check and see who made it out."

Holly closed her eyes and sighed deeply. Then she leaned over and plucked at Cody's sleeve. "What . . . what about Dorothea?"

"I just don't know. I didn't see her anywhere." As he spoke, the rest of the posse rode past them into the camp. Cody looked up as the men rode by and saw Edwin Perkins, with Baxter slumped in the saddle in front of him. Cody went on, "The marshal's been hurt. I'd better go see how badly."

Holly rode back into the camp beside him, worry etching lines into her face. Cody dismounted and hurried over to where Orion had placed Baxter by the embers of the fire. Orion knelt on one side of the injured lawman and was already unfastening his shirt.

Cody dropped to a knee on Baxter's other side as Orion stripped back his bloodstained shirt, exposing the wound. In the glow of the embers Cody could see a red-rimmed hole in Baxter's left shoulder where a bullet had punched into the flesh. Cody glanced up and realized that while the man's face was haggard and drawn, he was conscious and alert.

"How does it look?" Baxter asked through gritted teeth.

"Turn him on his side, Orion," Cody said. "Easy, now."

Gently, Orion raised Baxter's upper body and turned him so that Cody could see the the exit wound.

It appeared clean, too. Evidently the slug had not tumbled much in its path through Baxter's body.

"I'm no doctor, but it looks like you'll live," Cody told him. "You've lost plenty of blood, but when we get you cleaned up, you should be all right."

As Orion eased his body back to the ground, Baxter closed his eyes and nodded. "That's what I thought. I'll be ready to ride again in a little while."

"Where do you think you're going?" Cody snapped.

Opening his eyes again, Baxter glared up at Cody. "Why, back to Elysium, of course. We didn't get the lady out yet."

"We don't even know if she's still alive," Cody reminded him quietly.

"She's alive," Baxter declared. "Walsh wouldn't kill her yet. He's still playing the game."

Cody grimaced. "It did look like he was expecting you."

Orion went to his horse and took a roll of cloth and a small bottle from his saddlebags. When he returned to Baxter's side, he uncapped the bottle. "Scotch whisky," he said proudly, brandishing the liquor. "Th' finest medicine in th' world." He held the bottle to Baxter's lips and lifted it slowly as the marshal took a healthy swallow. He urged the marshal to take a second swallow, then poured a small amount of the amber liquid inside in the lawman's wounds. Baxter grimaced and bit his lower lip. Orion then unrolled the cloth and, tearing it into strips, began binding up Baxter's wound.

"I thought we had slipped past Walsh's guards," Baxter went on bitterly, his voice a little weaker now. "But he was just suckering us in. I figured Dorothea was probably in an old hotel down there. It's the biggest place in town, and if I know Walsh, he's got his headquarters there. But before we could even start to look for her, those varmints opened up on us, and then that fire started. . . ."

"Just take it easy and stay quiet," Cody told him. "We know what happened after that."

"Where's Perkins?" Baxter asked, trying to lift his head and look around. "I never thought that skinny galoot'd be the one to come for me like he did. Want to thank him."

"I'll tell him, don't worry," Cody assured him as he stood up. Now that Baxter was in Orion's care and would be all right, Cody turned to the other men, to find out how many of them were wounded. He moved slowly, speaking to each man and examining each injury.

There were several creases and nicks, and the side of one man's face was covered with blood from where part of his ear had been shot away. It soon became clear, though, that Baxter's wound was the most serious.

Cody looked for Richard Stockbridge but could find no sign of him. The deputy bit back a curse as soon as he realized that the young easterner was missing.

Holly, who had also been searching among the men, came up to Cody and said, "I can't find Richard. He's not here!"

Gently, Cody put his hands on her shoulders. "I'm sorry, Holly," he said softly. "I told you that we lost four men there in the town. I guess Richard must have been one of them."

Tears welled up in Holly's eyes, and she fell into Cody's arms, her head pressed against his chest. He tightened his arms around her as sobs began to shake her body.

Hearing someone calling his name, Cody turned his

head to see one of the townsmen from Abilene coming toward him. The man had a bandage wrapped around his forearm where a slug had burned him. He pushed his hat back and said, "Did I just hear you talkin' about that Stockbridge feller, Cody?"

"That's right, Clete. Did you see what happened to him?"

Holly lifted her head and blinked back tears as the man said, "No, I didn't rightly see what happened. But I know he wasn't one of the men who got hit while we was tryin' to get out of town. Just as the shootin' started, I saw him headin' down an alley next to that hotel."

Holly's fingers tightened their grip on Cody's shirt. "Then . . . then Richard might still be alive?" she asked in a choked voice.

"Don't know about that, ma'am," Clete replied. "I figger there was a bunch of Walsh's men in that old hotel, but I reckon there's a chance he could've got out."

"As long as there's a chance . . . " Holly looked up at Cody. "You're going back, aren't you? You're going to try to get Richard and Dorothea out?"

Cody hesitated. The way it looked to him, there was a very good chance that Richard had been killed in that alley, possibly in some attempt to rescue Dorothea. Dorothea might well be dead, too. They had already lost four men. What was Luke Travis going to say about the disaster this had become? More important, what would Travis do in a situation like this?

"Hello, the camp! Hey, you hear me in there?"

The shout made Cody's head snap around. The familiar voice was coming from the trail that led to Elysium.

He released Holly and turned toward the edge of the trees. "Give me that rifle," he snapped to one of the men. Taking the Winchester the man held out to him, Cody checked to be sure that it was loaded. Then he hurried to the edge of the trees and looked down the slope.

A single horseman rode out of the brush at the bottom of the ridge. Beyond him, on the other side of the valley, Cody could see the red glow of the burning bonfire in Elysium's main street, and the brightly lit large building.

Cody raised the rifle and called out, "Hold it, mister! Speak your piece, whatever it is!" In the darkness behind him, he heard the clicks of guns being cocked and the rustling of clothing as the posse prepared for more trouble.

The rider reined in, stopping his horse in the bright moonlight at the edge of the camp. Cody recognized him now as Walsh's messenger, the same man who had delivered the outlaw's earlier instructions.

"You in charge?" the man asked. "Reckon that old man's laid up, huh?"

"I'm in charge," Cody replied coldly. "Now get on with it."

"Take it easy, boy. Jake could've sent a whole bunch of us to wipe all of you out. Instead he just sent me to give you the word. Now listen up. That gal is still all right, no thanks to that stupid play you pulled! We got us another prisoner, too. Young blond fella, says his name is Stockbridge. Reckon he must be the gal's brother. That don't matter. What's important is that you don't try to pull anything like this again, or both of 'em will die. You understand?"

"We understand," Cody responded. Just in case

Walsh might be playing some trick, he kept the rifle trained on the messenger.

"Jake wants that ransom. He'd rather not have to kill nobody else, so the deal's still on, long as you stay out of Elysium."

"There won't be any more attacks," Cody assured him grimly.

"All right. That ransom comes, you bring it on in. One man, remember?" The hardcase laughed harshly. "'Course, if what you sent in tonight is the best you got, then it don't really matter. But you'd best do what Jake says, anyway."

He turned his horse and rode away. Cody stood watching the man until he had vanished into the shadows of a grove of trees a few hundred yards down in the valley.

Slowly Cody lowered the Winchester and turned to look at the rest of the posse clustered behind him. Now that she knew her brother and sister were still alive, Holly had stopped crying. That they had not been killed was the best the posse could hope for, under the circumstances. *As for the rest of it,* Cody thought bitterly, *we're right back where we started.*

The crack of a gunshot made him spin around.

The sound had come from the trees where Walsh's messenger had disappeared. As Cody stood listening tensely, he thought he heard a low moan of pain that was abruptly cut off. He muttered, "Now what the devil . . . ?"

Orion moved up beside him. The Scotsman slowly shook his head and said, "I dinna know, lad. But it kinna be anythin' good."

"If Walsh is up to something, I want to know about it," Cody said thoughtfully. "As shook up as they are right now, the men won't be taken by surprise. Orion, you and I better scout around, see what we can find out."

Orion nodded. "'Tis a fine idea." He held a rifle and lifted it to signal his readiness.

Cody chose two men to stand guard and instructed the rest to stay where they were and finish binding up the injuries. Then he and Orion slipped down the ridge on foot, moving quickly and using whatever cover they could find in the moonlight. Cody wished a cloud would come along to block the silvery glow that exposed them, but they were not that lucky. Still, no one shot at them, and Cody was thankful for that. Moving swiftly and stealthily, he and Orion reached the grove of trees and darted into the shadows.

Crouched in the brush, they waited in silence for a long moment, listening intently. Finally Cody whispered, "You hear horses?"

"Aye," Orion said softly.

With their rifles ready, they catfooted through the trees. The thick underbrush made it difficult to move swiftly without making too much noise, and the slowness of their progress ate at Cody. He sensed that something important was happening, but so far he had no idea what it was.

Abruptly Orion clamped a big hand heavily on his shoulder and forced him down. Both men sprawled on the ground and lay motionless. Cody squinted through the darkness as the sound of hooves grew louder. The earth vibrated under him as a fairly large body of riders moved through the night somewhere close by.

Suddenly, he sighted the men on horseback. They were dark, bulky shapes moving in the moonlight. Three men rode side by side, leading a party of at least another dozen men. All rode brazenly along, making no attempt to conceal their movement. Cody strained to overhear some of the conversation between the leaders.

"—hands on that fifty grand," one of the men was saying.

"We'll have it soon enough," another replied. "Remember all that shootin' we heard a while ago? Walsh won't be expectin' more trouble this soon."

Cody bit his lip to suppress a groan. *Another band of outlaws after the money Walsh had taken from the train . . .*

"—you reckon that fella we shot was?" another voice asked.

"Probably one of Walsh's scouts," the second man answered. "Walsh probably sent him out to make sure whoever hit them earlier was gone."

"Think we should have questioned him 'fore we killed him?"

"What for? We know where Walsh is, we know he's got that money. I've even heard tell he's got some girl with him that he's holdin' for ransom. We'll take her, too. Now come on."

The sounds gradually faded away. Cody and Orion waited for another moment, then stood up and faced each other. In the deep shadows of the grove it was too dark for Cody to see Orion's features, and he wondered if Orion looked as grim as he felt. Everything was going wrong!

"They're ginna attack the town," Orion rumbled.

"And Walsh will think it's us. He'll probably think that we killed his messenger, since that fella won't be coming back."

"This time he'll kill the lass, tha' is for certain."

Cody nodded. "Unless we stop him."

"But wha' can we do, lad? The men are shot up and worn out. They're no match for either Walsh's gang or tha' new band o' villains."

Cody's mind worked furiously. He turned toward the posse's camp and said over his shoulder, "Then we'll just have to get somebody else to do our work for us, won't we?"

Orion just frowned and shook his head. Then, as Cody broke into a desperate run, he raced after him.

Chapter Sixteen

———◆———

CODY HAD HIS PLAN WORKED OUT BY THE TIME HE AND Orion had dashed through the brush and rejoined the posse. As the men gathered around him, he broke the bad news about the group of renegades that was preparing to attack Elysium.

"But Walsh will think it's the posse!" Holly exclaimed. "You heard what that man said. He'll kill Dorothea and Richard!"

"I know," Cody said, trying to sound calmer than he felt. "That's why Orion and I are going to go in and get them out first."

A flurry of protests and questions burst spontaneously from the men, but Dan Baxter's voice cut them short. The federal marshal, his left arm in a makeshift sling and his shirt bulky with bandages, pushed the clustered posse members aside and went up to Cody. He moved a little unsteadily, but he did not look like a man who had suffered a fairly serious bullet wound only an hour or so earlier. His eyes burned intensely.

"Just the two of you, Cody?" Baxter hissed, his face an angry mask. "That's what you wanted all along, wasn't it?"

"I thought that was what we had agreed on in the first place, before you led half the posse into Walsh's trap!" Cody snapped harshly. The anger in his voice exposed only a fraction of the deep outrage he felt. Baxter's burning desire for revenge on Walsh, as understandable as it was, had created the dangerous situation in which they now found themselves.

"You really think you and Orion can pull it off?"

"Walsh is going to have his hands full with that other bunch," Cody pointed out angrily. "If we move fast enough, maybe Orion and I can be at the hotel in time to take advantage of the distraction."

Baxter took a deep breath. Cody watched as, after a long moment, the lines of anger in Baxter's face slowly dissolved. At last Baxter nodded and said, "You're right. It sounds like it could work. Sounds better than what I tried."

Cody did not know whether Baxter was trying to apologize or not, but there was no time to waste thinking about it, and he simply did not care. He turned to Orion and said, "Get your horse. Let's go."

A new voice broke into the conversation. "I'm going, too."

Cody glanced up to see Edwin Perkins pushing his way through the group of men. The lanky easterner had a pistol tucked in his belt and carried a Winchester. Cody shook his head and started to tell Perkins to forget it. Then he remembered the way the man had reacted under fire, the way he had overcome his lack of experience and ridden into that storm of bullets to rescue Baxter.

The deputy nodded abruptly. "Sure," he said. "I reckon you've got the right." Then he scanned the faces of the other men. "But everybody else is staying here. If we're not back in an hour, you pull out and head for Abilene. Understand?"

The possemen nodded. They knew as well as Cody that this was the last chance they had to save Dorothea Stockbridge. If this attempt failed, there would be no point in trying any more heroics.

During the frantic activity that had engrossed the camp since their return from Walsh's hideout, no one had tended to the horses, and they were still saddled. Cody, Orion, and Perkins mounted up quickly. Baxter strode over and extended his hand to Cody. "Good luck, son," he said. "We may not have seen things the same way, but I still think you're a fine lawman."

Despite his anger with Baxter, Cody was touched by the older man's words. Baxter had been a star packer for a long time and had seen plenty of good and bad lawmen. Cody softened, nodded, and said, "Thanks."

While Baxter was shaking hands with Orion and Perkins, Holly moved silently among the shadows, her face solemn. She stopped next to Cody's horse and, with her face averted, patted the animal's flank. Without looking up, she whispered to Cody, "I'll be praying for you, Cody. For you and all the others."

He reached out and stroked her silky blond hair for a moment. "We'll be back," he promised softly.

She quickly looked up at him, tears shining on her face in the moonlight that slanted through the trees. "I know," she said.

With a last glance at her, Cody swung his horse

around. He urged the animal into a trot and did not look back again. Orion and Perkins followed closely behind him.

The moon was in the western quadrant of the sky as the three men rode hard across the valley. The other men had quite a start on them, but the outlaws were a larger group, and there was always a chance that they did not know the territory as well. Cody was now pretty familiar with the trees, brush, and gullies of the trail to Elysium.

As they approached the town, Cody swung his group away from the trail, and they made their way around a small hill east of the settlement, which was now shrouded in darkness. This roundabout route took a little longer, but it enabled them to approach the hotel from the rear.

When they were still a couple of hundred yards from the buildings, Cody spotted some brush that would conceal them. Riding to it, he reined in, dismounted, and motioned for Orion and Perkins to follow. In a soft voice he said, "We'll leave the horses here and go ahead on foot. This is close enough. We can still get back to the horses in a hurry when we're ready to pull out."

Orion nodded and began tying his mount to a bush. Cody and Perkins did the same. When all the horses were secure, Cody drew his pistol and began silently picking his way through the brush toward the buildings.

He had been nervously awaiting the first blasts of gunfire for the last ten minutes, but so far all was quiet. Evidently the newly arrived hardcases were taking their time about starting their attack. That was all right with Cody: The closer they were to the hotel when the shooting started, the better. They were about fifty yards behind the two-story building when the firing finally broke out.

"Come on!" Cody rasped, breaking into a run.

A flurry of shots came from the north end of town, near the spot where the bonfire had finally burned itself out. *Some of Walsh's guards must have spotted the newcomers and are challenging them,* Cody thought.

No longer concerned with moving quietly, he lunged toward the building, concentrating on covering the ground between himself and the back door of the hotel as quickly as possible. He heard the pounding of Orion's boots close beside him and Perkins's hoarse breathing just behind him. The desperate sounds mixed with the beat of his own racing pulse and the now-steady hammering gunshots from the street.

There was a small porch on the back of the hotel, with several steps leading up to the door. Cody took the steps two at a time and hit the door with his shoulder, feeling the rotten wood splinter under the impact. It smashed open, and he all but fell through it into the hotel kitchen.

Shrewdly, Walsh had posted a guard there, but the firing from the front of the hotel had drawn the man away. Cody saw him returning to the kitchen, probably to see what had caused the crash. With a surprised look, the man tried to jerk the rifle in his hands around.

Cody triggered the Colt in his hand as he held it out at arm's length. He was off balance, but his aim was true, and the bullet smacked into the guard's chest. He grunted, fell back against the doorjamb, and dropping his rifle, collapsed in a twisted heap.

Cody crossed the kitchen in several quick strides and leaped over the guard's body. Weapons ready, Orion and Perkins were close behind him as he went down the hall toward the lobby.

Another of Walsh's men must have heard the shot in the kitchen, because he flashed into view toward the other end of the hall, a gun in his hand. He fired one wild shot before Cody's bullet punched through his throat and shattered his spine. Blood spurted from the wound, splattering the faded and peeling wallpaper in a vivid, gruesome pattern as the man collapsed to the floor.

Cody dove past the fallen gunman and launched himself into the hotel lobby. Landing in a crouch behind the old registration counter, he instantly took in the scene. There were several men at the front windows, firing steadily through the shattered glass toward the other side of the street. The men who had attacked the town must have taken cover in the buildings there.

Seconds later some of the men at the windows started to turn to meet the new threat, but just then Orion's rifle blasted from the hall, finding its target and knocking one of the outlaws backward. Cody began firing and dropped another man before he had to duck back behind the counter as bullets meant for him began to chew up the registration desk.

From the corner of his eye, Cody saw Edwin Perkins dart out of the hall and scan the lobby.

"Upstairs!" Perkins yelled. "Dorothea!"

Instantly Cody realized that Perkins was probably right: It was likely that Dorothea was being held prisoner in one of the second-story rooms. Perkins plunged behind the counter as a slug thumped into the wall close beside his head. As he scuttled along the floor toward Cody, the deputy twisted his head and started to say, "I'll go—"

"No!" Perkins cried. "You and Orion cover me!"

Before Cody could argue, Perkins was up and running again, vaulting the barrier at the other end of the counter and sprinting toward the stairs.

Cody knew he had to cover Perkins. Taking a deep breath, he stood up, abandoning the safety of the wooden desk. He squeezed the trigger of his Colt and began slapping the hammer back with the heel of his other hand. Fanning a gun was about the worst way in the world to hit something, but it got the bullets out in a hurry. In addition to the deafening roar of his own gun, he could hear Orion in the hallway, firing the rifle as fast as he could work the lever.

Abruptly glancing toward the man he was trying to cover, Cody saw Perkins reach the stairs and start up them. The easterner was moving so fast that he looked like an ungainly bird flying up the staircase. Then the hammer fell on an empty chamber in the deputy's Colt, and he did not have any more time to worry about Perkins.

Edwin Perkins felt a tug at his shirt as he went up the stairs. He assumed it was a bullet, but he ignored it and kept going. He was as frightened as he had ever been in his life, but the knowledge that Dorothea was probably just a few feet away from him propelled him on irresistibly. He was going to save her if he could— and die with her if he could not.

Unbalanced by the speed of his flight up the stairs, Perkins staggered as he reached the top. He looked frantically from right to left, wondering where to start searching. He knew he had only seconds.

Somewhere close by, a gun blasted. Perkins felt a

blow on his left arm, and the stunning impact spun him halfway around, disorienting him. He jerked his eyes from side to side, vaguely aware that he had been shot, and finally saw a man standing in the corridor in front of the door to one of the rooms. The man had a gun in his hand, and he was pointing it at Perkins.

Well, I have a gun, too, Perkins thought. *It would be rather foolish to just stand here and let that outlaw shoot me again.*

Edwin Perkins yelled involuntarily as he brought up his pistol and pressed the trigger. The sound of the shot blended with another explosion from the hardcase's gun. Perkins saw the flame flash from the muzzle of the man's gun and expected to feel the bullet smash into him at any second. Instead, the outlaw went reeling back against the wall of the corridor, clutching his chest. The gun slipped from his fingers, and he suddenly pitched forward, falling onto the floor.

Perkins could not feel his left arm now. He looked down and saw a red stain spreading from the wound in his upper arm. It did not hurt, so for the moment he decided he was going to ignore it. There had to be a reason the man had been standing guard in front of that door.

Perkins ran down the hall until he came to the room. Tucking his pistol behind his belt, he rattled the doorknob. "Dorothea!" he called urgently. "Dorothea, are you in there?"

"Edwin! Oh, my God, help me, Edwin!" a female voice shrieked from behind the door.

The voice was unmistakably Dorothea's. The door was locked, but that was not going to stop Perkins now. He braced himself, lifted a foot, and drove his heel against the door.

The flimsy wood around the lock shattered with the second kick, and the door slammed open. Perkins stumbled into the room and saw Dorothea writhing on the bed. She was wearing only her shift, and her hands were tied together above her head, the rope lashed to the bed frame. She was thrashing around and throwing her head from side to side, obviously hysterical with fear. As he rushed to her side, she stared wide-eyed at him but seemed not to believe that he could be real.

Frantically clawing at the knots, Perkins discovered right away that they were too much for him to undo with his fingers. He fumbled desperately in his pocket, searching for the clasp knife he had bought back in Abilene. Opening it with one hand was not easy; he had to use his teeth to hold the blade while he pulled it free of the handle. Then he slashed at the ropes that lashed her tied hands to the bedstead, sawing through the bonds in seconds. Dorothea's hands were still tied together, but at least she could get up off the bed now.

"Come on, Dorothea, come on," Perkins urged her. "We've got to get out of here."

Disheveled and wild-eyed, Dorothea stumbled as she tried to stand up. She caught at Perkins's shirt and lifted wondering eyes to his face. "Edwin?" she almost whispered. "Is it really you?"

"Of course it is, darling. You didn't think I'd leave you in the clutches of those . . . those fiends, did you?"

Dorothea gazed up at him for a long moment, then gave a sound that was half sob, half laugh. "Oh, Edwin," she cried. "You wonderful, stodgy man!"

Perkins frowned and patted her on the back with his good hand as she leaned against him.

"I'm sorry, Edwin," she said against his chest. "I'm

so sorry I . . . I treated you the way I did. I never should have done the things that I did—"

"Hush!" Perkins said sharply. "I love you, Dorothea, you know that. I don't care what happened before. Now, we really have to go. . . ."

"Richard!" Dorothea suddenly exclaimed. "Walsh told me Richard was here!"

"Have you seen him? Do you know where he is?"

Dorothea shook her head. "There's an old saloon down the street. Walsh and his men spent part of their time there. They might have taken Richard there!"

Perkins nodded and said, "We'll do what we can for him." Abruptly, a wave of pain washed through him. The shock of being shot was wearing off, and now the pain was asserting itself. "Come on," he whispered hoarsely.

Leaning on each other, the two people left the room and started toward the stairs. Perkins suddenly realized that although gunshots were still exploding elsewhere in the town, silence had fallen over the hotel.

What will we find waiting for us in the lobby? he wondered. Perkins put his good hand back on the butt of his gun, and then, together, he and Dorothea limped on.

Cody was thumbing the last of his fresh cartridges into the Colt when he heard the footsteps at the top of the stairs. He turned quickly, snapping the cylinder of the gun shut and bringing it up, then relaxed as Edwin Perkins and Dorothea Stockbridge came into view. Ashen and shaking, Perkins had a bullet wound in his left arm. Dorothea, dressed in her shift, held bound hands in front of her as she leaned against Perkins.

The stunned expression on Perkins's face as he stood at the top of the stairs and gazed down made

Cody stop reloading his gun. From where he stood behind the bullet-scarred registration desk, he followed Perkins's gaze and took in the carnage. At least half a dozen bloodied, unmoving men were sprawled around the lobby, most of them near the windows. Orion stood next to him, Winchester raised and ready for more trouble.

Cody grinned up at Perkins. "Looks like you found that woman of yours, Edwin," he said. "You all right, Dorothea?"

Dorothea nodded shakily. "I . . . I think so."

Perkins said, "You killed all of them!"

"Seemed like the thing to do," Cody said. The grin had vanished from his face. "They were sure doing their best to kill us."

While Perkins had been upstairs, Cody had spent a hectic few minutes—the seconds blending into a long, blurred nightmare of blood and smoke and explosions. The deputy remembered loading and firing, loading and firing, until there had been no one left to shoot at.

As Perkins and Dorothea limped down the stairs, Cody moved out from behind the counter and asked, "Was Richard Stockbridge up there?"

Perkins shook his head. "Walsh told Dorothea Richard was here, but she never saw him. There's a saloon down the street where he may be. Walsh and the rest of his men are probably there."

A fresh burst of firing shattered the night. "Shouldn't be hard to find them," Cody said dryly. "Orion, you and Perkins get Dorothea out of here. Head back to the camp and get the posse started toward Abilene as fast as you can."

Orion nodded. His thick hair was in disarray, and his features were grimy with gunpowder, but he seemed to be glorying in the fighting, as fierce a warrior as any of his highlander ancestors. "Aye! And wha' about ye, lad?"

"I'll try to get Stockbridge away from Walsh. We'll catch up as soon as we can." One corner of Cody's mouth twitched in a grimace. "If you don't see us in a couple of days . . . well, in that case I don't expect we'll be along at all."

"I could go wi' ye after Walsh—" Orion began.

Cody shook his head. "Perkins is hurt. You've got to go with them, Orion. But thanks anyway." Smiling broadly, he clapped the big Scotsman on the shoulder. They had been friends in Abilene, but if they both got out of this alive, they would be even closer than before.

Orion took Dorothea's arm. "Come along, lass." He steered the woman and Perkins toward the hall leading to the back of the hotel. Looking over his shoulder as a thought occurred to him, Orion asked, "But wha' about tha' strongbox o' money Walsh stole from the train?"

"I don't care about that," Cody said, shaking his head. "Those desperadoes can keep on fighting over it, as far as I'm concerned. I'm just going after Stockbridge."

"Good luck, Cody," Perkins said. He was beginning to wobble from shock and loss of blood, but he managed to shake hands with Cody before he followed Orion and Dorothea through the kitchen and out the back door of the hotel.

Cody covered them from the doorway in case anybody tried to take a shot at them, but the attention of everyone else in Elysium seemed to be centered on the other side of the building and the battle still raging along the main street. Cody watched as Orion hustled

Perkins and Dorothea away through the field behind the hotel. Within moments they would be in the brush where the horses had been left, and then they would be that much closer to the posse and relative safety.

When their fleeing shadows had vanished into the darkness, Cody turned and started down the alley that ran behind the buildings. The gunfire seemed to be slacking off a little. Cody wondered if one group of hardcases was on the verge of victory. If that was the case, it would not matter to him. Every hand in Elysium tonight was against him now.

Chapter Seventeen

———◆———

LISTENING CAREFULLY AND MOVING AS SILENTLY AS HE
could, Cody followed the alley behind the buildings
until he could tell from the sound of the shots that he
had reached the saloon housing the last of Jake
Walsh's men. Gunfire still blasted from inside the
ramshackle structure, but it was coming from only a
few guns now, instead of the many that had shattered
the night earlier. It looked as though Jake Walsh was
making his last stand.

Cody tried the back door of the building and found
it unlocked, but when he attempted to push it open, it
gave an inch or so and then stopped. Carefully sliding
his fingers through the gap, he encountered what he
had been afraid he would find—somebody inside had
blockaded the door with a heavy piece of furniture.

He stepped back and scanned the rear of the
building. There was one single window high above the

ground through which he could enter—if he could reach it and if he could get through it without calling too much attention to himself.

After spotting an old crate leaning against the building, Cody set it on its end under the window, hoping that the wood, which was weathered and partially rotten, would support his weight for a moment. He holstered his gun and stepped up, immediately reaching for the windowsill as he felt the sides of the crate starting to give.

His fingers caught the sill, and with a soft groan of effort he pulled himself up. Supporting himself with his left hand, he pushed at the window with his right. It slid up a few inches, stuck, then slid again as Cody put all of his strength into the push.

He caught hold of the sill again with both hands, then levered himself up and pitched himself headfirst through the open window. At the moment, he did not much care where he landed.

The gunfire covered up the sounds of his entrance as he fell to one corner of the big room and sprawled in a pile of debris. Evidently someone had broken up some of the saloon's tables and stacked them in this corner. One lantern was burning, and it had been placed on the floor in the center of the room, probably so that a stray bullet would be less likely to hit it.

Desperately searching the saloon for a place to hide, Cody saw a barrel to his right and, keeping low, rolled behind it. Hunkering down there in the deep shadow, he drew his gun and cautiously peered around the side of the barrel.

Three men were crouched at the front windows of the saloon, each of them firing toward the buildings across the street. Shots boomed in reply, the slugs whining past the heads of the men inside and punching through the faded wood of the saloon's walls. It was a desperate situation, one in which several other men had already lost their lives, judging from the bloody, sprawled bodies around the room.

Jake Walsh was in the center of the trio at the window, his burly, red-bearded figure unmistakable. To his left was one of his gang, a man Cody thought looked familiar. He had probably been one of the men who had helped kidnap Dorothea from the stable back in Abilene. The third man was crouching to Walsh's right, holding a pistol in each hand and firing them in turn through the bullet-shattered windows. He was Richard Stockbridge.

Cody stared, his jaw tight. No doubt about it, Richard was fighting right alongside Walsh, trying to drive off the rival bandit gang. *Maybe Walsh forced him to help,* Cody thought. *Richard's just trying to save his own skin.*

"Dammit, Stockbridge," Walsh yelled as he paused to jam fresh bullets into his pistol, "if that strongbox had been on the train like you said, none of this would've happened!"

"I told you it wasn't my fault!" Richard snapped back. "I never knew my father was playing games and moving it around."

"You still double-crossed me!"

Cody had been about to put a bullet into Walsh when the outlaw spoke up angrily. Now Cody waited, listening as the awful picture unfolded for him.

"You didn't have to steal my sister!" Richard punctuated the angry accusation with several shots.

Walsh laughed. "Once I knew that money wasn't on the train, our deal was off, Stockbridge. I was gettin' my payoff, one way or another. You didn't have to hire me to kill that union leader when you was bustin' up that strike a few years ago in Kansas City, neither, but you did."

"I knew you were a killer," Richard said coldly. "I never knew you were a damned blackmailer, too."

Cody's mind was racing. Now he understood why Richard had been so agreeable to Baxter's idea of a raid. More than anything else, he wanted Jake Walsh dead so that Walsh could not reveal his part in the scheme. That plan had backfired, though, leaving him Walsh's prisoner and now his reluctant ally.

"Cuss me all you want to, boy; just keep shootin' at those sons of bitches over there," Walsh said, rising up to shift his position and fire a couple of shots through the window. "We're all in this together now."

Richard edged back from the window. He reached into the open box of cartridges lying on the floor next to him and brought out a handful of shells. Walsh ignored him as Richard started reloading his pistols.

When the cylinders of both guns were full, Richard snapped them up and turned them toward Walsh. Crouching in his hiding place, Cody was astounded as he suddenly realized what was about to happen. Richard was going to try to kill both Walsh and the other man and attempt a getaway.

The other man must have spotted Richard's movement from the corner of his eye, because he spun around and yelled, "Look out, Jake!" The man fired at the same instant that Richard's guns exploded.

The outlaw's bullet tore through Richard's side, knocking him backward so that both of his shots went wild. Walsh whirled and brought his own gun up.

Cody lunged out of the darkness, aiming at the other outlaw. The man was dark featured and had a bushy beard, but that was all that Cody had time to notice—that and the fact that the outlaw was about to shoot Richard Stockbridge again. Cody fired first.

The bullet caught the hardcase in the chest. He went down, his gun blasting into the floor.

Walsh jerked his aim to the side to meet the new threat, instead of shooting at Richard as he had intended. The gun in his hand thundered, the roar blending with Cody's second shot.

Walsh's aim was better. Cody's bullet nicked his left arm, while the outlaw's slug slashed across the outside of Cody's left thigh. The crease was deep enough to send fire down the leg. It gave way; Cody felt himself falling but could do nothing to stop it.

Walsh was on him in a flash, kicking the gun from the deputy's hand, sending it skittering away across the dusty floor. Pointing his gun at Cody's chest, Walsh peered down at the deputy in the dim light and muttered, "Do I know you, boy? Hell, yes, you was in Abilene! The kid from the stable!"

Cody clutched his leg, feeling the blood seeping between his fingers. He glanced over at Richard Stockbridge. The young easterner still had his guns, and he was struggling to lift them. . . .

Jerking his head to follow Cody's glance, Walsh snorted. "Almost forgot about you, Stockbridge," he said. He lifted his pistol almost casually and fired. The bullet smacked into Richard's forehead, snapping his head back, killing him instantly.

Walsh turned back to Cody. "Don't know what you're doin' here, boy, but it ain't none of my business. Those bastards across the street are goin' to be rushin' this place any minute, soon as they realize we ain't puttin' up a fight no more. So I got to be gettin' out of here. Too bad about the gal, but I reckon they can have her. I got what I really want." He picked up a pair of saddlebags from the floor and slung them over his shoulder, then stepped to the rear door. With one hand, he shoved aside the heavy liquor cabinet that his men had used to barricade it.

Cody's gun was only about six feet away. He licked his lips. *I can roll that far,* he thought. Walsh would be able to put another slug in him, but Cody thought he could still manage to pull the trigger a time or two. . . . Jake Walsh was not going to ride away with that fifty thousand dollars.

Cody lunged for the pistol. Walsh spun around, raising his gun as he heard the movement.

"Walsh!" a voice cracked from the now-open back door.

The outlaw glanced over his shoulder and saw the same thing that a stunned Cody Fisher saw—a man in black, with an ivory-handled Colt in each hand.

Caught between two dangers, Walsh twisted, trying for a last desperate shot—

Dan Baxter's twin Colts roared, the slugs driving Walsh back against the liquor cabinet he had just moved. The cabinet leaned, then toppled with a crash, and Walsh went down with it. One foot twitched a couple of times, and then he did not move again.

Baxter strode briskly into the room, barely glancing at the man he had pursued for so long. The debt could never be paid, but at least justice had come for Jake Walsh.

The federal marshal bent over the astonished Cody and extended a hand to him. "Come on, son," Baxter said urgently. "Those other hardcases are all around the place. We've got to move."

Cody took Baxter's hand and pulled himself unsteadily to his feet. He had his Colt in his other hand again. If he and Baxter were not meant to get out of Elysium, at least they could go down fighting.

"What the devil are you doing here, Baxter?" he asked with a grin.

"Saving your bacon, it looks like." Pausing beside Walsh's body, Baxter nodded to the saddlebags. "Reckon that'd be the money. I guess we'd better try to take it back—though old man Stockbridge may not want it, what with all that blood on it, and the bullet holes and all."

Baxter stripped the pouches from Walsh and, wincing slightly, draped them over his left shoulder. Cody remembered that he had been wounded in that arm and said, "What about that bullet hole in you? Didn't look like it was bothering you much when you came in that door."

"I'm a tough old bird, son. Time you learned that about me." Baxter threw back his head and laughed, the booming, hearty laugh that had at first fooled Cody into thinking he was just a friendly, harmless old man.

About as harmless as a nest of rattlesnakes, Cody thought as he joined in the laughter.

Then the two lawmen stepped outside through the back door of the saloon.

Bullets thudded into the wall beside the door. "There's a couple of them!" a shadowy figure yelled as he fired again. "Come on, boys, they must have the money!"

The man ran forward, still firing wildy. Baxter smoothly raised one of his guns and shot him once, sending him flopping into the dirt of the alley. More figures appeared, running toward them down the alley behind the buildings, drawn by the man's cries and the shots.

"Head for the street!" Baxter rasped. "They won't expect us to go that way!" Baxter raced along the back of the saloon.

His leg throbbing, Cody forced himself to run after Baxter. The marshal ducked around a corner, and with Cody right behind him they hurried down the alley that ran beside the building, heading toward the street.

As they emerged onto the boardwalk, they saw at least six men crossing the street, converging on the building. There were several others behind them, pounding closer with every second. Cody realized that he and Baxter had nowhere left to run.

Baxter grinned and lifted his Colts. "Been nice riding with you, son," he said.

Cody returned the grin. There was nothing left to do now but sell their lives as dearly as possible.

With the thunder of pounding hoofbeats and the ear-shattering explosions of guns, riders swept into Elysium, galloping down the street, catching the outlaws in the open and cutting them down with a hail of bullets. Cody blinked at the suddenness of it, then fired instinctively as a slug whined close by his head. His shot hit one of the outlaws in the alley next to the saloon.

One of the men on horseback, a burly figure with a shaggy beard, aimed a shotgun toward the alley and fired it one-handed. Orion McCarthy thundered, "Have a taste o' buckshot, ye bloody-handed buzzards!"

Cody and Baxter sagged against each other, holding themselves up while the rescuers swarmed over the rest of the outlaws, killing most of them and capturing what few were left. When the shooting had died away, the man who had led the charge turned his horse and rode toward the saloon. Marshal Luke Travis reined in and, leaning forward in the saddle, grinned broadly. "Looks like you had a little trouble," he said.

Cody, realizing that he had been gaping at Travis in amazement, shook his head. "A little," he said. "Not that I'm complaining or anything, Marshal, but what the hell took you so long?"

Travis, still grinning, lightly slapped his leg. "Had to wait a couple of days for this bum leg to heal up enough for me to sneak out past Aileen. By that time the fella you sent back with the ransom note had gotten to Abilene, and so had a bunch of Pinkerton agents that Maxwell Stockbridge had sent for." Travis jerked a thumb at the mounted men behind him who were finishing up the chore of pacifying Elysium. "Stockbridge insisted he was going with the Pinks and the ransom money, so I figured I'd better come along, too."

"It's out of your jurisdiction," Cody pointed out.

At last, Baxter broke in and laughed. "You'd best learn to let your elders change their minds once in a while, Cody. Isn't that right, Marshal?"

"Right as rain, Marshal," Travis agreed.

Cody looked past Travis and saw Maxwell Stockbridge riding into town, surrounded by several heavily armed Pinkerton agents. Behind him came the rest of the posse that had originally left Abilene, and riding with them were Holly and Dorothea. Someone had loaned the older sister a duster to wear. Edwin Perkins rode close beside her, his arm in a sling and his eyes never leaving her. With the bloody bandage on his arm and a gun tucked in his belt, he looked nothing like the rather mild, dry executive who had come to Abilene on Maxwell Stockbridge's special train. And from the way Dorothea was looking at him, it was obvious she no longer found him at all boring.

"Where's Richard Stockbridge?" Travis asked, his face becoming solemn.

Cody nodded toward the saloon. "In there. Walsh killed him." Quickly and quietly, so that only Travis and Baxter could hear, Cody told them about Walsh's connection with Richard Stockbridge, revealing that Richard had been the one who set up the aborted train robbery with Walsh. "Everything fell apart after that," Cody finished. He saw that Maxwell Stockbridge, his daughters, and Edwin Perkins had dismounted and were walking toward the saloon. He took a deep breath and frowned. "Now, what do I say to them?"

"I reckon that's up to you, son," Baxter said.

"That's right," Travis agreed. "You make up your mind, Cody, and do whatever you think is right. Baxter and I will back you up."

"Thanks." Limping on his bullet-creased leg, Cody strode forward to meet the Stockbridges and Perkins. He saw the smile on Holly's face as her eyes met his, saw the looks of gratitude on the faces of Stockbridge, Dorothea, and Perkins. As he looked at their faces, he made his decision.

Holly ran ahead to meet him, and taking his arm, she drew it around her and let him lean on her. She looked up at him and said anxiously, "Are you all right, Cody?"

He smiled. "Reckon I'll be just fine, once I can get off this leg for a while."

"Have you seen Richard?"

Maxwell Stockbridge echoed the question.

Cody looked around at all of them, meeting their worried gazes, and then said slowly, "I'm sorry. I've got some bad news for you."

Epilogue

———◆———

Y OU DID THE RIGHT THING, CODY," LUKE TRAVIS TOLD
him the next morning as they were getting ready to
pull out of Elysium. "There was no need for any of
them to know the truth about the boy. That just would
have made the hurting worse."

Cody carefully hoisted his saddle onto his horse's
back. He knew there were plenty of people around
who would have been glad to handle the chore for
him, but he was going to have to learn to manage with
a sore leg for a while. *Might as well start now,* he
thought.

"You and Baxter knew what I'd do, didn't you?" he
asked.

"Let's just say we had a pretty good idea," Travis
replied with a grin. Already in the saddle, he turned
his horse to ride back among the other members of the

group and check their progress in getting ready to leave for Abilene.

Cody's leg was bandaged, and Baxter's arm was back in its sling. The two of them had spent most of the night sitting around a fire with Travis and Orion, talking about the violent events of the past week and trying to make some sense of them. They would never know the full story of Richard Stockbridge's treachery, but it was clear to Cody from some of the things that had been said that the young man had been consumed with ambition, a lust for power as much as money. And it was likely that he never would have had enough of either, having such a strong-willed man as Maxwell Stockbridge for a father.

There was some good in Richard, though, Cody thought. The main reason he had probably come with the posse in the first place was to get a chance to kill Walsh, but Cody felt sure that he had been partially motivated by his feelings for Dorothea, too.

No matter what he had been in life, Cody hoped his family could remember him well, and that was what counted.

During the conversation the night before, Cody had also had some of his suspicions confirmed by Dan Baxter.

"I followed you, Orion, and Perkins when you left the last time," Baxter had told Cody. "The more I thought about it, the more I realized that you'd been right all along, Cody. I was letting my hate get in the way of my brain, and that's not a good thing for a lawman. I'm sorry, son."

Cody had grinned across the fire and sipped his coffee. "I'm just glad you ran into Orion and the others when I sent them back to the horses. Walsh would have killed me for sure if you hadn't showed up when you did."

"Maybe, maybe not. You're pretty good with that gun." To Abilene's marshal, he said, "You'd best keep an eye on this one, Luke, or somebody's going to hire him away from you." Baxter nodded thoughtfully. "Why, with the proper training, we might even make a U.S. marshal out of him."

"Not likely." Cody had laughed heartily.

Now, as he pulled himself up into the saddle, the deputy glanced over and saw Baxter several yards away. The federal lawman was sitting on top of his white horse, the strap of his big black hat tight under his chin, that knowing grin on his face. Baxter laughed as Orion, who sat astride his horse next to him, said something.

Dan Baxter was a piece of work, all right. Cody was going to miss him once they got back to Abilene and Baxter went on to his next assignment.

"How do you feel this morning, Cody?" a gentle voice asked, drawing his attention the other way.

Holly Stockbridge had ridden up beside him. Although there was deep sadness in her eyes because of her brother's death, she had a sweet smile on her face for him.

"Why, I'm feeling fine," Cody said, grinning back at her. "Strong as can be, and ready to ride back to Kansas."

"Well, I'm glad to hear that. You can't be too careful with bullet wounds, though." Holly leaned over in the saddle, moving closer to him and lowering her voice. "I'm going to appoint myself your personal nurse, Cody Fisher. Anything you need, I'll be right there for you."

"I'll hold you to that," Cody replied softly.

Everyone was mounted now. It was a big group, what with the Pinkertons and the original posse members. Maxwell Stockbridge rode alone with his grief, but Dorothea and Perkins were side by side, the way Cody figured they would be from now on. Travis rode up to the front of the group and waved his arm, and slowly they got under way. Baxter joined Travis at the front, and with the two marshals leading, the riders left Elysium behind.

Cody glanced over at Holly Stockbridge and had to grin again. Getting back to Abilene promised to be a lot more pleasant than leaving it.